Twenty
Questions

Twenty Questions

Jerry Oltion

Twenty Questions

Published by

🌾 Wheatland Press

http://www.wheatlandpress.com
P. O. Box 1818
Wilsonville, OR 97070

Contents

PREFACE

When new acquaintances find out that I'm a writer, they almost invariably start asking questions. "Where do you get your ideas?" tops the list by a wide margin, followed by "How long does it take you to write a story?" People also want to know how I keep all the details straight (post-it notes), whether or not I've got an agent (I do), and how much I have to pay a magazine for them to publish one of my stories (I don't—they pay me...except when they don't, and that's why I have an agent).

It's apparently a fascinating career choice, probably because nobody can imagine a more lunatic way of making a living. I dream up stories— essentially cobbling together a pack of convincing lies—and then people pay me for them? Sounds pretty bizarre when you put it like that, but I do consider myself a professional liar, and I'm pretty proud of my track record in that regard. I've told some veritable whoppers in my time, and gotten a modest degree of acclaim for them. (Okay, that was a lie. I'm not that modest: one of those degrees of acclaim was the Nebula Award, of which I'm extremely proud.)

I tell lies for a living, but here's the odd thing about those lies: they're all told in pursuit of the truth. When I write a story, I'm asking questions of my own, and the stories, fiction though they may be, are the answers that come to me. They may not be *the* answers, but they're *some* answers, and occasionally they shed a little light on the subject.

My questions generally start with "What if...?" What if you could buy a life insurance policy that prevented you from dying? What if you could edit all the bad stuff out of your past? What if husbands and wives remember the same events differently because those events really did happen differently to each person?

I love asking those kinds of questions, and I love writing down my answers to them, but writing the stories is only half the fun. Seeing them in print is the other half. It's a kick to know that people are reading them and thinking, "Hmm. What if...?" But that joy is short-lived, because magazines are so ephemeral. You get this great idea, you write it down (he makes it sound so easy!), you go through the agonizing process of trying to sell it in a market that's already glutted with "slush" (which is what editors call the hundreds of unsolicited manuscripts they receive each month); eventually you do manage to sell it, the story shows up in a magazine...and a month later it's gone. You go into a bookstore to savor your moment in the sun and you find another issue of the magazine, with other people's stories in it. They don't even have your issue in the bargain bin. It's just gone, never to be seen again.

Authors live for collections like these. Collections give us a chance to share some of our favorite stories with people again, in a form that actually sticks around for a while. But they also force us to choose those favorites, which is not an easy task. I have over a hundred published stories—far too many for one volume. I had to sift through them in search of the ones I most wanted to share, the ones that most clearly define who I am and what goes on inside my head. At some point I realized that I was playing "twenty questions" with myself, using the underlying questions in the stories to dig for inner truth.

Coincidentally enough, I came up with twenty stories that I thought illustrated my work (so far, anyway) pretty well. I have no idea what the complete picture will look like to you, because readers bring their own experiences with them to a story, so the questions in your head will probably be different from the ones in my head when I wrote them. That's okay. I don't really have a message I want to convey.

No, that's a lie, too. I do have a message, but it's a pretty simple one:
Enjoy.

Jerry Oltion
Eugene, Oregon December 2003

Introduction to

The Love Song of Laura Morrison

This is one of my early stories, but it's still one of my favorites. I usually make up my characters to fit the idea, but this story was made up to fit the character. Laura Morrison is a little bit me, a little bit my mother, and a little bit an English teacher I had in college. I knew everything there was to know about her long before I started writing about her.

When this story was published, the readers of *Analog* magazine voted it the best of the year, and it was later turned into a pretty decent stage play. It was a surreal experience to sit in the audience and actually watch Laura and Teigh do the things I'd written about and say the words I'd put into their mouths. I still have one of their spacesuit helmets on a bookshelf in my living room. Every now and then I look at it and smile.

THE LOVE SONG OF LAURA MORRISON

Teigh was unpacking when he heard the sound at the window. He looked up from the pressure crate, but he could see nothing outside that might have made a noise; only the landscape curving upward in the distance. He looked out at it for a moment, then shrugged and turned back to the crate, lifting out a twist of gnarled wood that looked like a miniature oak tree in winter, which was in fact part of a pine's root system turned upside down. It had cost him nearly five hundred dollars to ship along, but ever since he had found it sticking out of an icy riverbank nearly ten years ago he had taken it with him wherever he went. Its weathered branches held for him the essence of Earth, a moment of life frozen in its struggle with the elements.

He stood with it cradled in his hands while he turned once around in search of an appropriate spot for his treasure, and he heard it again. A kind of high-pitched squeak, like a bearing going out, or...

Or a kitten, hanging onto the ivy that grew along the divider between his apartment and the next, looking down over one shoulder the way kittens do when they're thinking about jumping.

Teigh set his tree down on the bed and stepped to the window. He still wasn't used to the light gravity in the colony and he didn't know what the varying rate would do to a falling object's velocity, but he was pretty sure that a three-story fall wouldn't do a kitten any good even here. He opened the window gently so he wouldn't scare it into jumping, reached out from

3

below, and pulled it in, saying, "Well, little thing. Where did you come from?"

The kitten was gray and white and practically all fuzz. It looked up at him and meowed again.

Teigh stuck his head back out the window and looked along the building. The ivy originated from the apartment below and to the right; a perfect trellis for climbing kittens.

"So," he said as he pulled his head back in. "You're checking out your new neighbor. Hello. Nice to meet you." He let the kitten pull its legs up until it was standing in the palm of his hand. It couldn't have been much over two months old. "You're cute," he told it, "but I'll bet your mother wonders where you are."

He looked out the window again, but he saw nobody below and he didn't feel like shouting. "Well," he said, "I guess it's time I did a little visiting myself."

The nameplate on the door said Laura Morrison. Teigh looked down at the kitten in his hand and cocked an eyebrow. Single? He pushed the doorbell.

A voice from within said, "Just a minute," and there were some bumping sounds, then the door opened to reveal a white-haired woman in her seventies or so. Teigh tried to hide his disappointment.

"Hi, I'm Teigh Kuhlow, from upstairs in 308," he said. "I, uh, I found your kitten climbing on the ivy."

The woman nodded wearily and reached out for it. "Not surprising. Sorry. I'll close the window."

Teigh shook his head. "Oh, no. I didn't mean that. I didn't mind, really. I was just afraid he'd fall. I, uh, I like kittens."

She lowered her hand and looked at him through squinted eyes. "You do."

"Sure. Who doesn't?"

The woman smiled for the first time. "The last guy who lived up there, for one. Hah. Well, come on in, then. I've got a lot of 'em."

Indeed she had, Teigh discovered when he was inside. He counted six cats without looking hard, three of them from the same litter as the one that still purred in his hand. There might have been more, but if there were they were hidden in the lush foliage that grew almost everywhere. Laura led him to the kitchen table and moved a potted geranium from one of the chairs so he could sit.

"So you got the Hulk's apartment, eh?"

"The Hulk?"

"That's what I called him. Barbells. Always lifting them, banging them back down on the floor. Said he needed to keep in shape in the light gravity. Hah. What did he know? I've been here thirty years without lifting a barbell once and I'm still kicking." She took two cups down from a shelf and filled them with water. "Tea?"

"Uh, yes, please."

"Good, 'cause I don't have coffee. Horrid stuff. Should've left it on Earth. That where you're from?"

"I was. I guess I'm from here, now."

She nodded. "One-way ticket, huh? Me too. What do you do?"

Teigh set the kitten on his lap, where it promptly curled up to sleep. "I'm an architect. I'm working on the life support system for *Daedalus*."

"*Daedalus*?"

"The starship."

She put the cups in the microwave, punched a few buttons, and reached into a canister for a tea bag. "I use regular tea," she explained. "Don't like the aftertaste that heat-em-up stuff leaves. God knows what chemicals are in there anyway. Starship, you say. I didn't know they had one."

Teigh smiled involuntarily at her quick changes in subject. "Oh, come on now. You have to have heard. They're building it right outside. It's the biggest news in the solar system."

"Ah, well, I'm not much for news, you know. Full of wars and killing and such. I decided about twenty years ago that it wasn't worth listening to."

"Oh."

The microwave chimed softly and Laura took the steaming cups out. There was a silence while she dunked the teabag in one cup, swished it around, and dunked it in the other. Teigh used the opportunity to gaze out the glass door in wonder. He'd thought the view from his apartment was spectacular, but Laura's corner apartment had windows on two sides, and the side that faced along the colony's spin axis had an unobstructed view all the way down its length. Through the haze of distance Teigh could see the polar ice forming a bull's-eye in the middle of the endcap, melting at the edges to form the streams that ran outward from the center to the rim of the cylinder that was Spacehome. The three windows running the colony's length were strips of blue radiating from the pole, the blue fading to white overhead where the Sun's brilliance dominated the sky.

This would be a coveted apartment, he realized. He wondered who Laura Morrison was to have it. The mayor's mother? But certainly the mayor's mother would know about *Daedalus*.

"You like the view?" she asked.

"Yes, very much."

"David did, too. He was my husband."

Suddenly it all clicked into place. "David Morrison? The architect?"

Laura turned, surprised. "You knew him?"

"No," Teigh said. "But I wish I had. Everyone on the *Daedalus* project wishes so too. We could have used his genius in designing the ship."

She pretended no false modesty. "Ah. Yes, maybe so. He'd have liked that." She brought the two cups to the table and sat down beside him. "He was always pushing for a starship. Even building Spacehome wasn't enough. He wanted the stars."

"Then I wish he'd lived to see *Daedalus*."

Laura looked out toward the pole. "So do I," she said.

There was an uncomfortable silence. Teigh took a hesitant sip of the tea, wishing he could ask for sugar in it but knowing that he wouldn't, then feeling surprise to taste the honey she had stirred in while he was lost outside.

Laura took a sip of her own and winked at him over the cup. Teigh smiled, somehow embarrassed. This wasn't the sort of behavior he expected from a seventy-year-old woman.

"Yeah," she said, "I do miss the old coot. Hard as hell to live with, but I loved him anyway."

Teigh had read biographies of David Morrison, but none of them had portrayed him as being particularly hard to live with. But then none of his biographers had had to live with him, either.

"What was he like?" he asked.

With a fond shake of her head Laura said, "Oh, well, he was a real space

6

nut. One-track mind. 'Get our race into space' and 'Stay alive in L-5' and all that. When we first met he wouldn't take me out on a date unless I joined the L-5 Society. I didn't even know what the L-5 Society *was*, but David was so magnetic I went ahead and joined just to be with him. We were still in college then."

She took another sip of tea and gazed out over the colony. "He was always pushing. Made me take astronomy classes. Said that a person who couldn't find Cassiopeia without a map was as bad as someone who couldn't read. What do you think? Can you find Cassiopeia?"

Teigh felt the color rising in his ears. "Uh..."

"Shame on you. And you on the crew of a starship. Where are you taking it? Not Cassiopeia, I hope."

Her grin was contagious. "Nothing so ambitious," he said. "We're going to Alpha Centauri first. It'll take us about twenty years just to get that far."

Laura sighed. "You're a lot like David. He wasn't afraid of big projects either."

Teigh blushed again. Being compared to his personal hero—by his hero's wife, no less—was embarrassing. He stuttered a moment in search of something to say, then managed, "You must not be either. To come up here to live while they were still building it."

"Hah. No. I was terrified. But David was coming whether I did or not, so I didn't have much choice. I spent most of the first few months being sick, and then I got pregnant with Michael and spent *another* few months sick, but I guess you get used to anything after a while."

"I guess that's what it means to be a pioneer."

Laura said something that sounded like "Hrumph," and drained her teacup.

Teigh wasn't sure how to take that. He decided that a change of subject was probably safest, so he said, "What were you studying in college before you met David?"

"English literature," Laura said with a sudden smile. "Had my nose buried in a book almost all the time. I was going to be the greatest poet since Shakespeare, but I had to read everything that'd been written first, you know, and I never finished doing that. Do you like poetry?"

"What I've read of it," Teigh admitted. "I didn't have a whole lot of time for reading it in school, though. Just what we got in Freshman English."

"Ah, yes. 'In the room the women come and go/ Talking of Michelangelo.' T.S. Eliot. Remember him?"

Her words had loosed a tumble of images in his mind. "Yes! Yes, I do! *The Ballad of J. Edgar Prunecoat* or something like that, isn't it?"

"*The Love Song of J. Alfred Prufrock*," Laura said, laughing. "'Let us go then, you and I/ When the evening is spread out against the sky —' I think everybody gets that one. You know, I was going to be a teacher once, too."

"You were? Why didn't you?"

She looked away at the colony. "Oh, well, you know. David had his project, and we were moving all over those first years. And then we moved up here and I had the family to look after and it just never seemed to come together." She shook her head. "I don't even read as much as I used to anymore."

"Why not?"

Laura looked at Teigh as if she were sizing him up before she imparted a secret, then finally said, "'I grow old...I grow old...I shall wear the bottoms of my trousers rolled.'" She shrugged. "Same poem. It's hard for me to get to the library sometimes. Arthritis, tendonitis, you know. All the old-people stuff. You caught me on one of my good days."

"Can't you just download books onto your computer?"

Laura looked embarrassed. "I never could get the hang of working one of those things."

"I could show you. It's really easy."

She was definitely blushing now. "No," she said. "I don't get along too well with gadgets. Anything with buttons on it. Besides, there's nothing like having a real book in your hand when you're reading."

"I suppose not," said Teigh, who had never read a book on anything *but* a screen. He had a sudden thought. "How do you get your mail if you don't use a computer?"

"I go to the post office," Laura said in the voice a person uses to answer a dumb question, but her laugh was a quiet, little-girl sort of a laugh that carried no contempt. "On my way to the library. My grandkids think I'm crazy too," she added, "but they humor me. They're scattered out all over the solar system. I get letters from Ganymede and Vesta and Ceres all the time, but they come by regular mail, on paper."

More likely the post office printed them out for her from the digital transmission, Teigh thought, but he supposed they *could* still send letters by ship. People sent packages, after all. But it cost a fortune, even shuttling up from Earth. He shook his head. If Laura would learn to run a computer she could save herself a lot of trouble and a lot of money too. He didn't doubt that she could; she'd shown plenty of facility with buttons when she used the microwave.

But it didn't sound like she was interested. Teigh shrugged. "Everybody's got their own way of doing things," he said. "I'm certainly not the one to say what's crazy and what isn't." He finished his tea and set the cup on the table, scooped up the kitten in his hands, and said, "I should get back to unpacking. I've got to dig down as far as my socks before I go to work tomorrow. Thank you for the tea, and the lap-warmer."

"Any time." Laura stood and took the kitten from him, and followed him to the door. "Come back and visit again," she said.

"I will." Teigh stopped at the door to look at something he had missed on the way in: a fish bowl shaped like a pressure suit helmet. He bent down for a closer look, then laughed in surprise. It *was* a helmet. He looked up at Laura and asked, "What do you do for a suit when you go outside?"

"I haven't gone outside since David died," she replied. "There hasn't seemed much point."

"Oh." He stepped into the hall. "Well, maybe I can take you to see the ship sometime. And you can show me Cassiopeia."

She grinned. "Maybe so. We'll see."

As he unpacked, he thought about Laura and her husband. David had died almost twenty years ago in a construction accident, before Spacehome had been completed, but he had been the driving force behind it even after he was gone. It had been his plans that got the public funding for the project in the first place—his incredibly detailed plans that showed not just a cylinder with houses and forests and farms in it, but just where the houses and forests and farms ought to go and how to get them there. He had designed the entire colony right down to the last rivet and rock; he had written the manual on living in space, and then he had sold it to the world.

It was hard to imagine his wife as the kind of person who couldn't—or wouldn't—work a computer, but Teigh supposed it was just another sign of David Morrison's genius that he could build a high-tech world with room enough in it for someone like her. Maybe she was part of the reason why Spacehome was so liveable. She was a reminder that people were individuals and wouldn't all fit the same mold. She provided the human touch to David's technical expertise. Teigh would have to remember her while he helped design *Daedalus*'s lifesystem.

The starship was going together in a completely different way than the colony had. With Spacehome they had had the complete plans from the start, but *Deadalus*'s designers were barely a jump ahead of the builders. It was a reflection of the changing times; people were more impatient to get into space now that the first efforts had proved so successful, but the lack of an acknowledged genius for a designer was also part of the reason. Nobody had yet come up with a complete set of plans that somebody else couldn't tweak into a slightly better configuration. And now here was Teigh to add his own twist to the developing plans. Well, he thought, thanks to Laura he might at least have a direction to twist them.

The next few months were the most intense in his life. The problem of designing a closed environment that people could live in for twenty years was bigger than anything he had ever worked on before, and he found himself immersed in it from the start. He dreamed it at night and he lived it during the day, and slowly a picture began to emerge. It was a picture of mutability, gained from studying David's plans for the colony and noticing the changes that had been made in it since. In twenty years any lifesystem would become boring, so the answer to that was to make it changeable. Spacehome was by its very nature changeable and always changing; new housing replaced old, trees grew and forests expanded, and living styles from Earth and the outer colonies swept through in constant waves of variation. That wasn't as easy to do on a starship, but Teigh thought it might be possible. If the building materials were modular and if the modules were small enough to move around easily, then the crew could conceivably rebuild the entire lifesystem in transit, and they could do it as many times as they liked. The trick was not so much in designing the finished product, since there would be no true finished product, but in designing what the building blocks would look like and how they would go together.

Teigh took the idea to Laura after he had worked it out. He had visited with her a few times since their first meeting, and he had learned to value her quick insight into human nature. This time she listened to his explanation of building materials and mutable living quarters and looked at his drawings, and when he was done she said simply, "Not everybody will want to change things around."

"That's true," he said. "That's the beauty of it. If you like what you're living in then there's no reason why you have to change it, but the opportunity is always there. Just knowing that you *can* change it if you get bored will probably be enough to keep most people happy."

Laura nodded. "You know, this whole idea of yours sounds like something David showed me once. I'd forgotten all about it until now."

"He did a starship design?" Teigh had never heard of a David Morrison starship plan. Nor had anybody else, he was sure. But who was to say what David had worked on in his spare time? And if he had...

He felt like the carpenter who uncovers a fresco by one of the Old Masters behind a false ceiling. A David Morrison starship design!

"Do you think you could find it?"

"Me?" Laura said. "Hah. Not in a million years. It's on his computer. But you're welcome to give it a try if you want."

"I'd—" He swallowed. He couldn't speak.

"Come on, you said yourself that computers are easy."

"It's—" Teigh managed. "It's—that's—I mean, I'd be honored."

"Oh, cut that out. Next you'll be building monuments. Like as not my memory is playing me false and there's nothing there at all anyway." She got up and led the way into the study.

In the back of his mind Teigh still expected to find a shrine to the brilliant architect, kept exactly as David had left it the day he died and dusted carefully every day by his grieving widow, but when Laura flicked on the light that illusion fled with the darkness. Books and papers lay stacked on every horizontal surface, a blueprint that had been taped to the wall had come loose on one corner and dangled outward, and a stack of empty boxes threatened to fall over onto the desk. Laura gave them a shove in the other direction and waved at the computer sitting to the side of the desk. It was covered with dust, disturbed only by the footprints of kittens.

"Have at it," she said.

Some of Teigh's nervousness disappeared when he saw the computer. It was at least twenty-five years old, but he recognized it just the same. It had been an incredible machine for its time, the one that had reconciled all the other so-called "standards" into a single true standard that was still in use. He would be able to run it, provided it still worked.

He blew off the dust and sat down in front of it, fumbled for the power switch, and turned it on. The fountain of sparks he had half expected didn't happen; instead he got the normal sign-on message and a menu of choices. One of them was a directory, a listing of all the files in storage. Teigh chose that, and file names began to scroll onto the screen.

Ten minutes later he had it. There was an entire subdirectory entitled "starship" filled with drawings and specifications for not only the lifesystem but almost every other aspect of the ship as well. Teigh brought up one of the files on the lifesystem, wondering how close he had come to David's conception of it, and received his second shock of the day. The plans were almost identical to his. The only difference was in the degree of detail; David had once again put in every rivet and bolt.

"I can't believe it," Teigh said. "He did this twenty years ago and it's still better than anything we've come up with since."

"David understood how things work, and how people work," Laura said. "Time doesn't affect that."

Teigh nodded. "How do you feel about us using these plans?" he asked. "Would you let me show them to the design group?"

Laura thought about it a moment, then shrugged. "Why not? That's what he made them for, to use. If they'll do you some good, then you're welcome to them."

"More good than you can imagine," Teigh said. It was true. It would mean giving up the credit for the design, but having David Morrison's name on the plans would effectively cement them into place. They could get on with the job of building the ship instead of constantly changing the details, and the crew who flew in it would start the trip knowing that the design was right. Their confidence in it would go a long way toward making it work.

He sat with his hands resting lightly on the keyboard, marvelling at how much information had been locked up behind it all this time. He supposed this was how Laura felt when she blew the dust off a book and opened it for the first time in years. On impulse he said, "Why don't I show you how to get into the library with this?"

Laura's reaction was too immediate to be thought out. "No, I'm too old to be learning how to run one of these things."

"Nonsense," Teigh said. "If you can run a telephone you can run a computer. Watch." Explaining what he did at every point along the way, he returned to the opening screen, loaded the communications program, and accessed the colony library, all by picking options off menus. The library computer gave him another menu of choices, from which he picked the poetry index, and the author index under that.

"Okay," he said. "We're there. What do you want to read?"

Laura looked flustered. "I don't know. I usually just browse until I find something interesting."

"Easily done," Teigh said. He picked the first name off the index — Alan Aaron — and got another menu of titles. He picked the first title, and the first page of *After Gazing at Ganymede* scrolled onto the screen.

Laura leaned forward to read it, but after a few lines she straightened and said, "Hrumph. Doggerel."

Teigh laughed. "I'm afraid I wouldn't know the difference."

"No? Here, I'll show you." She turned away as if to go after a book, then stopped and turned back. "What am I doing? You've got the whole library right there. Okay, see if you can find Pope in there. Alexander Pope, his *Essay on Criticism*."

Teigh did, and within seconds was presented with the lines:

'Tis hard to say if greater want of skill

Appear in writing or in judging ill....

"There," Laura said. "Read that. He talks mostly about critics, but he's got a lot to say about good poetry, and the *Essay* is good poetry in itself. See here, this is called a couplet, and it's in iambic pentameter..."

Hours later, printouts of Laura's favorite poems in hand, Teigh made his way back to his apartment. He sat up well into the night reading them, laughing in delight at the crisp imagery and humor in her choices. He'd used to think that poetry was all stiff and formal and hard to follow, but not after reading Shakespeare's sonnets. Some of it was — he was going to have to read five or six more times through the *Essay on Criticism* before he could truly say he understood it, but he had to admit there was a certain attraction even to the difficult stuff.

He grinned when he realized what had happened. He had tried to get Laura excited about computers, and instead she had gotten him excited about poetry.

He stopped by the next afternoon to copy the starship files off of David's computer. Afterward, as he and Laura sat at the kitchen table over tea, he said, "You ought to go ahead and go into teaching. You're good at it."

Laura looked up at him in surprise. "Me? Hah. I've seen lots of seventy-year-old English instructors, but they were all on the way out, not in."

Teigh shook his head. "The best teacher I ever had was in her eighties. Late eighties. She was there because she liked what she was doing, and she made everybody in her classes like it too. You've got that same knack; you shouldn't waste it."

"No," Laura said, "I'd have to go back to school myself, get a teaching certificate, learn what's being *taught* these days—no, it's too late for all that, even if I wanted to."

"It's not too late. People live longer now than they used to, you included. You've got plenty of time to do anything you want." He paused, thinking, then said, "Remember J. Alfred Prufrock? I read about him again last night. He didn't act when he had the chance and he regretted it the rest of his life. That's kind of silly, don't you think? If you've got time to regret not doing something, then you've got time to go back and do it."

Laura looked out toward the axis, where a group of pedal planes were spiraling around one another in a near-weightless aerial dogfight. After a time Teigh realized she wasn't going to answer.

"Sorry," he said. "I guess it's none of my business."

She turned back to face him and said, "Yes it is. You're a friend, and friends are entitled to worry about each other. But remember, not everybody wants to change. Some of us are comfortable just the way we are."

Teigh nodded. "Point taken," he said. But at the same time he was thinking *but there's a difference between comfort and complacence.*

The lifesystem project was taking up even more of Teigh's time now that they had started construction on it, but he still made a point of coming

14

to visit Laura at least twice a week. He showed her a couple more times how to turn on the computer and call up books from the library and how to print them out on paper if she still wanted to read them that way, but even though she learned how he never saw any evidence that she had done it on her own.

It bothered him. He supposed everyone had the right to live their life the way they wanted to, but at the same time it seemed such a waste for her to sit around in her apartment with her cats and her plants and do nothing. She still had a good thirty years left—more if she would stay active—but it was obvious she'd already given up and was just watching herself grow old.

He tried to get her out more, going with her to the library since she wouldn't use the computer and taking her shopping when she felt like going and even taking her on the gondola around the curve of the colony on one particularly adventurous day. She seemed genuinely happy to get out, and that reinforced Teigh's conviction that even though she said she didn't want it, what she really needed was a change in scenery.

"You know," he said one day while he fended off a triple assault from the now-adolescent kittens, "you ought to come with us to Alpha Centauri."

Laura looked at him as if he'd suggested something obscene. "Me, on a starship? Forget it."

"No, I'm serious. The crew selection committee would jump at the chance to bring you along."

"What would they want with an old lady? Starships are for young people."

"Starships are for everybody. The human race isn't all under thirty, and it'd be a mistake to make a starship crew that way. They'd drive each other nuts."

"So you need a few coots and geezers to keep you all sane. Makes tons of sense to me."

Teigh thought of his pine root that he carried with him from apartment to apartment, how simply looking at its gnarled, aged branches could calm him down after a particularly hectic day, but he could think of no way to tell Laura about it without embarrassing them both. So he simply said, "It's true. We need interesting people no matter how old they are. You should apply for the crew."

Laura shook her head. "There's something my grandmother used to say; she was talking about airplanes, but it still applies. She said 'I want to keep my feet right on the old terra firma, and the more firma the less terra.' That's me too."

"You came here, to Spacehome," Teigh pointed out. "This isn't really what I'd call terra firma."

"David built it," she said, as if that ended the discussion.

"We're using his design on the ship too."

"Hrumph."

"At least come have a look at it. Remember, you've still got to show me Cassiopeia, too."

She smiled. "Maybe," she said. "Maybe I will."

"Today?"

"No."

"Oh come on. It's a good day for a trip outside."

"No, really, I—"

Teigh remembered what she was using for a fish bowl and said, "Don't worry about the goldfish. We can rent you a suit."

Laura laughed and shook her head. Without a word she got up and went into the living room for the helmet, brought it back, and pulled out the plastic bag that held the fish. "I'm an eccentric old coot," she said, "but I'm not about to ruin my spacesuit. All right. Show me your starship."

"That's the spirit," Teigh said, standing.

Laura dug the rest of her suit out of a closet and blew the dust off of it, checked to make sure she could still fit into it, and pronounced herself ready. They had to stop on the way to the airlock to fill her air tanks and put a new battery in the backpack, and as a precaution Teigh had the attendant pressure test the suit to two atmospheres while he was at it. It passed the test, and fifteen minutes later they were at the airlock, Teigh climbing into his own suit that he kept there.

"How do you feel?" he asked for about the tenth time. The colony's two main airlocks were at either end, at the center of the spin axis where someone going outside wouldn't be flung out into space, and he was concerned about her reaction to zero-gee.

She held out her hands thumbs up, and over the suit radio said, "Fine, for a terrified old lady. Let's hit vacuum before I decide to go back home and knit something instead."

"All right, here we go." Teigh checked the seals on both suits one last time, led the way into the airlock, and pressed the cycle button. Their suits stiffened with the drop in pressure, and the outer door opened to space.

"Take my hand," he said.

Laura did, and he led her out onto the surface of the colony. He could hear her breathing hard, but after a minute or so she said, "Hah. Hasn't changed much. Where's this ship of yours?"

Teigh smiled. She'd be all right. "Straight out," he said, pointing overhead.

She leaned back, tilting her head back still more, and said, "Oh. Doesn't look like much from here."

"It's twenty kilometers out. We'll take a car over."

"Okay. Lead on."

The cars were kept in a garage beside the airlock; Teigh checked one out and helped Laura inside, then set its autopilot for the starship and settled back for the five-minute trip. "So," he said, "where's Cassiopeia?"

Laura leaned forward and looked out the front windows for a minute, then turned to the side. "Got to be able to find the dipper first," she said. "What have they done with it? Not there; that's Sagittarius. Hah, that's a clue. Sagittarius there puts the dipper...there. Got it." She pointed out Teigh's window. "See it?"

"The *big* dipper?"

"Right. Now you follow the pointer stars north, past Polaris, right on over to—" There was a pop like a bursting balloon, and Laura's surprised exclamation was drowned out in the hiss of escaping air.

Teigh could see the blowout in her suit where the underarm seam had ripped when she stretched it to point. Pressure testing hadn't caught the weakness there. He felt panic closing in at the sight, but it receded when he remembered where they were. The car had its own air.

"Hold your arm tight to your side!" he said as he searched for the car's pressure control. Laura couldn't have heard him over the howl of air rushing through her suit, but she didn't need to be told to plug the leak. She pinned the arm down and doubled over to the side.

The car's controls seemed a sudden blur of switches and dials to Teigh. He had gotten a full briefing on them all when he had first come up to the colony, and he had passed his flying test with ease, but for the quick trips

17

back and forth to the ship he had never pressurized the cabin and now, months later, he had forgotten how to do it. He heard the hiss of Laura's air dwindling as her suit tanks bled dry, and still he hadn't found the right control. Fighting panic, he began to read the labels one by one and finally found the right switch, then almost broke it off in his haste to flip it on.

Air rushed into the car. Teigh reached out and pulled off Laura's helmet, but she wasn't breathing and there was blood on her lips.

He felt the gentle tug as the forward rockets fired to slow the car for docking with the starship. Looking up he saw its familiar shape growing nearer, and he switched his suit radio to the emergency channel and shouted, "Blowout! I've got someone with a suit blowout. Help me!"

"Where are you?" a calm voice asked.

"Coming in in a car. I've got the cabin pressurized now, but she was in vacuum for a while, and she's not breathing."

"I'm opening the emergency lock. Is your car on autopilot?"

"Yes."

"Switch to remote. The red switch on the upper right corner of the—"

"Got it."

"Hang on," the voice said, and at the same time the car's thrust doubled and it swung around past the aft of the ship and curved in toward a still-widening rectangle of light. The car shot in through the lock, still decelerating, the door slammed shut behind it, and within seconds people were pulling Laura out and ripping off the rest of her suit.

Teigh watched helplessly while the medics forced air into her lungs and tried to stimulate her heart into beating again, getting nothing, nothing, nothing...and then a faint beat that faltered and stopped again. More breathing and pushing on the chest and another heartbeat, this one holding for a while longer before it stopped. Again, this time with pure oxygen.

At last Laura was breathing on her own; a horrible, bubbling breathing that made Teigh sick to listen to it, but she was alive again.

As the medics carried her into the ship, one of them turned to Teigh. "Are you all right?"

He managed to nod.

"She's going to make it. You did good. She's lucky you were there."

Teigh shook his head. He found his voice and said, "Not so. If she was lucky she wouldn't have met me. Wouldn't have had some stupid kid dragging her around doing things she didn't want to do in the first place. I damn near got her killed."

He told her the same thing when they let him in to see her a few hours later. She was inside an oxygen bubble and her voice was barely a whisper, but her response was clear all the same. "Wrong. My suit blew because...it was too damned old...but that doesn't mean *I* am. I used to think I was, but I...had a lot of time to think about it...while my life flashed in front of me. You were right, it'd be silly...to die in a rocking chair. I'd rather go out in the middle...of something, like David did."

"You—" *almost did,* No. Wrong thing to say. Instead he said, "You're still invited on the trip to Alpha Centauri."

Laura was silent for a long time, so long that Teigh thought she had fallen asleep with her eyes open, but just as he was about to get up she nodded once and said, "So when do we leave?"

INTRODUCTION TO

SCHRÖDINGER'S LIFEBOAT

Einstein hated the paradoxes inherent in quantum physics. I love them. There's no richer source of ideas than the points where logic begins to break down and the universe starts misbehaving. And there might be some very practical applications for that odd behavior, too....

SCHRÖDINGER'S LIFEBOAT

The shrieking of alarms had quieted, but the crisis was not yet over. While computer-guided robots repaired the last of the damage left by the errant chunk of interplanetary debris, the four crewmembers of the astrophysical observation ship *Sagan* sat in the conference room and discussed their options.

"It's the classic lifeboat question," Aletha, the expedition leader, said. "Even accounting for reduced usage while asleep, we've only got air enough for two, but we've got four bodies using it. If any of us are going to make it back to base, two of us will have to stop breathing."

Tani, the quantum physicist, said, "We'll have to draw straws. Losers go out the airlock."

Gordon, the gravitational physicist, shook his head. "I don't think I could do that peacefully. If I drew a short straw, you'd have to kill me, and I warn you now, I'd struggle."

Aletha nodded. "We're scientists; we should be able to come up with a better system than that. Something humane, so the winners needn't kill the losers, and the losers needn't kill themselves, either."

"Who does the job, then?" asked Gordon.

"Chance," said Kharil, the astrophysicist.

His three crewmates looked at him in puzzlement. "Chance," he repeated. "A random event, triggering poison gas into a sleep chamber. We all take enough sleeping pills to put us under, and we leave the computer

23

set to target each sleep chamber in turn, say once every millisecond or so, while also sampling a radiation counter each time. With a normal background count it would take thousands of cycles before it detected an emitted particle. When it does, it triggers the gas in whatever chamber it's pointing to at the time. After it's gassed two of us, it stops sampling and the other two survive the trip."

There was a long silence while the other three crewmembers considered his plan. Finally Tani spoke. "We can do better than that. If we're careful, we can set it up so there's a fifty-fifty chance we all survive. Of course the drawback is there's a fifty-fifty chance we all die, but my way it's all one way or the other. Nobody has to die so the others can live."

"How can we do that?" Gordon asked. "We don't have the air to keep us all alive."

"No," Tani said, "but we do have the air to keep us all *half* alive. Now, here's the plan...."

The rescue crew boarding the research craft were prepared to find signs of a struggle. From the report they received before the telemetry had mysteriously stopped, they knew that the ship was short of air, and from human experience gained over thousands of sea and space accidents they knew what would most likely occur in such a situation. Therefore they were surprised to find all four crewmembers still alive, sleeping peacefully in their sealed chambers.

The poison gas canister hooked into the air system, but not opened, puzzled them still further. The sleeping drugs in the crewmembers' bloodstreams—enough to ensure that they slept until well beyond rescue but not enough to kill any of them—were also a puzzle. It wasn't until they cleaned the drug from Tani's system and woke her that she was able to enlighten them.

"It's Schrödinger's paradox," she explained, grinning wide and pinching herself to be sure she was really alive. "According to quantum theory, a single quantum event, like a radioactive atom's decay, is unpredictable. It's actually a probability wave, existing in both its possible states simultaneously until someone observes it and forces it to be one or the other. If you set up a situation in which a macroscopic event is tied to the quantum event, then the macroscopic event is indeterminate as well.

Schrödinger used a cat in his thought experiment; we used ourselves."

"What does that have to do with the poison gas and the sleeping pills?" one of the rescuers asked.

"Simple. We rigged the poison gas to kill us all if the computer detected a decay product in a radioactive sample. We chose the sampling time so it would have a fifty-fifty chance of finding one. The sleeping pills were to keep *us* from knowing which it had done and thus determining the state of the experiment too early. And that's why we shut off the telemetry: so *you* wouldn't know which way it went either."

"I still don't see how that kept you alive," the rescuer said.

"It didn't," Tani explained. "It kept us *half* alive. As long as nobody made an observation, we were in an indeterminate state. Half dead, half alive. That meant we were using only half the air we normally needed. When you boarded the ship you forced the universe to make a choice between states, and here we are."

Another member of the rescue squad entered the room, carrying a yellow cat in his arms. The cat gave a plaintive yowl when it saw Tani.

"Ginger!" she exclaimed. "We forgot all about you! Oh, poor thing; you must be half starved."

INTRODUCTION TO

DÉJÀ VIEW

I've never understood life insurance. You pay someone a lot of money, and they pay you back after you die. It seems to me you should get something a little more useful for your money, like protection from accidents. Life *assurance* rather than *insurance*. The only way to do that reliably, however, is to look at tomorrow's obituaries.

Time travel stories are a rich subgenre within science fiction. The concept quickly leads to paradoxes, and getting around them without introducing half a dozen more is a fun challenge. I wanted to see if I could have a character actually use a paradox to solve a problem, and once I started I realized that everybody in the story has their own problem. Of course, one person's problem is another's solution, and vice-versa.

Déjà View

"I think I'll create a new universe," George Fernwood announced as he selected a yellow push-pin to tack the obituary list onto the bulletin board. He stuck it carefully through the "d" on the "Amalgamated Mutual Life" letterhead and stood back to compare the board against the picture of it in his hand. The picture showed the same typewritten sheet of paper hanging at the same angle from the same spot on the otherwise blank board, but in it the pin stuck through the "d" was distinctly red.

He laughed a little maniacal laugh as he seated the pin firmly into the cork. "And thus do we loose Chaos upon the mortal world!" he said to the empty room.

That done, he seated himself at his desk and began sifting through the day's policies.

He had three adjustments to make today. Two were the usual traffic accidents, but the third one looked interesting. Tomorrow afternoon, while attending the President's press conference in the roof garden atop the Hanford Tower, his client had tripped—would trip—while trying to take a photograph and fall thirty stories to his death. Not your everyday sort of accident. George would enjoy watching the look on the client's face when he told him about it.

But he didn't suppose he should show him the pictures.

Barret, the city's Big Brother and George's link to the future, had sent pictures of the body along with the morning's obit list. He usually didn't do that, but George guessed with the President there he had naturally been watching the building, so it was a simple thing for him to zoom in for a look over the side when the client took his dive. The picture had been waiting for him on the phone screen when he arrived for work, along with a message.

"Take care of this one first," Barret had said.

Okay, George thought. Anything for a friend. He picked up the phone and dialed the number on the top of the life assurance policy.

After the sixth ring he got the answering machine. He frowned through the message, trying to decide how much to tell. He didn't want to blow the surprise, but he supposed he should still give some kind of warning. When the screen blinked "Recording..." at him he cleared his throat and said, "Hi. George Fernwood, Amalgamated Mutual Life. Your policy just paid off. I need you to call me as soon as possible to discuss the details, but I will advise you now to cancel your plans for President Sandoval's press conference tomorrow. It turns out not to be such a good idea. Call me." He punched in his number for the return call and hung up.

Calvin Tyson stared moodily out through the bars at the featureless white wall. It was built of concrete block. He had always wondered what they used to build jails, and now he knew. It wasn't particularly exciting, that knowledge, but you never knew what sort of information you might be able to use later. Gathering information was his job, and even after last night he couldn't stop noticing the details. The white concrete walls in the jail were just more data for the article that would eventually come of this whole mess.

It had seemed like a good idea at the time. Get himself arrested for an un-crime, get run through the system, then use that experience as the basis for another scathing article about the impending police state. Now, after a night in jail, it didn't seem quite such a bright idea. His first-hand experience had left him educated, oh yes. More so than he had ever expected or wanted. For the first time in his life, he had come face to face with Evil.

It wasn't the little man with the cherubic face and the terrified whine, nor the four who had beaten him until he couldn't even move, nor even the jailor who had kicked him into the cell with the words, "Here's a baby lover for you, boys." The evil was rooted more deeply than that, and as Calvin had cowered on his cot listening to the man screech, "I didn't do it! But I didn't do anything!" and the others mutter, "Yeah, but you were *gonna* do it," he had realized just where the source of it lay.

He had brushed with it himself. Not so directly as the wounded man in the corner, but he had felt its touch. His crime—failure to appear on a court summons—was now on his record. His employer was legally bound to withhold his pay for the day he had spent in jail, and he knew before he even tried it that he would be denied appeal, so he couldn't even take satisfaction in tying up the court system. No, he had only managed to tie up his own time, and scare himself to boot.

And like the child molester, all he had left to do was commit the crime.

Barret glanced nervously at the wall clock. Fifteen after eleven. Plenty of time for Fernwood to have taken care of Tyson. Yet the scene in the Déjà View still showed Tyson going over the edge, which meant that he hadn't adjusted the policy yet. Barret wished he would hurry up; Tyson's death was spoiling his view of the future.

He reached for the phone and punched in Fernwood's number.

Fernwood caught it on the first ring. "Amalgamated Mutual. Hi Barret. How're you going to be doing?"

"Ha. Lousy. What's holding up the adjustment on Calvin Tyson? He's still dead."

Fernwood shook his head. "He wasn't in when I called him. I left a message a couple hours ago, but he evidently hasn't gotten back yet."

"Great. He's messing up my seeing."

"Beg your pardon?"

"I can't see past his death. Oh, I can see all right, but anything after the change that you're going to introduce when you save him is a false future. It doesn't do me any good."

"I don't follow you."

Barret sighed. "It's simple. The moment Tyson changes his mind about going to the press conference—or even decides to stay away from the edge of the building—the future will change to account for it, and the Déjà View will show the new reality. But until then I'm as good as blind beyond the point of change. That's why I told you to take care of him first."

"Oh." Fernwood nodded. "Well, it's still a day away. Don't worry. He'll get the message soon enough."

"Don't worry, he says. George, this is the President's time line we're talking about here. I'm supposed to be watching for trouble and your man is a walking random factor right in the middle of the field. I want you to get him straightened out and I want you to do it soon, all right?"

Fernwood shrugged. "All right. I'll try to catch up with him. But hey, I wanted to tell you something. You know the other clients on this morning's list? One was a guy due to kick it tomorrow on the highway, way the hell out in Colorado. When I called him he said I was nuts. He didn't have any plans to go out of town, much less Colorado. He refused to pay the deductible on his policy."

"He did?"

"He did. I did some checking and found that an agency in Denver adjusted a policy on his mother yesterday afternoon. That was why he was going out there, to her funeral. I feel like sending them a bill for half the deductible on *her* policy instead. If they hadn't adjusted hers, I'd have made it on mine."

Barret laughed. "The first alternate-future lawsuit. I knew it would happen sooner or later."

Fernwood smiled. "Hey, I'm kidding. It's not that big a deal. I just thought it was kind of strange, their adjustment saving both the mother and the kid like that."

"You might as well get used to it," Barret said. "Every time somebody makes a change, the effects spread out. Everybody they come in contact with that they wouldn't have before is changed, and everybody *they* come in contact with is changed, and so on until eventually the whole world is different."

"I'm glad it's you keeping track of it and not me."

"I bet you are. Every time I look in the path of a change I see the wrong future until the change works its way past where I'm looking. Since there's only three Déjà Views on the coast so far we haven't had too many people making changes, but when more people start using them the seeing's going to be terrible. Even if we keep them restricted to just the police departments, we're going to have a reliability of about ten minutes."

Fernwood blinked. "I hadn't thought of that. What happens then?"

"Déjà Viewing becomes useless. Don't sweat it; they'll pass laws before then. But you'll probably have to work with less than a day's advance notice before they do." Barret shook his head. "No more posting obituaries on the bulletin board for me to peep. You'll have to set up a faster system than that."

"Wonderful." Fernwood stared off into space a moment. "I, uh, I guess I should put a red push-pin back in the board."

"What?"

He described what he had done with the yellow push-pin that morning. "I wanted to see what would happen. I thought I would split the timeline in two or something, but if it screws up your seeing, I guess I shouldn't do it. What's funny?"

Barret's chuckle went on for an embarrassingly long time. "You're great, George. Whoo—wonderful! You've been duplicating the list I send over every day?"

"Yes," Fernwood said coldly. "Shouldn't I?"

"It doesn't matter. Well, it does really, but so far we've just been lucky. Nothing we've done has caused an additional death. But George, you've got to make up a new list every day, based on real up-to-the-minute deaths. Somebody could slip through the cracks on you if you don't. Reality's had two days to change on us since I peeped that list you tacked up today."

"But if I don't put up the same list, then where does this picture come from?" Fernwood pulled open his desk drawer and dug out the photo he had printed off his phone screen two mornings ago, the one he had used to prepare today's list.

"It's a picture of an alternate reality. One that disappeared when you stepped in to change it. It's an artifact from nowhere, if you want to think of it that way."

Fernwood looked still more puzzled. "What if I don't put up a list at all?"

"To the people you've already saved, nothing. The past is solid; whatever you've done there is done. Today exists the way it does only because you did what you did yesterday and the day before. But if somebody else needs saving between the time I View the list and now, then you'd better put their name up, or they won't get saved."

"If the past is solid, what difference would it make? They're already dead."

"True. But as long as you *agree* to put their name on the board, then I can look ahead and see what you would have done and warn you before you have to. We're dealing with free will here. If you really intend to list every client death when it happens, then I can look ahead and see which ones you *would* list if we didn't change anything. Then we make the change and you don't have to make a list. But it's vital that you *intend* to make one whenever you have to. You follow?"

"Barely. You're saying that I could completely leave off putting up lists, as long as I agree to put one up whenever someone really dies on me?"

"Right. Barring catastrophe, like a change that reveals another death too late to do anything about it, you shouldn't ever have to list a name, but you have to intend to do it or I'll never be able to look into a future where you do. But look, I didn't call to discuss theory. I need Tyson taken care of right away."

Fernwood smiled again. "Hey, I *intend* to find Tyson as soon as I can. So, shouldn't your Déjà View show you that future no matter when I actually do it?"

Barret thought about it, frowning. "It should, but it isn't. Maybe you aren't intending to be serious enough about it."

"All right, I get the hint. I'll track him down."

"Thanks. Bye." Barret hung up and leaned back to look in the View screen. It still showed Tyson going over the edge. But Fernwood was right; his intention to warn him should have been enough to change the timetrack around. That it didn't was significant, but Barret didn't know just how.

There were times, he thought, when he wished that the Déjà View had never been invented.

The date on the speeding ticket said Thursday at two o'clock. At the appointed time the jailor unlocked Calvin's cell and led him from the jail through the labyrinth of City Hall to the courtroom, where he waited on a hard wooden bench for forty-five minutes before the bailiff called his case.

The judge looked up briefly from his copy of the docket and said, "The charge is speeding, eighty-seven miles per hour in a seventy zone. How do you plead?"

Calvin could hardly believe what he'd heard. He said, "What? I thought it was failure to appear."

"That matter has already been taken care of. You have been sentenced to one day in prison, which you have already served."

"But the ticket said two o'clock. I was here at two o'clock. I've appeared. I'm innocent!"

"You appeared under duress, Mr. Tyson. Routine prognostication indicated that you would not have been here had not the state compelled you to be so. Hence your claim that you are here now has no bearing on that case."

Calvin shook his head angrily. "How can it have no bearing? That's the whole question!"

"Mr. Tyson, this court has no time to explain the intricacies of prognostic criminal law. It is sufficient to note that before your arrest you did not intend to appear before this court, nor did you intend to pay the appearance bond customarily referred to as the 'fine' for your speeding infraction. Thus you were arrested and detained for trial. Now as to the speeding charge; how do you plead?"

"Now wait just a damned minute. You're saying I don't even get a trial for the failure to appear?"

"No, you don't. Failure to appear is a form of contempt of court, which by its nature is not a triable offense. And if I may say so, you are dangerously close to being in contempt once again. I ask you one final time: to the charge of speeding eighty-seven miles per hour in a seventy zone, how do you plead?"

Calvin took a deep breath. Protesting his innocence wasn't going to help him any. It hadn't helped the child molester. Make that the *potential* child molester. *He* hadn't done anything either. No, the smartest thing Calvin could do would be to get out of here now and cause as little trouble as he could on the way out. This was rapidly becoming much more than the simple tour through the judicial system that he had originally intended. He was right in his fears about the Déjà View—it was an even worse threat to individual freedom than he had thought possible—but he couldn't fight it from here. Maybe he couldn't fight it at all.

He looked at the flag behind the judge, wondering what it stood for now, as he said, "Guilty."

The judge nodded. "A wise decision, Mr. Tyson. The fine is forty-four dollars plus fifteen dollars court costs. You may pay the clerk on your way out." He banged his gavel on the block. "Next case."

Barret fumed under the glare of the camera lights. He hated television. He hated the mindless intrusion of the screen at home, and he hated the intrusion of the cameras at work. He had better things to do than explain on camera how the Déjà View worked to a public that would maybe understand one word in ten.

But the President was coming to town, and she was campaigning hard for the Déjà View, so of course the networks needed footage for the nightly news.

Having Sandoval give her press conference in his district was bad enough, but she had to complicate things by relying completely on the Déjà View for security. It was her way of showing faith in the system, she said. Barret felt that it was her way of giving him an ulcer, but he knew why she was doing it. There was a key case coming up in the Supreme Court over the use of the Déjà View, and the doomsayers who moaned about the loss of personal freedom would have their argument dealt a heavy blow when the nation saw the President standing out in public without a platoon of Special Servicemen around her.

There was one such doomsayer in the gaggle of reporters surrounding him now.

"Doesn't this whole setup constitute an invasion of privacy?" she asked in her concerned-investigative-reporter voice.

"Not so," Barret said. "We only View public events, which as television reporters I'm sure you would agree is not an invasion of privacy, and crimes in progress, which are not protected by privacy laws even if they occur in private areas."

"But how do you spot those crimes, unless you invade someone's privacy to watch for them?"

"Oh, we watch for them, but the watch is kept right here in this building. That bulletin board you see through the glass, to be specific. Crime reports are posted there for the operator to View, and only after the area has been legally declared the scene of a crime can he actually scan for evidence. And only after enough evidence for a conviction has been gathered can officers make the arrest. So you see, your privacy is still protected by law and very much respected by the Déjà View operator." Barret smiled wide.

One of the others said, "What sort of effect does your watching have on the future? Does it alter it in any way?"

Barret looked at him quizzically. "Well, sure. That's the whole point. We spot crimes before they happen in order to prevent them. Of course that changes the future."

"I meant the act of observing in itself. Say you focus on someone walking down the street some time tomorrow. Does just your watching have any effect on that person?"

"Hmm. Theoretically, yes. That's the Heisenberg principle; the act of observation has to affect what's being observed. In simple terms, the Déjà View works by projecting a field into the target area and sensing what bumps into it, so I suppose you could say that it affects its target. But the effect is minuscule."

"Projecting a field for someone to bump into doesn't sound minuscule to me."

"Oh but it is. You're doing it right now yourself. See?" Barret held his hand out toward the spotlight. "Projecting streams of particles to bounce off my hand and travel to your sensing device. Its effect is to raise my skin temperature to an uncomfortable point."

"So what's the Déjà View's effect, then?"

Barret scratched his head. "I don't know for sure. Since it's more of a barrier than a beam, I'd guess that it slows down the atoms it comes in contact with instead of speeding them up. That would make them colder. But don't quote me on that."

Before he even had a chance to breathe, the first reporter asked, "How far into the future can you see?"

Barret shifted gears. "Theoretically there's no limit, but in practice we usually don't scan beyond a few days. It takes more energy the farther we go, and what we see isn't as reliable because of the possibility of changes between now and then." He pointed to a wire cage enclosing a slide control. "But that's what I call the overdrive. Every so often we do long-range scans for things like weather and crop analysis. That sort of thing is hard to change, so it can be Viewed fairly accurately even a year or so ahead."

"Really? You mean you could tell me whether it's going to rain or not on my birthday next year?"

"Certainly." Barret turned to the control panel. "What day is it?"

"July twentieth."

"July twentieth it is." He set the date on the dial. The scene on the monitor blew away into a howl of static until he unlatched the cage over the intensity control and slid it slowly forward. A scene began to resolve out of the static.

"That's the Hanford building," Barret said. "I didn't change the spatial coordinates, so it's still focused there. But it looks like you're going to have a sunny day."

Calvin decided to walk home from the grocery store. He needed to clear out his head after the contortions he had gone through today. Contempt of court. Hah. Contempt was a mild term for what he felt about it all. He could scarcely believe that American justice had come to this in so short a time. Arresting a person before they even committed a crime! All their explanations about what you *would* have done came to nothing in the face of one simple truth: they were prosecuting people for thought-crime.

And it would get worse before it got better. The man who had been beaten for molesting a child he had never even touched was just the beginning.

Calvin could see very clearly now how Sherry Sandoval had orchestrated the entire situation. Putting Déjà Views in high-crime areas so there would be an immediate drop in the crime rate, and so that the first test cases would involve habitual criminals; appointing carefully picked judges to the Supreme Court to ensure that those test cases would go in favor of the new surveillance—oh yes. Her plan was clear enough. Even to allowing life insurance companies access to the future. That was great for her image. Think of the lives saved! And as the Déjà View won greater and greater public acceptance it would be simple to use it to keep track of all sorts of potential criminals, including political dissidents.

Someone should try to get rid of her while it was still possible. If it *was* still possible. It might be too late already. Calvin looked behind him, half expecting to see the police pulling up to arrest him for assassinating the President, but he was alone. He had gotten away with it, this time.

Besides, he wasn't the assassin type. He was a journalist. Killing wasn't his style.

What he needed was a way to discredit the Déjà View. Use it to *commit* a crime, for instance. That would open a few eyes. But how? With the police watching his every move, what could he do? He thought about it, glancing over his shoulder from time to time, the rest of the way home.

He heard the phone ringing as he fitted his key in the lock. It rang twice while he juggled the grocery sack and opened the door, once more as he crossed the room and put the sack on the bar, then the answering machine caught it before he could reach to turn it on.

George Fernwood's face appeared on the screen. "It's urgent that you return my call as soon as you get in," he said, and blanked out.

What was he talking about? Calvin backed the tape up to the beginning and played his first message. He thought about it for a long time, rolling it around in his mind. Then, slowly, he began to smile.

Barret sighed in relief as the camera crew packed up their equipment and left him to do his job again. He set the View on the press conference, but there was Calvin Tyson still going over the edge. He rubbed his temple where he was developing a headache, leaned over, and called Fernwood again.

Fernwood didn't bother with preliminaries. "I just called," he said when he recognized Barret. "Still no answer."

"Can't you get him at work or something?"

"I tried that too. They said that they don't talk with him more than once a week or so. He mostly just sends his articles in by modem. I left a message there too, but I don't think it'll do any more good than the message I left him at home."

"Great. Well keep trying, okay?"

"Right."

Barret hung up and leaned back in his chair. What to do? He couldn't let the President hold the press conference if he couldn't see all the way through to the end of it. Not without security guards, anyway. She wouldn't like that, but he couldn't think of an alternative, short of letting Tyson go on over the edge, and he didn't imagine she'd like that either.

Reluctantly, he called the number he had been given for her chief of security and explained the situation to him. Within minutes he wished he hadn't.

George could hardly believe the face peering out of his phone screen. It looked like—no. Impossible.

"Has anybody ever told you that you have an uncanny resemblance to President Sandoval?" he asked.

She smiled that famous smile and he knew he'd screwed up. But she kept smiling. "Yes, as a matter of fact. Hello. Barret Addison, your Déjà View observer, tells me you have a client due for an accident at my press conference tomorrow."

"Uh...yes, Madam President. That's correct."

"He also tells me you're having trouble getting hold of him."

"That's also correct."

"Well I thought the simplest solution to the whole thing would be to invite you to the press conference. We know he's going to be there, so if you're there too, that should solve the problem, shouldn't it?"

"I suppose it would, yes."

"Glad to hear that. But could I get you to do me a special favor?"

"Certainly, Madam President. What can I do for you?"

"It's nothing, really. Just wait until Mr. Tyson climbs up on the wall to take the picture before you stop him, and make plenty of noise when you do, okay?"

George didn't like the sound of that. He said, "Wouldn't that be cutting it a little close?"

"Oh, but think of the reaction. You'd be a hero. And I'd take it as a personal favor." She flashed her smile again.

He didn't see that he had any choice. "Of course, Madam President. As a favor to you."

"Thank you. I'll see you then." She blinked out.

George stared at the screen a moment longer, the shock slowly fading. He had felt this same feeling once before, just after agreeing to a blind date. That had been a disaster too.

Calvin watched from behind a column as George Fernwood stood before the entrance to the roof garden. Fernwood was sweating a little under his suit, either at the prospect of bungling a preventable death and thus having to pay the death indemnity or at the prospect of having to crash the press conference to prevent it. A couple of Secret Service agents had noticed him and were whispering into their walkie-talkies, but they didn't approach. Evidently someone had vouched for him.

He walked on through and disappeared from sight.

Calvin couldn't believe his luck. He had expected to have to avoid Fernwood right up to the end, but instead Fernwood seemed to be avoiding *him*. He was nearly sure that Fernwood had spotted him in the lobby, but before Calvin could even begin to lose himself in the crowd Fernwood had turned away and pushed the elevator call button. He couldn't figure it out, but he hadn't been anxious to go ask him why, either.

This was the tricky part. He didn't know how much time he would have after Fernwood's warning before they arrested him. It seemed likely that he would have at least thirty seconds, but he doubted if he would get a minute. If he let Fernwood catch him too soon, then the whole thing would be for nothing. But it looked like he was in the clear now.

Or as much in the clear as a man could be who was about to throw himself off a building. He had to *intend* to jump, or none of it would work. And that meant more than just going through the motions. If Fernwood didn't rescue him, then he would actually have to do it, for there would be nothing to rescue him from unless he did. Calvin had thought it through very carefully—all through the night, since he couldn't sleep—and he had slowly puzzled out the rules to this game. As long as he really intended to jump he wouldn't have to, but as soon as his resolve slipped none of it would work. He had weighed the possibilities, his own death against the death of the Déjà View, and he had made his decision. This morning he had gone out and bought a gun.

He waited until he saw the President enter the garden from the other side and the door guard began to close the door, then stepped out and said, "Hold that a second."

The guard looked up, saw Calvin's camera and the portable word-processor, and said, "Hurry up."

Calvin slipped through the door just as the governor said, "Ladies and gentlemen, the President of the United States."

He looked out of the corner of his eye for Fernwood, and saw him standing clear across on the other side of the garden. What was the deal? He should have been standing right beside the door, ready to nab Calvin as soon as he stepped through. Something wasn't right. The thought of abandoning the whole project pushed its way forward in his mind. He hadn't committed himself yet.

Or had he? Fernwood was here; that meant that the police had already seen him fall. No, he was going to have to go through with it.

He moved toward the back, where a single waist-high wall was all that separated the rooftop from empty air. Now he saw Fernwood move toward the back too. He was dimly aware of Sandoval saying something from the podium, but his entire concentration was on the spot where he and Fernwood would converge. It was almost time. As soon as Fernwood said anything at all...

He stopped at a point almost directly opposite Sandoval. Any time now — any time — but a glance toward Fernwood showed him stopped a few feet away, sweating freely now, but not making a move toward Calvin. Why didn't he say something? He had to know what Calvin was about to do.

Calvin looked up at Sandoval. She was looking directly at him, and smiling. Saying something about all the wonderful things the Déjà View had done for us. And suddenly it all made sense. She was in on it. She and Fernwood. They were waiting for him to take his dive so he could save him and she would have yet another example of how wonderful the new police state was.

Well she was about to get the biggest surprise of her life. Calvin smiled back and, unslinging his camera to look as if he was about to take a picture, climbed up to stand on the wall.

Barret had the Déjà View aimed straight at the President. He was watching five minutes ahead, hoping that any problems Fernwood revealed wouldn't occur sooner than that and cursing the President for her stupid stunt. She had entirely too much faith in gadgets. He had tried to warn her that he wouldn't be able to see at all until Fernwood actually saved the man, but she had insisted on doing it her way. Saving Tyson in the middle of her press conference was too big an opportunity to pass up.

The scene flickered. For just an instant Barret got a view of something else, but it shifted back before he could make sense of it. He scowled. Somebody up there had changed their mind about something, then changed it back. Was Fernwood having second thoughts?

The scene flickered again, but this time it settled down to show the new future. Barret leaned forward to see what it looked like, but he could already tell that something had gone wrong. Reporters huddled around the podium, completely hiding the President, but from their postures Barret knew that she was down. Others streamed for the doors, while Fernwood and four or five more fought with a twisting, shouting Tyson, a gun still held in his hand.

"Emergency!" he yelled into the radio. "Tyson has a gun!"

He frantically turned the scan back toward the present, watching the people in the scene scurry around in speeded-up motion, backwards, searching for the moment when Tyson pulled the trigger. He watched the backwards struggle, the shouting, the shock on the faces turning away from Tyson—there. Three, four, five shots, then aim, then the gun going back under the jacket. But that was only ten seconds from reality! Nine!

Barret shouted, "Shoot him! No time for anything else!" but he knew that it was too late. There was no time for anything at all. By Sandoval's own orders, none of the Secret Service agents were in the roof garden. If the conference had been inside they might have still been able to kill the lights, but out in the open there was no way to do even that. He watched helplessly as Tyson reached into his coat for the gun, only a second or two ahead of real time.

He had to do something. He couldn't just sit and watch. But he was miles away; he had no influence from that distance.

Or did he? He remembered his answer to the reporter during the interview. The Heisenberg principle still applied, even to viewing through time. He did influence what he Viewed, if only a minuscule amount.

But if he turned up the intensity of the scan? It wouldn't be minuscule anymore. In fact, if he was right in his guess, it would slow down molecular activity. Dangerous, and possibly fatal.

But he couldn't let him shoot the President! With a silent prayer, Barret yanked open the cover and shoved the overdrive all the way up.

George had carefully rehearsed it in his mind. His "favor" to the President be damned, he wasn't about to let Tyson actually climb up on that wall. He'd let him get a start, and then—there he went.

"Wait!"

A few people turned to look. George raised his voice. "Don't climb up there!" He was about to shout, "George Fernwood, Amalgamated Mutual Life," like a television cop, but the look on Tyson's face when he turned stopped him.

"What the—"

Tyson's expression was that of pure satisfaction. George watched, fascinated, as he reached into his jacket and pulled out a shiny, snub-nosed revolver, raised it up over his head, and brought it down toward the President.

George was just beginning to think about going for the gun, but the next moment he lost his chance. With no warning at all, the Sun dropped from the sky like a meteor. In the instant of darkness that followed, he saw the city's lights blink on as if controlled by a single switch, then the searing pain of spotlights in his eyes washed the entire scene away.

He blinked. Tyson lay sprawled on the ground. A policeman had materialized on the wall and was holding a gun that trailed tiny wires from its barrel out to Tyson.

"Taser," the policeman said with a smile, as if that explained everything.

"I was wrong about the Déjà View's effect on the future," Barret said with a laugh. He had calmed down considerably now that the President was on her way back to Washington. "I thought it would freeze everything solid, but instead it slowed everything down in time. Once we realized what was happening we just waited for the Sun to go down so Tyson couldn't take aim, and stationed men outside the field to take him out as soon as I shut it down."

George was glad he was sitting down. "You mean you thought it would freeze everyone to death and you still went ahead and did it?"

"Not to death, George. They've been freezing medical patients for years."

"But not thawing them. No one knows how to do that yet."

"They will. But I didn't have time to think it all the way through. I just saw what I had to do and did it. Cheer up, George! It worked. And it makes you one of the world's first time travelers."

"I feel like the world's first Guinea pig. I'm beginning to wonder if this playing around with the future is such a good thing."

Barret sobered somewhat. "Well you're not alone. Sandoval's got something new to think about now. She never imagined that her pet project could be turned against her. You know, I think Tyson accomplished more this way than if he'd actually shot her."

"Maybe so. What do you suppose is going to happen to him?"

"Not much. Turns out he had blanks in the gun. What I saw in the View was Sandoval fainting. So about all we can really get him for is scaring the hell out of everyone." Barret smiled again. "Except you. I've got some great shots of you grappling with him for the gun. You just dived right in there. I didn't think you were the type."

George blushed. "I didn't do anything."

"Ah, but you *would* have."

"Let's not get into that."

"Right. But hey, since the next few days have been so screwed up by all that, I went ahead and Viewed your board for you again. Here's an updated list." Barret held it up to the camera while George pressed the copy button. When it slid from the printer slot a moment later, George picked it up and scanned it for changes.

"Is this supposed to be a joke?" he asked.

"What? No, no jokes. I didn't even read it. What've you got?"

George read from the bottom of the list. "'Note to self: Don't even *think* about leaving this note to yourself.' Now what the hell is that supposed to mean?"

Barret laughed. "You figure it out."

"Barret!"

"Sorry. I've got to go. There's a lot of work to catch up on." Barret's laughter cut off with his image.

George stared at the note. After a few minutes he laid it aside and reached into his desk for the bottle of aspirin. "And thus do we loose Chaos upon the mortal world," he said to the empty room.

INTRODUCTION TO

PEACE ON EARTH

I grew up with the threat of nuclear annihilation hanging over my head. All through childhood, my generation was told that the Soviet Union was just a sneeze away from launching a first strike on the U.S., and that the U.S. would retaliate and probably wipe out all life on Earth in the process. (Except cockroaches. Those were supposed to survive.)

Then the Berlin Wall came down, and the Soviets admitted that socialism was a total repressive failure. Overnight our former enemy became a neighbor in need, and the threat of nuclear war liftted away like a bad dream.

And like a bad dream, the memory of it went away just as quickly. I had to write this story before I forgot what it felt like. Of course now, thanks to inept leadership right here in the U.S., we're closer to nuclear war than ever before, but for a little while this is what the future looked like to people from my generation.

PEACE ON EARTH

We were out at the mall—supposedly looking for last minute Christmas presents but actually looking at girls—when Pinky said, "Hey, check out this old babe. She looks like a time traveler or something."

We all glanced at him to see where he was looking, then followed his gaze to see a short, gray-haired woman in black leather and slashed pants. She stood by one of the mall's central columns, just in front of the garbage cans, handing out some kind of pamphlet to anybody who'd take one. I could tell by her attitude she wasn't just handing out advertising; she was protesting something. Probably the skystalk, I figured. All the old-timers are afraid the ground-to-orbit elevator cable's gonna break and fall down right on *their* heads. Paranoid, every one of 'em. I wanted to go over and ask her just how she wanted to build the power satellites without a skystalk, but I didn't.

Instead, I said to Ivan, "She's just your type." Ivan's the worrier in our group. He's always the designated driver, 'cause he can't trust anybody else to stay straight at a party.

He looked at me like to say, "What?" He didn't make the connection. Course he wouldn't. Most of it was in my head.

Pinky saved me from having to explain. He guffawed and said, "I saw her first."

Rachel gave him a shove. "Go make a pass, then."

"Why don't you?"

"Maybe I will." Rachel could have, and probably succeeded, too. She's good at it, but then she knows how girls think. We don't mind—sometimes she helps one of us out if we need it—but it pisses Pinky off when she goes after one he wants, cause he always loses.

She wasn't into old punks, though. In fact, she wasn't much into girls at all just then, and she said so. "Hey," she said, "I'm tired of this; let's watch a movie."

"Which one?" Ivan asked, blowing a little bubble about a centimeter across with his gum and snapping it.

"I don't care," Rachel said. "I just want to look at something flat for a while."

"Huh," Pinky said. He wasn't going to touch that one.

Rachel didn't wait for an answer, just walked off toward the theater without looking back. She knew we'd follow. We caught up to her at the catalog and packed around to read over her shoulder as she paged through the selections.

"Let's see *Batman Forty*," Pinky said.

"We've seen that," Ivan said, blowing another bubble.

Not looking around, Rachel said, "I'm in the mood for something different." She looked over at the old punker and grinned. "Something old."

"*Bat Forty*'s old," Pinky said. "It came out this summer."

"Older. And funny."

"Oh."

She poked at the menu bars on the screen a few times and got a new page of titles: old comedies. She rapped on the glass a few more times and got a different list. *Really* old comedies. Stuff like Marx Brothers and Eddie Murphy and Sylvester Stallone. I scanned down the title side of the screen and one jumped out at me.

"*Dr. Strangelove*," I said, pointing.

Rachel snorted. "Hah. Porno comedy from—God, from the sixties. Sure, what the hell." She rapped the screen next to the title, took out her cash card and stuck it in the turnstile slot, and pushed through. The rest of us poked our cash cards in the slot one at a time and followed her into the theater.

There was a four-seater already open, so we trooped right on in and dropped into the chairs and by the time I'd squirmed around and gotten comfortable the movie was starting.

It was in black and white. The sound was scratchy and the video was full of spots and stuff, and when the title screen came up we read the subtitle: *How I Learned to Stop Worrying and Love the Bomb*.

"We've been had," Ivan whispered. He was beside me on my right.

"Cheeze," Pinky said from beyond him. "People actually *watched* this stuff?"

Rachel, sitting to my left, said, "Yeah, and so am I, so shut up and let me do it."

So we watched the movie. It was about the crew of a plane carrying nuclear bombs and how this dumb mix-up made them fly into the Soviet Union with it. I had a bitch of a time making sense of it until Ivan said, "Oh, this was before we joined the States," but even then I didn't get half the jokes. The whole damn movie looked pretty grim to me.

It must have looked pretty grim to Rachel, too, because about halfway through, when the National Guard started shooting up a military base, she reached over and grabbed my hand and squeezed. I looked over at her and I'm sure my eyes were big as dollars, but she just pulled my hand down on her side of the arm rest so Ivan and Pinky couldn't see and kept holding on. I wasn't going to argue, but I wondered what got her so scared. Then I started paying more attention to the movie and before I knew it I'd grabbed Ivan's hand, too, and he didn't even flinch.

This wasn't any comedy. Oh, sure, black comedy, but what it was making fun of was dead serious. It was making fun of the way people thought back then. The Soviets were the Big Enemy, or the U.S. was, depending on where you were born. They had all these missiles aimed at each other, and bombers and submarines ready to deliver nuclear warheads to every major city in the world, and all of them were on a hair-trigger.

And people lived like that, knowing that any time, day or night, a cosmic ray could hit the wrong computer somewhere and blow them all to bits.

We were getting it second hand, but that was plenty. By the time the cowboy pilot went out the bomb bay with the nuke I thought I was going to throw up, and Ivan had swallowed his gum.

None of us got up until after the credits were all done and the lights came up again, and even then we didn't say anything, just got up and sort of shuffled for the door. As soon as he heard the familiar noise of the mall,

Pinky headed for it like a shot, but Ivan and Rachel and I hung back, trying to work the horror off our faces before we ventured out in public again. Ivan looked back into the empty room with its four seats and blank screen and whispered, "Jesus Christ." He shook his head, then turned away and followed after Pinky.

Rachel and I took a few deep breaths and went out after them. They were already halfway toward the main doors.

We passed by the old punker on our way out. She waved a pamphlet at me and I took it. Sure enough, she was worried that the skystalk was going to come down. I just about launched into a defense of it, but I stopped myself, thinking, *She lived through what we just saw. No wonder she's afraid of things falling out of the sky.*

So I winked at her and said, "Merry Christmas," and waited until I was out of the mall to throw the pamphlet away.

INTRODUCTION TO

NEITHER RAIN NOR SLEET NOR WEIRDNESS

Writers' lives are intimately tied to the mail. All our business is done by mail. Each day's delivery could mean another sale or a royalty check—or another rejection. We tend to hang around the mailbox and wait like puppies eager for treats. My mailman in Cody, Wyoming was a friendly guy; he used to stop and visit for a few minutes whenever I was out, and eventually we struck up a pretty good friendship. He joked about the strange covers on the science fiction magazines he delivered to me, but he insisted that if I wanted to write about something *really* strange, I should write about his job. So I got him to describe it to me, and I realized he was right.

This one was—and always will be—for O.J. the mailman, who put up with my hovering anticipation of his arrival six days a week for over four years.

NEITHER RAIN NOR SLEET NOR WEIRDNESS

Greg had seen some strange names in his sixteen years as a mail carrier. Most of the ones on his route were familiar enough to seem normal to him now: Dinkie Winkel on Aspen Drive and Khanibrostu Khan on Cedar Lane and even Normel Strainge over on Tenth Street, but every now and then he'd run across a new one. Like the one he held before him now: Iptch Tswana, 1014 Meadow Lane.

He looked at the envelope. It was a plain number ten, lick-stamped and hand addressed, so it wasn't likely that a computer somewhere had mangled a name like Ivan Tanner to get that spelling. No, whoever had written it had either mangled it on purpose or had copied the name from someone who had. And they'd mangled the address in the process. There was no 1014 on Meadow Lane.

But the city was right, and the zip code. It must be somebody staying with the Fraleys, he thought. They were 1012. Probably a foreign student by the name, though the letter was postmarked New Jersey.

He rapped the envelope against his sorting case while he tried to decide what to do. Technically when he got mail for a nonexistent address he was supposed to return it to the sender, but if it *was* for somebody staying with the Fraleys then he should probably just deliver it, bad address or not. He supposed he could take it along and ask, and if it wasn't for anyone there then he could send it back tomorrow. Yeah, that was what he would do.

But Iptch Tswana. That was a good one.

He forgot all about the letter until three o'clock that afternoon. Normally he would have reached Meadow Lane by two or two thirty, but his jeep had gotten a flat tire just after he'd left the post office and no matter how hard he tried he couldn't seem to make up for the time he had lost changing it. He wasn't so late that he would have to put in overtime to finish the route—he usually had time left at the end of the day—but all the same it bothered him to be behind his normal pace.

The reason it bothered him waited behind every curtain and screen door on his route. He delivered in the older part of town, still a nice neighborhood but given over mostly to retired couples or widows who had little else to do with their day than wait for the mail, and when he was late Greg could sense their heightened expectation and he could feel their eyes following him up the street when he finally did arrive. And what was worse, the mailboxes were up on the houses instead of out on the sidewalk like they were in the newer parts of town, so he had to open the gate in the picket fence that guarded nearly every house, walk all the way up to the porch and put the mail in the box, and walk back to the street under the watchful eye of the house's silent occupants.

It was spooky. They never came out while he was there, but waited until he was walking down the walk away from the next house down before they ventured out to see what he had brought them. He heard a steady progression of screen doors banging and mailbox lids clunking down behind him, but he never saw the people in the houses. They could be aliens for all he knew.

He was tempted to turn around and look occasionally, but he never did. It would be violating some sort of unspoken agreement. He could almost imagine the squeal as women in bathrobes, their hair in curlers, scurried back inside their houses in indignation. Then they would probably call the postmaster and tell him that their mailman was "looking at them," and there would be no end to the ribbing he'd get from the other guys at work.

No, it didn't pay to be too curious. A lot of people were already sure that you read their mail; there was no sense giving them provocation to call you a Peeping Tom, too.

Besides, he did see some of them on occasion, like when a package was too big for the box or when somebody got a certified letter. The court had taken to certifying their jury summonses in order to have proof that they were delivered, so every now and then he had to ring the doorbell and get a signature. It was a trick of sorts. People could always refuse mail, even certified letters from the court, but they had to come to the door to do it and that at least told the court—and Greg—that somebody was home. People seldom refused mail anyway, especially if it was certified. Their curiosity wouldn't let them.

But there were no certified letters today. He parked the jeep at the corner of Eleventh and Meadow Lane, shouldered his bag, and headed off up the odd side of the tree-lined street, feeling the eyes watching him all the while. The sensation seemed stronger than usual today, even stronger than the tingling at the back of his neck that he usually felt as he approached Ginger, the Kovarichs' aging Doberman at 1006. He'd read somewhere that a Doberman's brain never stopped growing, that as they grew older the pressure in their skull drove them crazy, making them even more likely than usual to tear your throat out. Like most carriers he had a can of Mace clipped to his belt, but he dreaded having to use it. Mace just made a dog madder, made him that much more likely to go for you. The way to treat a dog was to ignore it, treat it like a tree or a tricycle or any other piece of lawn junk. Don't acknowledge it. Most of all, don't *fear* it. Dogs could smell fear. He tried to ignore the feeling of being watched the same way he ignored Ginger, but the more he thought about it the worse it got until it seemed he could hear every whisper of movement behind him as people abandoned their posts by the windows and crept out to sneak the mail out of their boxes.

I will not look back, he thought. He forced himself to smell the flowers in the neatly planted beds alongside the walks, to listen to the leaves rustling in the enormous cottonwoods that lined both sides of the street— anything to avoid letting it get to him. It seemed to be working, too, until he reached Seventh Street, crossed over to the even side of Meadow Lane, and started back. There, instead of weakening still more, the sensation grew stronger, which made no sense since he was headed back toward the jeep and relative sanctuary. But his determination to ignore it grew proportionately, so much so that he was only one door down from the Fraleys when he noticed the new house.

It hadn't been there yesterday. He stopped and stared at it in open surprise: a light eggshell blue house nestled in between the Fraleys and the Douglasses. It had that boxy look common to pre-fab houses, but if it had come in on a trailer there was no sign of wheels now. Not even tire-marks in the grass. There was already a picket fence around it, and yes, a mailbox beside the screen door, right under the numbers 1014.

That had to be the fastest he had ever seen a house go up. A single day from bare ground to picket fence. Evidently the Fraleys and the Douglasses had each had a lot and a half, and this new person—he took out the letter as he began walking again and read the name—this Iptch Tswana had bought the middle ground.

Well, that solved the problem of delivering the letter. It created a problem back at the office—he would have to rearrange all the slots in his sorting case after 1012 to accommodate the new house, and for a couple of weeks until he got used to the new arrangement he would be putting mail in the old slots out of habit—but that was part of the job.

Just like this sensation of being watched was part of the job. He was feeling it more than ever now as he walked away from the Fraleys and toward the new house. It was almost a physical presence in his mind, a tension that grew with each step toward the gate. The tingling at the back of his neck was almost an itch, demanding that he whirl around and face the monsters sneaking up on him...

When he put his hand on the gate it was as if an electric shock went through him. He lurched, steadied himself on the post and straightened up, shaking his head. This is ridiculous, he told himself. The fence is just a wooden picket fence. The house is just a house. The shadowy figures peeking around the curtains are the same shadowy figures that you see in every house on the street. No big deal. Deliver the mail.

He even managed a soft whistle as he walked up to the porch, realizing belatedly that it was the repetitive dum-Do-dum, dum-Do-dum of the *Jaws* theme. He stopped whistling and opened the mailbox lid, dropped the letter inside and let the lid bang shut, then turned around and walked the distance back to the street while the back of his neck tried to crawl up under his scalp. At the gate he felt the same shock as before, but this time he didn't stumble.

Six more houses to the jeep. Then five. Four. The farther he got from the new house the less he felt the presence in his mind. He began to relax. He'd been about to say to heck with being late and take a break over in the park for a few minutes, but now he decided to go ahead and finish the route first. Get it over with and then go wiggle his toes in the grass before he went back to the post office.

He delivered the last bit for Meadow Lane, crossed back over to the jeep, and unlocked the door. He looked back down the quiet street with its shade trees and its picket fences and laughed at his reaction to it, but his laughter dwindled to a stop and he leaned against the jeep for support when he realized what he was seeing. Or rather, what he wasn't seeing. The new house was no longer there.

He climbed into the jeep and drove slowly down the street, thinking that it must be a trick of the light and shadow, or that it really sat farther back on the lot than he'd supposed, but when he came abreast of where it had been he could see no sign of a house, only the neat white picket fence dividing the lot neatly between the Fraleys' and the Douglasses' gardens. Without further thought he flipped a U-turn in the middle of the street and headed for the park.

Ted Songerman was late, too. He was pulling the empty mail trays out of his jeep and stacking them on a cart when Greg pulled into the garage at the end of the day. Ted was the rotating shift person, the one who covered a route when the normal carrier was on his day off. He never had time to really get used to a route, so he was always a little later getting back in. He grinned as Greg got out and began stacking his own trays, and said, "You look like a Pony Express rider after the Indians got him. Rough one, huh?"

"Yeah," Greg admitted.

"Feel like knocking back a couple on the way home?"

Greg looked up, surprised. He hardly ever went out for a drink after work, and never with Ted. He and Ted had never gotten along well. Ted was the sort of person who thought practical jokes were funny, and Greg was not. Greg usually just avoided him, but a frosty mug of beer suddenly sounded like the best idea he'd heard all day. He nodded. "Sure. Let's do it."

They picked up another couple of carriers by quitting time: enough to fill a table at the Silver Dollar. As Ted poured the first round, Sue Windermere asked, "So what's the occasion, Greg? I haven't seen you out drinking since you got promoted to carrier."

Greg shook his head and said, "Just a long day."

Dennis Cook laughed. "I didn't think you *had* long days. That's Ted's job."

"Yeah, laugh all you want," Ted said. "You guys all did the rotating route once too."

Greg took a long pull at his beer. It was exactly as good as he'd hoped it would be. He nodded and said, "And I'm damned glad I'm off it. It used to drive me nuts, having people staring at me from behind the curtains every day. It's bad enough when you're on time, but when you're late it's like the whole neighborhood gets cranked up with about a megawatt of anticipation. I feel like a bug under a microscope."

Sue nodded. "I know what you mean. I feel it too."

"Me too," Dennis said. "That what happened to you today?"

Greg nodded. "Yeah. Got so bad I actually started hallucinating."

"Hallucinating? How?"

"I had a letter for a nonexistent address, and when I got to where it would have been, I saw the house."

"You're kidding," Ted said. "What'd you do?"

"I delivered the letter."

Sue and Dennis erupted in laughter. Ted slowly turned red, realizing he'd been had. Greg realized what he'd done, and tried to squelch it before Ted could start scheming a joke to play in return. "No," he said. "Really, I did. I thought there was a house there. I put the letter in the mailbox and everything. And then when I got to the jeep and looked back, it was gone."

Sue laughed again. "It was a trailer house, right?"

Ted lifted his glass and eyed Greg over the rim.

"I once delivered a letter to a manhole," Dennis said. "There was a crew working on a water line or something, and they'd been there for like a month, blocking this guy's driveway every day, so as kind of a hint that maybe they ought to get moving he sent them a 'get well soon' card, and..."

Greg drove down Meadow Lane on the way home, but the house was still not there. *I delivered a letter to a nonexistent address,* he thought, and the sudden absurdity of the whole situation made him laugh out loud. They hadn't believed him in the bar, and now he was beginning to doubt it himself. He'd probably dropped the letter in the Fraleys' box and imagined the whole thing when he'd had that dizzy spell there at the gate. Must have been the ham he'd had on his sandwich for lunch; it was probably spoiled and that's what gave him the shakes and everything else. Just a touch of food poisoning. Yeah. The letter probably *was* for someone staying with the Fraleys, and if it wasn't then they'd just put it back in the box so there was no problem there, either. Forget it.

The next day he had enough to keep his mind occupied anyway. It was Wednesday, *Buyers' Guide* day, which meant a stop at every house on the route. And on top of that he had a box of ladybugs to deliver and the box had a hole in it that he hadn't discovered right away. He'd taped it up, but not before a couple hundred of them had gotten loose in his jeep. Now he was seeing bright orange spots wherever he looked.

He was so busy with the *Buyers' Guide* and the ladybugs that he didn't even notice the shadowy shapes behind the curtains today, and he didn't feel the prickling at the back of his neck until just before he turned onto Meadow Lane. Even when it came it was more of an isolated event, a wave of sensation that passed over him and was gone almost as soon as he noticed it. He rounded the corner and parked the jeep, looking surreptitiously down the block for the phantom house, but he saw only the shady walk and soft pastel houses that had always been there.

He set off down the odd side of the street with a feeling of relief, glancing casually across when he came abreast of the spot where yesterday he had thought he had seen a house, but today there were two vegetable gardens back-to-back against the dividing fence. A rain-bird sprinkler clicked its way around in a circle, watering them both. *Definitely the ham sandwich,* he thought, putting it out of his mind completely.

But back at the post office he learned that the story had gotten around. For a change Ted had had a fast day, and to get back at him for suckering him in the bar, he'd evidently been telling everybody else Greg's story, complete with Greg's assurance that it was true. As Greg parked his jeep and started unloading trays Ted called out from the door, "Hey Greg, see anymore disappearing houses today?"

Heads turned, faces smiled. Ted grinned, *gotcha.* "Here, maybe this will help," he said, holding out a scroll of paper tied with a ribbon. Greg took it reluctantly and opened it. It was a street map with his route marked in orange. Ted said, "The postmaster says anything that's not on the map, you don't have to deliver to it."

Greg forced a smile. "Thanks, Ted. I appreciate it." He made a show of putting it in his jeep's glove box, then finished unloading his jeep, mistakenly assuming that the joke would die out faster if he didn't let it get to him.

But Thursday there was a package for Iptch Tswana, 1014 Meadow Lane. It was just a plain brown-paper rectangle about the size of a video tape, not insured or anything. At first Greg thought that it was probably another of Ted's little digs, but the return address was from someone or something called PBW, Newark, New Jersey, and the postmark was real. Ted might have gone to the trouble to arrange a mail drop for a particularly good joke, but he hadn't had enough time for this one. So, it was real.

PBW — Plain Brown Wrapper, Greg thought with a grin. He had seen a million packages just like it, from a million different innocuous-sounding companies. It used to be magazines in manila envelopes, but more and more lately it was becoming video tapes. You never knew who was going to start getting them. There was that preacher over on...

But that was none of Greg's business. So the Fraleys' foreign student wanted to check out American porn, what difference did it make to him? None at all. But he'd better tell the kid to correct his address. That *was* Greg's business.

He was still chasing ladybugs out of his jeep today, but the mail was mercifully light, light enough that he was a half-hour earlier than usual when he turned the corner at Eleventh and Meadow Lane. All the same he felt that same wave of sensation that he had felt yesterday, that tingling at the back of the neck like someone was watching him, but today it didn't go away like it had yesterday. It was just like it had been Tuesday, as if there was a physical presence in his mind, someone watching him from within instead of from behind the curtain.

Reluctantly, he looked down the street. The blue pre-fab house was there again, just as it had been on Tuesday. And from this distance it seemed to shimmer slightly, as if heat waves off the pavement were blurring it. But Meadow Lane was a shady street.

And what's more, that house had definitely not been there yesterday.

Greg took the package for Ipswitch Whoever out of the back of the jeep and juggled it in his hand, trying to decide what to do. He felt a moment of absolute blankness wherein no ideas surfaced, then with a shrug he stuck the package in his bag and checked for others on this relay. The address said 1014 and there was a house with the number 1014 on it, so there was at least one thing he could do. He could deliver the mail.

The feeling of being watched faded out about the middle of the 700 block. It was a distinct absence down here three blocks from the mysterious disappearing house, but as soon as he crossed the street and started back toward it the sensation began to return, until when he got about a block away it was back to full hair-raising strength. He walked on toward it, practically oblivious to the other houses, relying on force of habit to deliver the mail while he wrestled with his fear.

The cottonwoods were closing in on him. Tenth Street became some kind of symbolic barrier that he crossed by strength of character as much as by power of legs and feet. He was barely aware of stopping at 1002 and putting their outgoing mail in his bag, leaving a magazine and a sweepstakes notice in the box, walking down the walk, up to 1006's gate where Ginger waited with bared fangs and —

"Yeow!" He slammed the gate in the dog's face and backed slowly away, fumbling for his can of Mace while Ginger clawed at the fence and barked in mindless fury. But it looked like the dog wasn't going to come over it after him. He took a deep breath, wondering why the stupid dog had chosen today to go berserk, then suddenly realized what it was: it had sensed his fear. Not of the dog, but of the blue house, but that didn't matter. Fear was fear in Ginger's tiny but expanding brain.

"Bad dog," Greg said in what he hoped was an authoritative voice and not the squeak it sounded like to him. "Calm down. Nice Ginger." He risked a glance over at the blue house — it was still there — then turned his full attention to Ginger.

"Pipe down!"

The doberman stopped barking, looked up at him with its head tilted to the side, then wagged its stump of a tail. From behind the screen door came a voice saying "Ginger, go to your place," and the dog obediently trotted over to a patch of bare dirt worn in the lawn and lay down. A few seconds later Mrs. Feigelman pushed open the screen and said with a shake of her head, "Don't mind him; he won't bite. He's just a big softie, aren't you, Ginger?"

The dog wagged its stump of a tail again and *whuffed* softly at her.

"Any mail today?"

"Uh, yeah." A little shudder ran down Greg's spine as he stepped through the gate again, extending two letters out to her. He was turning to go when she said, "Whoops, this one's for Fraleys."

He took it back and looked at the address. "So it is. Thanks."

"You're welcome. I guess Ginger's little joke must have rattled you a little, huh?"

Joke. Right. "Yeah," Greg said. "I guess so." He turned away again and made it through the gate, then turned back again.

"Yes?" Mrs. Feigelman asked.

"Can you—" *see a blue house two doors down?* he wanted to ask, but he suddenly realized that if she couldn't then she'd think he was more than just a little rattled. "—maybe keep an eye on him around this time of day?" he finished lamely. "I don't think he likes me much."

"Oh, he likes everybody. But I'll watch him."

"Thanks." Greg turned and walked on toward 1012, Ginger already forgotten.

He delivered Fraleys' letter without taking his eye off the blue house. It was sitting square over the top of the garden he had seen yesterday. For a moment he thought he could still see stalks of corn too, as if one eye saw the garden while the other saw the house, but when he blinked the garden was gone. He hesitated at the Fraleys' mailbox, wondering if he should ring the doorbell and ask if they had a foreign student staying with them, but he knew they didn't. Iptsch Tswana lived right there, wherever there was.

He took the package out of his bag and advanced on the house. The feeling of being watched was back as strong as ever. He knew there was someone inside, and now he seemed to be getting some kind of sixth-sense feeling about them in return. Just as Ginger had sensed it in him, he felt fear emanating from inside the house.

They're afraid of me? he thought, barely stifling a hysterical laugh. *What am I going to do, report them to the postmaster?* He sensed a sudden surge of fear from inside at that thought, fading slowly as he shook his head. The postmaster wouldn't believe a word of it, and Greg would be lucky if he got off without a psychiatric exam. Especially with Ted's joke circulating around. Mail carriers had cracked before.

Not a reassuring thought. Well, he wasn't going to crack; he was going to find out what the hell was going on here. He put his hand out to push open the gate, remembered the shock from the time before, and pushed it open anyway. He got shocked again, but it was no worse than an ordinary static shock, of about the magnitude you'd get scuffing four or five times across a new carpet and then touching a light switch. To get shocked by a picket fence was definitely strange, but it was in keeping with the rest of the place.

He marched up to the door, ignoring the mailbox, and pushed the bell button, but if it rang anything inside he couldn't hear it. He knocked on the door frame and, clearing his throat, said through the screen, "Hello, is anybody home?"

No answer, but he still got that feeling of being watched, still felt the sensation of fear.

"Package for —" he looked at the package " — Iptwitch Tiswana," he said, beginning to feel a little foolish. After all, the damn thing would fit easily in the box.

The sudden wave of — what? Hope? — that washed over him was even stronger than the fear. It was almost as if someone had spoken to him, saying, "Yes, put it in the box!"

You are reading my mind, aren't you? he thought.

The sensation cut off abruptly. No fear, no hope, nothing.

"Hello," he called again.

Nothing.

With a shrug, he opened the lid and dropped the package in the box, turned, and walked back down to the gate. On sudden impulse he swung the mail bag over and used it to pull the gate open, stepped through, and pulled it closed behind him with the bag. But when the latch clicked, he still felt a shock.

He looked up, but the house was gone. In its place stood Mr. Douglass, his back turned to Greg, calmly watering his garden with a hose sprayer.

Greg took a deep breath, let it out, then nodded. Okay. He'd just delivered a pornographic video tape to a corn patch. He reached in his bag and pulled out a *Prevention* magazine and a *Reader's Digest*, then shouted,

"Good afternoon!"

Mr. Douglass's start sent out a wave in the water stream, then he turned and squinted at Greg. "Afternoon," he admitted.

"Got your mail here," Greg said, holding out the magazines.

The old man nodded, twisted the valve on the sprayer until it stopped and set it down, then walked over to the fence.

"No bills, I hope," he said with a smile that revealed a missing front tooth.

"Not a one," Greg said, handing the magazines across the fence.

"Think it'll rain?"

Greg looked up at the canopy of leaves overhead. "Not under here."

"Never does."

"I don't suppose." Greg cleared his throat. "I, uh, was wondering, did there used to be a house here before yours? Right in the middle here?" He waved at the two gardens on either side of the fence.

Mr. Douglass shook his head. "Nope. This here was all sagebrush when we built on it. Why?"

"I just—well, for a second there I thought I saw something. Like a ghost house. Must have been a trick of the light."

The old man turned to look at the gardens, then back at Greg, who was blushing by now. He laughed. "Must've been. Any ghost house you'd see out here'd just about have to be a teepee."

"That's what I thought. You, uh, you didn't see anything just now, did you? Flickering at the corner of your eyes, maybe?"

"You get my age, son, everything flickers. But no, I didn't see nothing diff'rent, if that's what you mean."

"Must've just been my contact lenses, then," Greg said. "Every now and then they do that."

"That so?"

"Yeah, seems like you never get used to them." Greg rubbed at his left eye and started to walk on down the street. "Thanks," he said in parting.

He could feel eyes on him as he walked on past the Douglass's house, but this time he knew whose they were. *Boy, that was stupid,* he thought. *Now Douglass thinks you're a kook too.*

And maybe he was right, hmm? Ghost houses, and people who read minds! Maybe he should call the *National Enquirer* and have them come do a story on him.

He made it back to his jeep without seeing any more disappearing houses and drove up Eleventh to Willow Lane, where he loaded his bag again for his next relay. As he walked from house to house he thought about what had just happened to him, and decided that he was not crazy. There had been a letter on Tuesday, and a package today, and both of them had gone *somewhere*. Where? Wherever the house at 1014 had gone when they blipped it out of Douglass's corn patch.

And that shock; it wasn't electricity he was feeling, not from a wooden fence that he hadn't even been touching that last time. It was more likely the momentary disorientation of matter transmission when they blipped *him* wherever *they* were all along. They certainly weren't really in the corn patch.

And then there was that mind-reading bit. Purely subjective, that, so not reliable as evidence, but it was something to remember.

All right, suppose the gate was a Gate, a doorway into someplace else. Somebody on the other side obviously needed something from this side, and they were getting it by mail. Why? Because they couldn't let themselves be seen here. Why not? Because they had green skin and tentacles instead of arms? And they liked human pornography?

It started to fall apart about there. Greg thought about it a while more while he walked down to Eighth Street and back again along Willow Lane, and he finally came up with a flaw in his reasoning. He didn't know for sure that the package held a porno tape, or even a video tape for that matter. It could be anything: books, Swiss chocolate, or repair parts for a nuclear reactor. It was *something*, and that was what was important.

The admission that the package and the house were real brought a little sanity back into the situation. Not much, but it made the difference between admitting he was crazy and trying to prove that he was not.

The next day there was no letter, and no blue house on Meadow Lane. The watching sensation hit him while he was still on Aspen, a block away, and faded out again in a few seconds, but that was the only bit of strangeness that whole day. *They were just checking,* Greg thought. *They read minds; so they know when there's no mail and they don't have to open the gateway for me.*

Saturday Ted drove the route. Friday afternoon he made a big thing of asking Greg where the disappearing house was, but Greg just shrugged it off and let him go on about it until he'd run himself down. There was no delivery on Sunday. When he got to work Monday Greg resisted the urge to ask Ted if he'd had a package for 1014, but he was almost glad to see another videotape-sized package waiting for him today. He'd been thinking about it over the weekend, and he'd come up with an idea.

When he felt the first glimmerings of someone watching him he concentrated on keeping a clear image of the package in his mind. Nothing else but the package, don't give them a clue to what else you're carrying...

The presence in his mind settled down to a steady Watchfulness. Greg ignored it as best he could, delivering the mail as he always had when it was just people watching him. He turned the corner onto Meadow Lane and glanced quickly down at the blue house—yes, there it was, shimmering slightly—then pointedly ignored it and delivered the mail all the way down the odd side to Ninth Street, then back up the even side. Ginger stayed in his place, and Greg smiled. *No fear this time.*

He paused at the Gate, reached in his bag for the package, and held it before him like an offering while he pushed his way through. He was ready for the shock; as soon as he felt it he turned around and looked back at the street. Yes, it was definitely shimmering out *there* now.

Keeping his mind firmly on the package, he walked up the walk, put the package in the box, and walked back down to the Gate. But instead of going through, he reached into his bag again and took out the pocket Instamatic camera he'd tucked into it this morning and one-handedly fired off the whole roll of film in a shaky panorama, making sure he got some of the neighboring houses in the picture along with the blue one. Then he tucked the camera back in the bag, took out the compass, noted the direction of magnetic north and the direction of the Sun in relation to the other houses, and put that back in the bag too. *Then* he stepped through the Gate.

It took fifteen seconds, maximum. He'd practiced with an empty camera until he'd gotten it down. Now, as he walked purposefully down the sidewalk away from the Gate, he felt a rush of alarm in his mind, a rush that suddenly blinked out of existence along with the house.

He couldn't help grinning as he worked his way back to the jeep. Score one for curious mailmen! There was one customer who wouldn't be calling the postmaster to complain.

Back in the jeep he took out the compass again, and sure enough, local North at the house was at least sixty degrees west of true. That put the Sun, which had appeared an hour or two lower than normal, in the northern sky, which put the house somewhere in the southern hemisphere.

Assuming, of course, that it was still on Earth.

Aha! Tomorrow he would bring a spring scale and measure the local gravity. And maybe a bottle for an air sample? Who could he get to analyze it for him?

Or would he get the chance? He might have scared them off with the camera and the compass. He had thought about it last night while he was practicing with the camera, but somehow it didn't seem likely that they would scare that easily. They were more afraid of scaring *him*. They needed whatever he was delivering, needed it bad enough to come up with this whole business of the house, and as long as they could read his mind and know that he hadn't told anyone else about them, they wouldn't do anything to jeopardize their supply.

What *was* he delivering to them? He had thought about just opening the next package and finding out—for about half a second before he realized what he was considering. Opening people's mail was just about the worst thing a carrier could do. Start doing that and you might as well just quit the job; you wouldn't have it much longer anyway. Taking pictures of someone's house was bad enough.

Feeling somewhat guilty, but not guilty enough to throw out the film, he made a detour past the one-hour fast photo shop and dropped it off before he went on with the rest of the route.

He half expected to find that his film had been mysteriously fogged, or that he would have a dozen shots of Meadow Lane, the Fraleys house, the Douglasses house, and a corn patch; but what he got back from the photo shop was exactly what he had seen while he was taking the pictures. So, here was physical evidence that something out of the ordinary was going on. He thought momentarily about showing the photos to Ted, but he knew that was the wrong approach the moment he thought of it. Let Ted know that he was getting under his skin and he'd never let up. The photos would just make it worse.

Part of him said *look, here's proof that you're not nuts, so just leave it alone and deliver the mail,* but another part of him said *not yet.* He was still too curious.

He waited four days for another package. The anticipation was getting to him; he didn't sleep well, and he was distracted at work. Ted took advantage of the opportunity, rolling his eyes and making spirals beside his head with his finger when he thought Greg wasn't looking, but Greg ignored him. He knew he was doing too good a job, that he was driving Ted to do something truly bizzare just to get a reaction, but he didn't care. He had something bigger than Ted on his mind.

Each day he felt the probe of inquiry as he neared Meadow Lane, and each day he concentrated on the image of a package, but not until he actually had the real item with him did the house reappear. They could tell when he was faking it.

He tried knocking on the door again when he delivered it, but still nobody answered. So with a shrug he reached into his mail bag right there on the porch and took out a fisherman's scale with a ten pound weight hooked to it.

At least it had been a ten pound weight that morning. Now it was about eight and three-quarters. Not a big difference, not enough to notice in the soles of the feet, but measurable.

And suddenly, standing there with the scale dangling from his hand, Greg's composure cracked. There wasn't anyplace in the solar system with nine-tenths of a gravity and a breathable atmosphere. Wherever they had brought him to, it was a *long* ways away. He stuffed the scale back in his bag, jammed the package into the mailbox, and rushed back through the Gate to Earth.

He staggered diagonally across the street to his jeep, fumbled with the key to unlock it, and collapsed inside. Heart racing and breath coming in short gasps, he sat in the seat and tried to get control of himself again, and after a few minutes he was able to sit up and take a few deep breaths. He looked back down the street to where the blue house was no longer visible. He wanted to go back to the post office, tell them that he was sick and to get somebody else to finish the route. Nobody should have to deliver mail after being yanked halfway across the universe and back. But he knew if he did that he would call in sick in the morning too, and the day after, and when he

70

had used up his sick time and all of his vacation time he would go for early retirement rather than face that house again.

And Ted, damn him, Ted would be right.

No, he had too many years invested in this job to give it up now, strange house or no. He took another couple of deep breaths, got back out of the jeep, and finished the even side of the street.

There was no package for 1014 on Friday. Even so, as he made his deliveries Greg tried to reconcile himself to the truth: he had an alien house on his route. He tried again and again to tell himself that it was none of his business who they were, but nobody — not even the most unimaginative mailman in the world — could go on delivering to that address without some kind of explanation. Postal Creed be damned; that was beyond the call of duty.

If only they would talk to him! All he wanted was an explanation. If they would just talk to him once, tell him what was going on and why, he could deliver their mail until he retired. But how could he get them to talk? He thought briefly about just opening the door and walking in on them, but that seemed a little reckless. After all, his theories about them were just wild speculation; they could be anybody, or anything. He remembered a cartoon he had once seen tacked up on the bulletin board at the post office: a predatory life form disguised as a mailbox, flag up to attract mailmen.

No, just barging in on them wouldn't do. What he needed was some sort of remote sensing device, some way to tell if they were friendly *before* he risked his skin trying to talk with them. He needed to bug them.

He tried to imagine how to do that. He had a couple days to figure it out; his weekend was coming up. Ted would be driving the route tomorrow, and — wait a minute.

Something clicked in his mind. Yeah. It worked for the court house, why not for him?

The next morning Ted left the post office with a certified letter in his bag and a puzzled frown on his face. Greg, following him slowly a few blocks behind, was sure that his expression would change before the day was out. Oh yes, it would change.

TWENTY QUESTIONS

INTRODUCTION TO

ABRIDGED EDITION

"Where do you get your ideas, Jerry?"

"From reading the ingredient labels on boxes of tea, of course. Where else?"

ABRIDGED EDITION

Quinoa wasn't in the dictionary. Owen checked twice, but the listings went straight from quinine to quinoid.

Thinking he must have misspelled it, he looked back to the box of Bengal Spice tea where he'd read quinoa among the list of ingredients, but now he couldn't locate it there, either. He'd have sworn he'd seen it after nutmeg and cloves, but now cloves was the last ingredient.

Nor could he find anything he could have misread to produce the word. That was odd. Must be the stress, he thought. Seeing words that weren't there wouldn't be the first strange thing he'd done since losing both Richard and his job.

He set the dictionary down on the countertop separating the kitchen from the living room. The walls above the loveseat and the stereo didn't look so bare anymore—he had stapled up Van Gogh poster prints where Richard's paintings had been—but the bookshelves and the CD rack were still full of gaps. Those would take a while to refill.

The tea's spicy aroma filled the kitchen. Owen lifted the cup, blew across the top, and took a sip. Something about it *did* suggest India, or Arabia. Foreign, anyway. It tasted fine even without quinoa.

He took both cup and dictionary down the hallway into his study. Spreading the morning newspaper out on his drafting table, he pulled aside the curtain on the street-facing window to give him more light and began the morning ritual of looking through the want ads. He found the usual glut of accounting and auto body jobs, but once again no draftsmen. Plenty of restaurant jobs and sales positions, but no openings for surveyors, either. If this kept up, he was going to run out of unemployment compensation before he found anything.

Another ad caught his attention: Stevedore. There was no job description, just a number to call. Owen tried to remember what a stevedore did, but if he'd ever known, he'd forgotten it. Well, no problem; he had the dictionary right there. He flipped it open and paged through the S's.

No stevedore. The listing went from stethoscope to stew.

Hmm, he thought. Wasn't much of a dictionary, was it? He shook his head sadly. The dictionary — like the tea — had belonged to his housemate, until Richard had left for Calcutta three months ago to join an eastern religion Owen couldn't even pronounce. Owen had sneaked it out of a packing box so he'd have something of Richard's to remember him by, but until lately he hadn't felt the need to actually use it. Good thing; even now the disappointment was intense, like being rejected all over again.

That was silly. It was just a dictionary, and not a very good one at that. He was trying hard not to be vengeful about it, but even so, a dictionary without "stevedore" was missing something.

He flipped to the F's, remembering how as a kid he used to look up dirty words for fun, but "fuck" wasn't there. Nor was "fornicate." Well, that was somehow appropriate. Since Richard had left, Owen hadn't had so much as a date. Not that he hadn't tried, but one of the people he'd attempted to strike up a relationship with had turned out to be his boss's nephew, and now he was out of a job.

He closed the dictionary and looked back to the paper. Maybe he would just call the number and ask what a stevedore was. But when he looked for the ad, he couldn't find that, either.

What the heck? He traced the columns of jobs. They were alphabetized; he saw sales, screen printers, steelworkers, then summer jobs. No stevedore. But it had been there just a minute ago. He wouldn't have made up a whole job listing, not for something as unlikely as "stevedore."

There was another explanation, of course. An easily testable one, too, save that it was completely crazy to imagine it could be true.

Owen didn't mind. Right now he felt as if he were at least halfway insane anyway. So he picked another ad from the paper — taxi driver — and flipped through the dictionary to the T's. No listing for taxi.

He'd kept his finger on the ad for taxi drivers, but when he looked back down, it now pointed to "teachers."

Owen stared at the newspaper for a long while, not really seeing anything printed there. He shifted his gaze to the dictionary. It looked like a standard collegiate, hardbound in red cloth, but instead of Webster's, the name read, "Drake's Deleting Dictionary."

Where had Richard gotten it? Owen had no idea. He looked for a publisher's mark on the copyright page, but there was no copyright page. Good grief, did it contain *anything* it was supposed to?

Of course it did. It was full of definitions. Owen opened it at random — the pages parted to the same F's he'd been at before — and read the first entry he saw: fundamentalist, noun: an adherent of fundamentalism. He closed the dictionary, wondering why it would have fundamentalist but not stevedore, then a sudden suspicion made him open it to the F's again. No fundamentalist. There was fundament, and fundus, but no fundamentalist. Or fundamentalism either, for that matter. Evidently whatever he intentionally looked up, disappeared.

Too bad I couldn't get rid of the real thing that easily, he thought. The fundies and their anti-gay attitudes had been a thorn in his side ever since...ever since when? Come to think of it, they'd never really amounted to much after their "no special rights" ballot measure had died at the polls. Owen hadn't heard much about them for over a year.

Or had he? There was a fuzziness to his thoughts that bothered him. Hadn't he just read in today's paper that they were planning to introduce another bill in the state senate? He dug out the front page and scanned the headlines. Nothing about it. Just an article on the chronic public transportation problems, another about a mysterious crop failure in the Peruvian Andes, and another about a new automated cargo-handling system for unloading ships.

The hair was beginning to stand up on the back of his neck. Had he somehow wiped out the entire *concept* of fundamentalism just by looking it up in Richard's dictionary? It seemed impossible, but so did want ads vanishing, and ingredients from his tea.

He needed something he could test. Something physical that he knew was there, like the teacup. Good enough: Teacup. He opened the dictionary to the T's and ran his finger down the column past "teacher."

He heard a wet *sploosh* beside him, and hot tea flooded the drafting table. It ran off the edge onto his lap, and he leaped up, howling in pain and fear. Jesus, the cup had just vanished. He ran for the kitchen and pulled a handful of paper towels off the roll beneath the cupboard, then ran back and sopped up what hadn't already soaked into the newspaper or dripped to the floor.

The dictionary had been splashed, too. Owen wiped off the wet pages and fluttered them until they were dry, then threw away the towels and the soggy newspaper and sat back down at the table.

Richard's dictionary could make things disappear.

Why hadn't he used it? Owen wondered, then he thought, Maybe he had. Who could say what the world had been like before Richard started tinkering with it? Unless Owen had been involved directly, he probably wouldn't have remembered the changes.

Whatever Richard might have done, there was still plenty left for Owen to do. The possibilities were endless. He quickly looked up "prejudice" and "bigotry." Neither one was listed, and presumably neither concept existed now, either. He shuffled through the papers on his drafting table and found the envelope his last paycheck had come in, but the pink slip was still there. Too subtle, maybe? He tried "unemployment," and that time he got results.

The pink slip had disappeared, but so had his paycheck. And something had changed down by his feet. Owen looked down and found a chain connecting his left ankle to his drafting table. What the—?

A loud crack came from outside, and someone screamed. Owen scooted over to the window—he had to stretch out his leg to reach it—and looked out. A line of convicts shuffled past on the sidewalk, chained together at the ankles just like he was chained to his desk, and a burly guard paced along beside them, flicking a whip to lash the back of anyone who stumbled.

"Holy shit," Owen whispered. "Those aren't convicts; they're slaves." And so was he. He'd eliminated unemployment, all right.

Frantically, he looked up "slavery," and sighed in relief when the chain vanished from his ankle. He looked out the window again and was reassured to see just the normal pedestrian traffic. Well, not necessarily "normal"; everyone seemed to be striding along with much more determination than usual, as if they had places to go and no time to waste.

Better than dragging chains, though.

Owen looked back to his drafting table. He didn't recognize the half-finished and now tea-stained topographic map taped there...but the longer he looked at it, the more familiar it became. A freelance job? Yes, that was it. He dug through the papers until he found the job order, complete with a check for half the work in advance.

All right. He'd squeaked through on that one. Maybe it was time to put the dictionary away before he got into worse trouble. But he still had one problem...

He considered looking up "abandonment," but he wasn't so sure he wanted Richard back. What he wanted was a new companion, someone who wouldn't leave him for an eastern religion. What he wanted was not to be lonely anymore.

Yes, of course! He eagerly flipped through the L's, looking—for the last time in his life—for "loneliness."

It wasn't there, of course.

He heard a soft noise from the other side of the house. A sigh? Good God, had the mysterious dictionary actually created a companion for him already? Without his even having to go out? He stood up from his drafting table and walked hesitantly down the hallway into the living room, at once hopeful and afraid of what he might find, but his trepidation melted away when he saw the soft, fuzzy golden labrador puppy.

Hmm. Not exactly what he'd been expecting, but when the puppy tilted its head sideways and blinked at him with its big round eyes, he couldn't help smiling. He hefted the dictionary in his hand, then laid it down on the coffee table. Plenty of time for fine-tuning later.

But by the time the puppy had messed on the carpet and chewed up his shoes, it had already eaten the dictionary.

Introduction to

A Star is Born

I'm always amazed at where an idea winds up taking me, but this time was even more amazing than usual because I started with a single image that wasn't even my own. Alan Clark, the artist, was putting together an anthology called *Imagination Fully Dilated* in which authors would write stories based on his paintings, rather than the other way around, which is how it's usually done. He posted a bunch of his artwork on his web site and invited his authors to pick one and write about it.

I chose one in which an insectile...something—maybe a spaceship?—is racing away from the surface of a sun while great billowing clouds of purple nebulosity roil ominously in the background. I had to ask myself what was happening, and why, and what it meant to the people on board (if there *were* any people on board). Slowly a story emerged, and it turned out to be much more complex than I expected. This may be one of my most profound stories, and it all started with the question, "What is that dang deal, anyway?"

A Star is Born

When traveling with aliens, it's always a good idea to bring your own toilet paper. There's nothing more frustrating than finding yourself a thousand light-years from home without the bare necessities, so I usually tuck a few rolls in my luggage just in case.

With the Darefta I should have brought my own toilet as well. Not that it mattered to anybody but me. The rest of the crew were content to do their business wherever it was convenient, and those who even acknowledged my existence expected me to do the same.

They're not lousy hosts. The problem is they're *hosts*, in the biological sense of the word. They're huge; imagine a 150-foot snake that has eaten a whale, with six legs — the front two of which could be used for clumsy arms — sticking out beneath the lump. Creatures that big can't help but attract a following. They evolved with half a dozen smaller species who took advantage of their size and less-than-fastidious nature for a free meal ticket, so they never had to worry about cleaning up; their hangers-on were happy to do it for them. They found more and more uses for their companions as they developed higher intelligence, using them for everything from fine manipulation to an emergency food supply, but they grew so dependent on them that by the time they went into space, they had to take the whole ecosystem along for the ride. That meant a shipful of animals, not all of them housetrained or even trainable, run by a crew of 70-ton behemoths who didn't care much where they stepped.

I could have stayed in my room—really just a packing crate tucked into a protected alcove in the ship's lifeboat—but I was here to observe the crew in action. To do that I had to mingle with them, so I wore high boots, learned to breathe through my mouth, and carried climbing gear with me wherever I went.

That often meant hanging out—literally—at head elevation in the nursery while my main contact among the crew, Dajef, nursed her babies. She had to do it five times a day, so she was happy to visit with me while the crew's four children slurped away at the barrel-sized nipples on her underside.

My rope sling was not the most comfortable nor the most dignified place to be, but it was by far the safest. The children, who looked like six-legged worms about twenty feet long, were omnivorous and not very choosy, so I was happy to be fifty feet above their heads. That put me in danakak territory, so I had to watch out for the aerial scavengers who fluttered around Dajef's teeth and snout, but it was better than fending for myself on the floor.

It smelled better, too, but my nose had pretty much burned out by then so that didn't matter as much as it might have. Not all of the smells were bad anyway. Dajef's milk had a gingery aroma that I actually kind of liked. It had the consistency of honey and it was bright orange, which made the children look even more ghastly than usual while they fed, but it smelled okay.

It was my fourth day on board. Dajef was telling me a joke about a Vipri, a Grath, and a Nonshweiller all stuck together on a derelict ship when the intercom clicked on with a thump like an asteroid strike and the pilot's amplified voice said, "We have reached the Inbazi nebula." What he actually said was "Da rinoge da bara da Inbazi," but my earphones translated it into English for me, while incidentally muting the intercom's 150-decibel thunder to a less painful vibration that only rattled my bones.

The "Da" part was a meaningless noise the Dareftans all made when opening their mouths, sort of like professional videogame players back on Earth. I suppose that meant Dajef's name was actually just "Jeff," but it weirded me out to refer to something so alien by such a human name so I made sure to pronounce the "duh" part as well. She called me Darobert, so I guess it evened out.

"Fated displeasure," she said when she heard the pilot's announcement. She looked down at her distended udder. "I've still got a couple hundred gallons to go."

"It's a big nebula," I said. "We'll still be in it when you're done." She didn't need earphones; she had uploaded a translation program directly into her mind. The Dareftan ability to do that was one of the many things I wanted to understand by the time I left their ship.

"Yes," she replied, "but I won't get to see the surface structure. I wanted to examine how starlight sculpts the outer edges."

"Won't that be recorded?"

"It's not the same as seeing it with my own eyes."

Dangling as I was like a spider from the ceiling just for the privilege of watching alien rearing habits, I could only agree. "How important is the outer edge to what you're studying?" I asked. "I thought we were here to watch a protostar ignite."

"We are. But who knows what will prove to be important? That's the nature of research. I observe everything, and with luck and enough data it will all eventually make sense."

Spoken like a true optimist, I thought, but I didn't say that. I was counting on the same thing.

The Darefta were studying stellar evolution. I was studying Dareftan evolution, and I planned to tag along and watch them in action for a few weeks as they flew from star to star. A spaceship is a perfect microcosm for examining an ecosystem in detail; it's a closed environment, so unless everyone dies for lack of some vital nutrient you can be reasonably assured that everything important to survival is on board. Also, you don't have to put radio collars on your subjects and you don't have to add more variables as new species migrate in with the changes of season. Most of my work had already been done for me by the Darefta themselves when they'd chosen what to bring with them; my job was really just to catalog it all and see how it interacted.

A lot of people back home thought it was a total waste of time. Why study a bunch of alien dinosaurs, anyway? Especially when there were other alien species so much closer to the human model. I had to answer that question a lot while I was applying for financial support, and I told everyone who asked it that the more we learned about species interaction in general, the more we would know about our own selves when we finally killed off everything on Earth and had to patch the ecosystem back together artificially. We thought we knew how ecosystems worked, but studying only terrestrial models was a little like expecting to learn quantum physics by studying only leptons. The Darefta were my hadrons; if they also followed the rules as we understood them, then we would know we were on the right track.

That was my official reason. My real reason was much more personal. Nobody had ever ridden with the Darefta before, and I thought it might be fun. I kept telling myself that as I dodged leviathans in the corridors and scraped dung off my boots. It was supposed to be fun.

My invitation had come about because of an argument Dajef and I had gotten into about evolution back on Tennerif station. She had promised to show me proof that evolution didn't affect some of the biggest lifeforms in the galaxy, but she had refused to tell me more, saying I would never believe her until I saw it with my own eyes. I had assumed she was talking about her own species, but so far I had found no contradictions.

Dajef was neither male nor female in the usual sense, but that didn't disprove anything. My translator called her a "trimom," apparently cobbling together the closest words it could find to match the concept. Her genetic contribution to the children was transferred through her milk in an ongoing viral infection that slowly replaced the biological parents' genes — the other crewmembers' — with her own as long as she continued to let the babies nurse. It made perfect sense, evolutionarily speaking, because the more she nurtured them, the more of her own genes they would carry.

She complained about the inconvenience just the same. She was the chief astronomer, and there she was stuck inside a mud-encrusted brood chamber half the time with nothing to do but suckle babies and talk to a foreigner who hung from the ceiling on a rope beside her ear.

The ship shuddered as we punched through a particularly thick part of the nebula. "So," I said, "What do you expect to learn once we get to the protostar?"

86

"I think my translation program must have a bug in it," she said. "It asked me to tell you what I didn't know."

I laughed. "It was pretty close. I asked what you're looking for. What kind of information can you get here that you can't get anywhere else?"

"Dah. I see." She turned her head, looking at me first with one eye, then the other. "I had thought to make it a surprise, but I suppose I can tell you now. We hope to contact the stellar mind at the moment of its birth, to steer its development, and to record it before it dies."

I tried not to let my mouth hang open. There were too many dazazies — little wormlike flies — around. "The stellar mind? You think stars are alive?"

"I know they are. The magnetic fields within the protostar grow incredibly complex as it collapses. I have already proven in simulations that they can achieve consciousness, but that condition only lasts for a few days before the nuclear ignition in the core wipes it out again. I have developed a network of probes that will let me record the state of the magnetic field before that moment, and then I should be able to replace my simulation with the real thing. I will learn to talk with it, and later I will download its mind into future protostars so I can communicate with them, too, in the short time they are alive."

She wanted to catch a star in a bottle. I wondered if she thought on such a large scale because she was so big herself, or if she was ambitious even by Dareftan standards.

I also wondered how close this meant we would be to the star when it ignited. I had assumed we would stand off a few light-hours at least, but it sounded like we would need to be closer than that to make our recording in real-time. Much closer. "How, uh, how dangerous is this?" I asked.

"Define dangerous," she said. "Our ship is designed to withstand the heat and radiation near the stellar surface. We will only be there a few hours at most. Even if that time coincides with the moment of nuclear ignition in the core, the actual shock wave takes years to propagate to the surface. We will be long gone before that happens."

I relaxed a bit. I had imagined the ignition to be like a small nova.

She belched, setting off a flurry of danakaks and dazazies around her mouth. "On the other hand, we will be skimming the surface of a star. If something goes wrong, we will probably die."

I tried to keep my voice calm. "What are the odds?"

She snapped at a danakak who strayed too close to her left eye. "Who knows? Nobody has ever done this before. Probably worse than half, though."

"Worse than half! Why didn't you tell me that back on Tennerif station?"

"I thought I did."

"You said, 'Come watch us in action if you'd like. It'll be a life-expanding experience.' You didn't tell me I might be expanding as part of a plasma cloud. And you've got children on board. What was I supposed to think?"

She snaked her tiny head—tiny only in proportion to her body—around so she was facing me straight on when she said, "What difference do children make?"

I felt the hair stand up on the back of my neck at the sight of her cavernous mouth so close to me, but it would have been standing up anyway at the news that our lives were in danger. "They could be killed, that's what difference. It's reckless endangerment, and furthermore, it makes no evolutionary sense."

"Da, evolution again. Are you still clinging to that theory? I grant it may explain the actions of primitive creatures, but not those of a being capable of directing its own behavior."

"Of course it does."

"Da, da, da. Despite the many contradictions you have observed on board?"

"There are no contradictions," I told her. "Everything I've seen so far can be explained once I learn the whole picture."

"Even reckless endangerment of our children?"

"Maybe," I said. Anger made me add, "Then again, maybe you're just insane."

She made a cat-purring sound deep in her long, sinuous throat that vibrated the walls, and my teeth. Laughter. "I am probably that. After all, I'm the one who believes she can talk to a star."

I looked at the nursery around me. Three hundred feet across, with mud walls dripping from condensation. A couple feet of dung mashed underfoot, mixed with hay the size of bamboo stalks and crawling with "darats" and "daspiders" and "dabeetles" the size of coyotes. The place stank like a cattle dome. On the other hand, Dajef may have had the appearance of a clumsy, six-legged mountain of flesh, but the three-foot squids she called "dabaras" that hung like tentacled remoras from her flanks were remote-controlled hands, programmed before their release by a brain the size of an elephant in the forward part of that immense body. There was plenty of gray matter left for abstract thought. That didn't guarantee sanity, but I didn't think she was suicidal, either.

She was merely adventurous. Just my luck. I had figured my worst danger on board the Dareftan ship would be from clumsy leviathan feet, not from their careless sense of derring-do.

"Do you want to leave?" she asked. "You could take the lifeboat now and wait for us outside the nebula."

The expedition ship was nearly half a mile long, and shaped like a blunt teardrop. About halfway down its curved topside, a lifeboat bigger than most human-built starships stuck like a tick on a dog's back. It was my temporary home while I was on board, and I actually thought about fleeing in it while I had the chance, but not for long. "Oh, sure," I said, "and strand you on the surface of a collapsing star with no chance of escape if something goes wrong."

"Was that a yes or a no?" she asked.

Translation problem again. Never trust language software to do your thinking for you, even if it's part of your brain.

"That was a no," I snapped. "If I lived and you died, I'd feel guilty the rest of my life."

"You prefer death to guilt? Yet you continue to believe in evolution?"

"It's not that simple," I said. I took a deep breath, trying to calm down. "If I *knew* we'd die in there, I'd take the lifeboat in an instant. But since there's a possibility we'll all survive it, maybe in that same lifeboat, I can't lower your chances just to increase mine. That's—well, I guess that's called honor. It's a long-term survival trait. Benefits the race rather than the individual."

"I fail to see how."

"It increases the status of my offspring," I said. "That improves their chances for reproductive success, so the race gets more copies of the genes that make people help each other in an emergency."

"I thought you had no offspring."

"I don't," I said. "But if I did—"

"Evolution makes such theoretical leaps? I am making a pretense of being impressed."

Was that the translator again, or had she made a joke? I didn't know, and I wasn't in the mood to pursue it. Neither was she, apparently. She rolled to her feet, pushing her young ones aside so she wouldn't step on them, and said, "I must go ready the magnetic sensors."

"You do that," I replied, looking down to where the children squalled and snarled at each other, their orange-stained mouths and pointed fangs matching my mood. One of them looked up at me, then stretched to its full length, trying to reach me. Just like any child, it wanted to touch everything it saw. It probably wanted to put everything in its mouth, too. I shivered and reeled myself closer to the ceiling, but I wondered why I didn't just do a swan dive into their midst instead. What difference did it make if I was vaporized in a star or eaten by a twenty-foot grub and then vaporized in a star? Dead was dead.

The cavernous door irised open to let Dajef out. My path back to my room or wherever I wanted to go would be through the air duct overhead, but I didn't crawl through the grate just yet. As long as I was there, I might as well watch the children play now that they had been fed. It seemed stupid to just continue on with my research while the ship plowed deeper and deeper into trouble, but it would be even more stupid to go sulk in the domesticated packing crate I called a stateroom and wait for the end. If we didn't go up in flames, I would look pretty foolish.

The young ones were just starting to develop the swelling in the middle of their bodies that would become the digestive system and muscle mass they would need to support a heavier body. It wasn't yet big enough to keep them on all sixes, especially in the half-gravity the Darefta maintained on board. They could still rear up on their coiled tails and reach for me, and when they grew bored with that they dropped on each other, the solid meaty *smacks* and their happy squeals echoing in the brood chamber. They tumbled together into one big, writhing heap, tugging on each other's heads and biting each other's tails like kittens.

How could rational parents expose their offspring to a worse-than-even chance of death? Even if Dajef was crazy, each of the kids had two other parents among the crew. They couldn't all be nuts. There had to be some advantage I wasn't seeing, some potential gain that made the risk worth taking. Maybe it was the same as my own reason for not taking the lifeboat. If we succeeded in recording the mind of a star and returned home with the evidence, everyone on board would be instantly famous. In Dareftan society, that might be worth the risk.

Hell, it might be worth it in mine. I smiled grimly at the thought. If I lived through this, I could come out of it smelling like a rose. After I took a week-long shower.

We came to a stop a quarter million miles from the surface of the protostar. It looked pretty much like a regular star to me, glowing bright yellow and surrounded by a wispy white corona. That corona was gas falling *in*, however, not blowing outward, and all the light was from frictional heating as the star contracted. The neutrino flux was still negligible, though it spiked occasionally as small pockets of hydrogen at the core went critical.

The nebula from which the star had formed was still drawn tight like a blanket around it. The inner surface was deep violet and bumpy, roiled like the underside of a thundercloud.

"Is that caused by turbulence or light pressure or what?" I asked. I was standing on the control console, up near the top edge where I had a good view out the forward window and where I wouldn't get squashed if the pilot, Dalapek, started pushing buttons in a hurry.

"Yes to all three," Dajef said without looking away from her monitors. She stood off to the right, also facing the window, but with a curved theater of holo tanks surrounding her on the other three sides. From my angle she was just a shadow behind a ghostly line drawing of the magnetic field lines, which were winding tighter and tighter as the star gained rotational speed from infalling matter.

Two of the other crewmembers were running the probe guidance controls and the computer that would collect the incoming data. The rest were in the cargo bays, waiting to start feeding probes into the launch tubes when Dajef gave the word.

"What's the 'or what' part?" I asked.

"Magnetic effects. Gravity. Planets are forming out there. Some of them might even be habitable in a billion years or so, if the star chooses the right evolutionary path."

"Say what?" I asked. "Evolution? I thought you didn't believe in that."

"Translation glitch," she replied. "Apparently you use the same word for two different things. To me, stellar evolution means what happens to an individual star over its own lifetime. I'm talking about the decision to flare early and drive off the rest of the nebula with light pressure so it becomes a smaller, more steady-burning star, or to hold off as long as possible and collect as much mass as it can, which will ultimately shorten its life or even turn it into a variable."

"You talk like the star has a choice. I thought the density of the gas cloud determined that sort of thing."

"Largely, yes. But the last-minute infall is significant. The moment of ignition determines everything from stellar composition to planetary formation, and that moment happens while the star is alive."

"Provided your magnetic plasma brain theory is true," I said. "But even if the star is awake, that doesn't mean it has a choice, or the ability to do anything about it anyway."

"It does. It just doesn't realize it. That's why I'm trying to learn how to communicate with them."

One of the monitors flickered and went out. Dajef growled, and my translator said, "Typically perverse." She yanked one of her squid-like dabaras loose from her flank and shoved it through an access hatch, then continued working at the controls for the magnetic field probes.

"What do you mean, that's why you want to talk with them?" I asked. "You want to coax them into holding on?"

"No," she said. "I want to ask them to commit suicide." She stuck her head through the hologram between us to look at me. "The sooner they ignite, the more steadily they burn. The more steadily they burn, the more conducive their planets will be to life. I plan to ask them for a favor. But to do that, I have to learn how to talk to them."

I didn't know what to say. Did she really think she could talk a being who only lived for a few days into killing itself early so someone could get a tan under its light a billion years hence? What difference would that

92

make to the star? Why should it care?

I almost started that argument, but the dead monitor came back on and Dajef got busy at the controls below it. She slapped an intercom button the size of a dinner plate and said, "Begin launching."

I could feel the faintest of vibrations as the probes blew free. There were just over a thousand of them, each the size of a railroad car. The optical monitor showed their paths as they accelerated away to surround the star and skim along just above its surface.

We weren't so far away from it ourselves. "What's our hull temperature?" I asked.

She had to ask Dalapek, the pilot, but my earphones translated his reply directly: "Three thousand degrees."

"How, uh, how dangerous is that?"

"Don't touch it," Dajef said.

"Duh," I replied, but she didn't respond. Of course not.

The ship's hull had been designed to burn away slowly and carry off built-up heat as it did, but there was a limit to what it could withstand. And how long.

I retraced the path to the lifeboat in my mind. Back along the central corridor, jog left toward the nursery, then up to the outer hull. It would be in the main ship's shadow, so it should be relatively cool until it cast off, after which its underside would start to heat just as badly in the intense light this close to the protostar. It would actually heat worse, because the lifeboat's hull wasn't built to ablate nor shaped to deflect intense light. It had a concave underside designed to conform to the main ship's round surface, plus engine ports and access hatches and leg-like instrument housings all along its length. If it was exposed to the protostar for more than a few minutes, it would vaporize. But we wouldn't stay close to the star if we needed the lifeboat. The moment we launched it, we would be fleeing for our lives.

Dajef's dabara popped out of the access panel and slithered back to her side. Dajef paid it no attention. She was focusing on the magnetic field display, which was knotting up like a ball of string in a blender. The level of detail grew finer and finer as the probes started reporting in, and I could see how it continued its fine structure as small as my eyes could resolve it, like a fractal.

"It's getting complex," she said. "It could become self-aware at any moment."

"How will you know?"

"Watch."

"We'll be able to *see* it?"

"If it follows the simulations."

I watched, looking from the magnetic field display to the window, where the surface of the star curved gently away from us, the nebula like a mottled stage curtain behind it. The stellar surface was beginning to swirl and flare as the magnetic fields dragged huge volumes of charged plasma around in their embrace.

"There it goes!" Dajef shouted. I covered my ears a second too late, but I looked back to the monitors. The optical ones didn't show much, but the magnetic image suddenly locked into place, then began to vibrate with a million tiny waves that propagated back and forth through it. They built up and flattened out in three-dimensional interference patterns that looked way too regular to be accidental.

"Holy shit," I said. Those looked like brain waves.

"Yes," Dajef said. "It is a pitifully low-resolution map. I would need millions of probes to gather every nuance of the star's mind. But with luck, it will be good enough to retain its intelligence in a simulator."

"That's—" *not what I meant,* I started to say, but I stopped when I saw the lines of force shift again. They reached upward like amoebae, little loops peeling off and reaching still farther, clear up to the surface.

"It senses the probes!" Dajef said.

"Probes, hell, it senses *us!*" I yelled, because I could see the side of the hologram she couldn't, and one of the magnetic loops—the one pointing straight at our ship—didn't stop at the surface.

Out the window huge flares arched out from the photosphere, following the field lines. The magnetic map lost resolution as the probes failed one after another.

"Get us out of here!" I shouted at Dalapek. He couldn't understand me, but he didn't need to. He could see the obvious just as well as I could. Like any newborn child, the star was reaching out to touch the only thing it could feel, using the only sense and the only appendages it had available: magnetism. It probably didn't even know that it was trailing million-mile-long limbs of superheated plasma behind it, or what it would do to us if it touched us. It probably didn't know anything at all, except that it existed, and something else did too.

Dalapek mashed a big yellow button under his three-fingered hand. The ship lurched as the artificial gravity fought to cancel the forward thrust, then lurched again when the magnetic field swept through us.

I had never actually seen a control panel erupt in a shower of sparks before. Vids show it happening all the time, but it's usually a load of hooey. Impacts don't cause voltage surges. On the other hand, magnetic fields certainly do, especially ones strong enough to drag a solar flare along after them. The control panel became a very bad place to be just then; at the first sign of trouble I took a running leap and jumped the ten feet of space to Dalapek's forearm while fireballs blew through the plastic buttons right behind me. I pulled myself upward until I was closer to his body, then grabbed hold of his rubbery skin with both hands.

He reached forward to do something; switch off the power, run the throttles up to full, I'll never know. His head and forearm were right over the panel when it exploded upward like a bomb had gone off inside it, and the impact knocked him backward hard enough to lift him off the deck.

It also flung me upward, arcing through the holographic display that tracked our destruction. I felt a moment's hilarity at the realization that it was the star's life, not my own, that flashed before my eyes in my final moments; then I hit Dajef's side, bounced off, fell about twenty feet, and lurched to a stop with my head just a couple of feet off the floor. One of her dabaras had snagged me by my right foot.

"Thanks," I managed to croak. It looked at me with three or four of its multiple eyes, blinked one of them, and stretched its tentacle to lower me to the floor.

I promptly ducked for cover under the holo tank, because Dajef was jerking around like a fish on the end of a tight line. She'd gotten hit by some high voltage.

A major quake shook the floor, and by the wet, heavy thud that accompanied it I guessed that Dalapek had fallen. By the looks of his head as I'd flown past it, I didn't think he'd be getting up again.

The star was still reaching for us, dragging its magnetic field back through the ship. The lights flared bright as sunlight for a second, and the gravity suddenly tripled. I sagged to the floor, but Dajef did worse than that; I heard bones break and saw her body flatten out like a water balloon just before it bursts.

The generators failed before she did. She rebounded toward the ceiling, and I heard her scream when she hit it head first.

Then the lights blew out. The control room didn't go dark; there was plenty of the real thing just outside, and the forward window was a real window rather than a viewscreen.

It was also melting. It was an ablative insulator like the rest of the hull, but at least half of it had already vaporized. I could see it bubbling just a foot or so from the inner surface.

"Time to go!" I yelled. I pulled myself out from under the holo tank and shoved my way up the side of it, grabbing the lip to pull myself to a stop. "Dajef!" I shouted. "Dajef!" She was a blimp overhead, adrift.

She quit screaming, but she didn't answer me. I doubted if she'd heard me over her own voice anyway, so I yelled again, "We've got to get to the lifeboat!"

"I'm...injured," she said. Her voice was barely a whisper. The only reason I could hear her was because there weren't any other noises in the control room at all. The ship was dead.

So were her other crewmates. They hadn't been as lucky as she was when the gravity generators had overloaded.

"Can you move?" I asked, kicking off and floating up toward her head.

She tried, screamed again. "No! Save yourself. Go."

I thought about dragging her through the ship. We were in free-fall, after all. Once I got her moving, it wouldn't matter how big she was.

There was the rub, though. Getting her moving would take half an hour, and stopping her at the other end of the corridor would take just as long. Not to mention the two turns on the way. We had maybe five minutes before the window weakened enough to blow out. Less if the star tried to touch us again.

I grasped the side of her neck and looked back toward the doorway, thanking luck it had been open when the power failed.

"Save the data," Dajef whispered. A dabara wriggled free, jumped to the computer, and disappeared inside. A moment later it reappeared and launched itself carefully toward me. I flinched away, but it reached out with a tentacle and snagged my leg, then slithered up to grip me around the waist. I saw no memory cards in its grip. Had it downloaded the star's mind into its own?

"Data schmata," I said. "What about the children?"

"You...would risk your life for...an alien's offspring?"

"If I knew how to get them into the lander."

She thought about it. "They wouldn't listen to you. Forget them. Save yourself."

"I can't just leave you—"

The window started to squeal. With a cry of pure agony, Dajef flicked her neck like a whip, throwing me straight through the doorway. I sailed past the portal with dozens of feet to spare on all sides and continued on down the corridor at about fifty miles an hour, wondering how I was going to stop, but the window solved that problem for me. It blew out while I was halfway down to the end. Air roared past, pelting me with debris I didn't even want to think about, but it slowed my flight to practically nothing before the corridor suddenly got very dark and the wind cut off. I twisted around to see if the pressure door had closed, but it was still wide open.

Dajef's body was wedged in the window. Air still whistled out around the edges, and sunlight still leaked in, but the worst of the hole was plugged. I had no idea how long that would last, but I didn't wait to find out. I hit the end of the corridor feet-first, took two running steps to the left and kicked hard for the side corridor before I bounced away. My balance was off with the dabara on my back, but it helped steady us with its tentacles.

This corridor was short, less than a hundred yards. At the end of it, the nursery door was sealed tight. Straight up, in a shaft that never had gravity generators to begin with, was the direct access tube to the lifeboat. The circular doorway up there was wide open, and soft light glowed from beyond it. The boat had its own power supply, and the bulk of the starship had spared it the worst of the flare's effects.

I wanted nothing more than to jump into that light, but the nursery was right there. I had to at least try. I braced myself against the jamb and pounded on the "open" button with my fist. It was at least a foot across and spring-loaded for giants, but it slid into the wall for a second before popping back out.

Nothing happened. I hit it again, making sure it bottomed out against the contacts this time, but still nothing. The door had no power.

There had to be a way to open it manually. I leaned back, careful not to lose my grip on the jamb, and looked for it. It was easy to spot: a crank overhead with a shaft as big around as my thigh. I wasn't going to get that door open anytime soon.

I tried it anyway, jumping up and grabbing it in my hands, then planting my feet against the ceiling and shoving. It didn't budge, so I tried to tug it the other way, but of course I had nothing to hold onto, so I just managed to pull myself toward the crank.

Then the dabara slid around and stuck half its tentacles to the ceiling, and pulled on the crank with the other. It turned smoothly, and the door irised open a few feet. When the dabara got the crank around so I could push, I helped it along, letting it tug the handle around again.

We had opened the door about halfway when I suddenly realized it was big enough. One of the children stuck its head out of the hole in the middle, coming straight at me with a toothy mouth about five feet across.

I yelled "Yaaa!" and kicked off toward the lifeboat. I didn't have to tell the children to follow me. As soon as they saw me, they all swarmed out into the corridor, trailing a cloud of debris behind them. They'd have had me at first leap if they'd had any experience with free-fall, but they were even more clumsy at it than me. The dabara landed on my back again and with its help I managed to stay ahead of them all the way up the corridor, and I ducked to the side just inside the door.

They went roaring past like shuttles late for dock. I climbed up the curved frame and slapped the door-close button while they were still nosing around the controls, then yelled "Hey, over here!" and waited until they were airborne again before I jumped over their heads and bounced off the ceiling toward the forward window. I risked a glance outside; we were still in the shadow of the main ship, but huge flares arched overhead and ionized gas streamed upward around all sides, glowing like liquid neon light. That was our hull boiling away.

My packing crate home was tied to a girder just above the door. I'd put it there so it would be out of the way in case of an emergency. Its open doorway offered familiar sanctuary, but I couldn't go for it yet.

There was one big yellow button in the middle of the control panel. I hoped to hell that was the "go" button, and that the autopilot was smart enough to fly us out of here on its own, because that was the only chance I was going to get. I took aim, leaped for it, kicked it with both feet, and let the rebound send me back to the ceiling again. One of the children clipped my heel with its outstretched hand as it tried to intercept me, but I kept going, tumbling end over end until I hit one of the open girders on the ceiling. I kicked off for my crate just as the autopilot said "Prepare for boost," but I made it through the doorway and grabbed my zero-gee sleeping net for support, then peered cautiously outside.

There were vertical panels rising from the floor behind the control console. Back rests, I guessed, which meant there wasn't any artificial gravity in here even during boost, and the direction of thrust would be from behind. I clung to my net and waited for it to hit. The dabara looped a couple of tentacles around the net and a couple around me as well.

Two of the children leaped toward us.

"Launch!" I screamed.

Nothing happened. I ducked inside just as they hit. The plastic crate was designed to take a beating, but not an assault; one side caved in and a big split popped open right beside my feet. The door was too narrow for the children to stick their heads through, but it wouldn't take them long to try reaching in with their hands.

I looked wildly around for a weapon, but there was only my duffel bag and some of my personal junk held in place behind another drift net. Nothing there would even slow down a Dareftan child, but I started throwing things at them anyway, determined not to give up without a fight. Data disks, my book reader, my razor—I threw practically everything I owned at them, including a roll of toilet paper which bounced off one of the children's nose and caromed away, spilling a long fluttering tail out behind it as it unrolled.

The crate rocked as both kids shoved off after the bright white streamer. A second later the lifeboat shuddered as the docking clamps released, then a gentle push shoved me against the back wall. The door was right in front of me; I stuck my head out and watched the flying mouths drop back to the floor to land among their siblings.

The thrust built up to a full gee and then some as we streaked away from the melting starship. The deep violet nebula reached toward us like a flat wall, and I gasped as we plowed into it with a shudder and a groan from the hull. The sunlight grew dimmer, then faded out entirely when the overdrive kicked in. I had no idea where it was taking us, but wherever it was had to be better than here.

The dabara on my back wriggled free and dropped down into the tangle of children, who were voicing their frustration at being pinned to the deck while I dangled out of reach overhead. The dabara attached itself to the topmost one, which shivered as if it had been bitten. The baby Dareftan looked up and squeaked at me, and I was surprised when my translator said, "Who are you?"

"Dajef?" I asked. Could she have downloaded her own personality into the dabara? Or was this the star's mind overlaid on the Dareftan child's? Their brains were programmable, after all.

"Dajef?" it echoed. Apparently the name wasn't familiar. That meant I was talking to a star. A star in a baby's mind. I wondered if that was why Dajef had brought children along.

"Dajef is your trimom's name," I told the gestalt being below me. "And your savior's. And maybe your jailor's and your executioner's as well, depending on how things turn out." I didn't know if it had the translation software it needed to understand me, but I thought maybe the sound of a voice might be soothing.

It looked at the window, then back at me, clearly puzzled by this sudden odd turn of events.

So was I. Why had I risked my life to rescue these children? For that matter, I was still risking it. There were undoubtedly rations on board for Dareftan passengers, but I could easily end up as a snack if I wasn't careful.

"It was the least I could do," I said, more to myself than to the child. "She was trying to make liveable solar systems for people a billion years in the future. I couldn't let genes like that go to waste."

It occurred to me that I was living proof of Dajef's argument that rational beings could think themselves into counter-evolutionary strategies. I had put an abstract higher cause above my own safety, just as she was hoping to someday convince stars to do. I hadn't consciously intended it, but that's what I had done. Which meant, I supposed, that convincing a star to do the same might not be so difficult after all.

I looked out the window at the darkness. There were hundreds of protostars in this nebula alone, all of which could become life-supporting solar systems for our descendants. Maybe even some of my own, if I survived to have any.

I looked back inside my crate, taking inventory of what I had left. Plenty of food. Extra clothing. And two more rolls of toilet paper, which might just come in handy before we got back to civilization.

INTRODUCTION TO

UNCERTAINTY

I've always maintained that quantum physics is easier to understand than marriage. The Heisenberg Uncertainty Principle and the Schrödinger's cat paradox are nothing compared to the complexity of spousal interaction. Only a fool would try to explain marriage in a short story, yet this is the first of two stories that attempt to do just that. What can I say? Love makes fools of us all.

UNCERTAINTY

Jason is excited as he parks the demonstrator LeBaron in front of his house. He parks on the street so his neighbors can see it, and maybe decide to buy one. That's not likely, but it's possible, and a car salesman plays the odds. If you greet enough customers, put the cars in front of enough people, someone will buy one. As they have done today. A brand new Imperial, cash, and Jason already has the commission check in his breast pocket.

He fingers the crisp paper as he walks up the driveway to the door. Yes, still there. And just before Christmas. Ginny will be pleased. He tries the doorknob before he goes for his house keys, but it is locked. Not a good sign. If Ginny were home, she would have left it open for him, maybe even met him at the door. Unless she got caught up in something and forgot the time. That's happened before. So Jason sets his briefcase on the concrete step and fishes in his pocket for the keys, unlocks the door, and as he steps into the darkened house he says loudly, hopefully, "Honey, I'm home!"

The silent house returns not even an echo. Jason switches on the kitchen light and takes a cautious sniff. No aroma of freshly baked bread, no meaty heaviness of a roast or even a hamburger casserole. The wave function has collapsed; the universe has chosen. Ginny is not home today.

She might have been. That's the most frustrating aspect of the whole thing. Until Jason checked to see, she might have been right here in this kitchen, wanting him as eagerly as he wanted her, but the very act of arriving was enough to set the universal dice in motion and tonight they came up snake-eyes.

105

He turns around and steps outside again, closing the door behind him. A virtual couple pops into being on the sidewalk beside his car, a teenage boy and girl walking arm-in-arm. She nods at something he says, then laughs. They take three steps before vanishing, their very existence swallowed in the quantum foam.

Jason shivers and opens the door again, but Ginny is still gone. He knew she would be; the universe can't be fooled that easily.

He sets the commission check on the kitchen table and plods through the house, shedding briefcase, shoes, tie, and the rest of his clothing along the way into the bedroom, where he collapses backward on the bed and stares at the ceiling. The lunar landscape of its textured surface is dimly lit from the evening light filtering through the window overlooking the back yard. Jason tells himself that the ceiling is a good metaphor for his life, that the even pattern of bumps up there results from the same randomness that haunts his marriage. The carpenter who made the ceiling had no idea where each speck of grout would go; he just sprayed them upward in a great shower of mud, and the overall, aggregate pattern of those thousands of flying particles turned out to have a kind of order to them. Even though it was theoretically possible, the carpenter probably didn't worry about them all landing in the same place, or inexplicably avoiding an area shaped like, say, the face of the Madonna.

It's a lousy metaphor and Jason knows it. Yes, overall he and Ginny have a happy marriage, but he wants her *now*. Now, this instant, warm and cuddly with her auburn hair dancing in loopy curls around her ears, her smile wide and inviting...

Jason gets up abruptly, pads into the bathroom, and takes a shower. He scrubs off the day's sweat first, then closes his eyes and satisfies his other need as best he can. It isn't enough. He opens his eyes, looking at the bright white tiles with the beads of water forming and falling from them. Thousands of drops, spraying randomly off his chest, yet forming an even distribution along the wall. A Gaussian distribution, named after Karl F. Gauss, the German mathematician who studied randomness before Schrödinger, the other doyen of particle behavior, was even a boy. Jason knows these things. He has read up on the subject. Yet as so many physicists have learned, knowing how a phenomenon works doesn't mean he can control it.

Jason still needs some kind of release. He reaches forward and turns the faucet slowly to cold, gritting his teeth until the primal whoop bursts from his lungs. This time the whole house echoes.

The next evening she is home. Jason knows that last night has nothing to do with tonight, that random events by definition cannot influence one another. A tossed coin can come up tails a dozen times in a row and still have a fifty-fifty chance on the next throw.

But tonight it's heads. For Jason. Trouble is, evidently Ginny is having a tails sort of day, because the moment he opens the door he feels himself fading away. He gets a glimpse of her talking on the phone, but when she turns she looks right through him and Jason goes where virtual particles go when they annihilate.

When awareness returns, he is sitting on a stool at the end of a polished mahogany bar. A tall glass in front of him holds ice and a straw, and smells of gin. Jason groans. Of all the places he could go, why does he keep coming here? Only a cheap motel would be worse. But either way, whether he reeked of gin or perfume, if he were to go home now his marriage would be ruined. Jason knows this with instinctive certainty. Ginny may suspect where he goes, but she must never know.

He orders coffee from the gray-haired bartender, slurps down two cups while watching the other patrons in the mirror. How many of them came here voluntarily? he wonders. How many are victims of chance?

In one of those random moments when all the voices are silent but one, he hears: "Okay, a Frenchman, a Mexican, and a Texan are in a balloon..."

Jason laughs, but not at the punch line.

When he gets home, Ginny is gone. This time it works in Jason's favor; there will be no argument tonight, no attempt to explain the inexplicable. No warm wife to snuggle with either, though. On the whole, Jason doesn't like the trade.

He looks in the bedroom closet, but her suitcase is still there. Sometimes it and some of her clothing is gone and he knows she is at her mother's, but tonight she could be anywhere. She could even be right here at home, simply phase-shifted so they cannot interact.

He goes to bed and holds her pillow, imagining that it is her.

The next day he considers calling her from work to find out what he'll be facing when he goes home, but he has tried that before and it doesn't work. Early knowledge gives him no more satisfaction than none, and finding her home during the day doesn't guarantee anything anyway; she is indeterminate again by the time he arrives.

He imagines one of his co-workers overhearing him on the phone, maybe even saying something like, "Checking up on the little woman, eh?" but he knows that will never happen. Such a statement might be misconstrued, and even if the meaning could somehow be made unambiguous, whether or not their wives are home to greet them at night is not something men talk about. Not these men, at least. Yet Jason wonders if they all struggle with the same uncertainty. Some of them even have kids; Jason shudders to think what it must be like to go to bed without knowing that your child is safe in his room. Always wondering, as Jason wonders on the lonely nights, whether this time your loved ones are lost for good. Or whether *you* are lost to your family.

He and Ginny have decided to wait until they solve their problem before they have kids of their own. It's one of the few things about which they both agree perfectly.

But the problem has no solution. Heisenberg proved that. You can never know both the position and the disposition of your spouse to infinite accuracy.

That night he takes a pickup from the lot and brings home a Christmas tree. He backs into the driveway so he can unload it easily, and as he gets out of the pickup he sees Ginny smiling at him through the kitchen window. A great weight slides away from him, and as he takes the few steps to the door he squares his shoulders, shakes his head so his hair will fall into that slightly mussed state she likes so much, and opens the door. "I'm ho-ome," he calls playfully, and she smiles, comes to him, kisses him with lips warm and soft and tasting of cookie dough. She is baking snickerdoodles, Jason's favorite.

"Tell me how they are," she says, handing him one still hot out of the oven.

He blows on it to cool it, takes a bite, feels it melt into a burst of sweetness and spice in his mouth. "Mmmm," he says, then kissing her again with crumbs still on his lips, "*Mmmmmm.*"

In the bedroom she helps him change out of his suit, running her hands over his body and kneading the sore muscles in his back just as he'd wished she would for the last two nights. He rubs her back as well, and is about to unbutton her shirt when the oven timer goes off. Laughing, she twists away, and he feels a momentary pang of regret, but then he laughs and dresses in his casual clothes. There will be time enough for that later.

They decorate the tree, he hanging the gold balls and she the silver. They're careful not to let the antiparticles touch. Ginny suggests using just one kind, for safety, but Jason shakes his head and says, "If we did that, the energy balance would be off."

When the tree is decorated, heavy with cosmic strings and shimmering gamma rays, Jason goes into his study to wrap presents. He has bought many small things, not wanting to repeat the fiasco of two years ago when he bought Ginny a single diamond necklace. Of course when she opened the box, it was empty. Fifty-fifty chance. This year she'll get a few empty boxes, but half of them will be full.

He has even bought multiple presents for the cat, though he hasn't seen it for days.

After dinner they cuddle on the sofa. They whisper, they tickle, they laugh. Jason kisses her, softly at first, then more deeply. In the rush of excitement that follows, her shirt makes a quantum shift to the floor; then in a quick chain reaction the rest of their clothing follows. Inexorable pressure brings them together, the heat between them building and building until they undergo fusion.

Jason wishes they could remain in this state forever, but the isotope is unstable, as it always is. Fission inevitably follows. They move to the bed when bare skin begins to cool.

Later still, as they lie side by side under the covers, moonlight softening the shadows, he realizes this is the time he loves the most. The quiet time at the end of a perfect day. Hesitantly, he asks, "Do you—do you ever wish it could always be like this?"

She nods, an almost imperceptible tilt of her head. "Of course I do. But it can't be."

"Why not?" he asks.

"Because it isn't. The universe doesn't work that way." She turns on her side, away from him.

He knows he is treading on thin ice now, but he can't leave it alone. "I just wish—" he begins, but she says, "Jason, I can't always be your fantasy lover."

The moment has become as fragile as a uranium atom. Jason pauses, his mind seething with the possibilities. Virtual particles come into being, annihilate, while he tries to decide. Should he fire a neutron into the nucleus, directly into the heart of the matter? Increase its weight with questions until it splits apart, and in splitting yields its secrets? Or should he shield it, preserve its glittering presence for as long as possible? Jason feels the entire universe quiver with anticipation as he considers the ramifications. Weighs the options. Decides.

"Oh, but you are," he says, kissing her earlobe and nestling up against her like one spoon behind another. He holds her, and as she drifts off to sleep he thinks, You are my fantasy lover. And all the craziness, all the uncertainty, is worth it for these moments when it's fantastic.

INTRODUCTION TO

IF YOU WISH UPON A STAR

Have you ever wondered why two people who went through the same experience will have different memories of how it happened? Anybody who's been married for more than a week has noticed the phenomenon, and probably argued fruitlessly about it for hours. There can only be one good explanation for it, but the implications are terrifying.

The idea for this story came to me in a flash while packing the car for a picnic in the Shoshone River canyon between Cody, Wyoming and Yellowstone Park. I didn't speak a word of it to Kathy until after we'd made it back home, safe. Then I wrote it all down, knocking wood and clutching a rabbit's foot the whole time.

If You Wish Upon a Star

"You ever wonder about luck?" he asked.

They were driving up the winding canyon road into the mountains, out for an afternoon drive and a walk in the woods and the chance to get away from town and time and people for a few hours. "Looking for meteorites," he called outings like these, because he'd always thought it would be neat to find one and he supposed that if he got out and walked around enough the odds would eventually work in his favor. Of course he didn't much like prairie, which would have been a better place to look than in a forest with its steady accumulation of duff on the forest floor covering all but the freshest falls, but then meteorites weren't really the reason he went out walking anyway. They were just the excuse. By the time he got into the woods he had usually forgotten meteorites completely, and spent most of his time there looking up into the trees instead of down at the ground.

"What about luck?" she replied. She'd been looking out the window, watching the canyon walls slide past and wondering how many dinosaurs were buried in the sedimentary strata exposed by the road's construction, and whether the sudden boundary that she could see between colors of rock might be the 65 million year old Cretaceous-Tertiary boundary that marked the extinction of the dinosaurs. *They* certainly hadn't been lucky.

"I was just thinking how it seems sometimes that you and I are luckier than most people."

"What makes you think that?" she asked, but she asked it with a smile. Of course they were luckier than most. They had each other, didn't they?

He looked over and saw her smile, and they both laughed. He looked back to the road, shifted down and gave the car a little more gas going into the next curve. The smooth hum of the engine was like the car laughing with them. It was a '72 Datsun 240-Z, still in beautiful condition, and they'd bought it for a song when the previous owner — the one who'd done all the restoration — had thought the engine was about to blow. The problem had turned out to be a plugged fuel filter making it lurch and cough like a dying Pinto; they had replaced it with a two dollar and forty-nine cent generic filter from K-mart and the car had run like a dream ever since. Yeah, they were lucky.

"So what got you thinking about luck?"

"Oh, I was putting the cooler in back before we left, and I'd left the hatch locked. Of course I forgot to bring the key with me. I was standing there with the cooler in my arms, wondering whether to just stuff it in through the front or if I should set it down and go back inside for the key, and I thought `hey, wouldn't it be great if I hadn't slammed it hard enough when I closed it last time and I could just lift up the hatch?' So I gave a tug on the hatch and sure enough, it opened right up. That got me to wondering if it would've been unlatched if I hadn't thought about it first."

"How could that make any difference? It was either latched or it wasn't."

He grinned again and shook his head. "Maybe not. Quantum theorists believe that a subatomic particle doesn't necessarily have a `true' state without an observer. It's just a probablity wave until someone makes a measurement and collapses the wave into a certain state. Who's to say luck isn't the same way?"

She looked at him with head tilted. "Quantum luck?"

"Right! We can call the particles `luck-ons,' and — "

He waited until she'd quit laughing before he said, "Don't you wonder, though, how come so many things happen the way we hope they will?"

"Don't talk about it; you'll jinx it."

"Hah. We're making a scientific examination into the nature of luck. Now just for a minute suppose that luck-ons are real. Every time you're in a situation that could go two ways, there's this immense probability wave hanging around. It doesn't collapse until you force it, in this case by tugging on the hatch to see if it's open or not. But if you imagine ahead of time a chain of events that could lead to the luckier of the two possible outcomes, then you bias the universe toward that side of the question, and then when you check it out that's the way the probability wave naturally collapses."

"Uh huh." She wasn't buying it. But she could still appreciate the argument, so she said, "I suppose that's what people mean when they talk about making their own luck. The power of positive thinking and all that."

He knew when he was being ribbed, but if he'd let that sort of thing stop him he'd have been silenced on their first date. "Exactly," he said. "No doubt people have noticed it before, but until we discovered the actual operating principle it's been nothing more than a folk myth."

He looked in the mirror and instinctively let off the gas, then sighed in relief as a police car with lights flashing sped past and skidded around the corner ahead.

They looked at one another for a moment before she said, "Let me guess; you saw him in the mirror and immediately hoped he was after someone else, right?"

"How'd you guess?"

"Luck."

"*Touché.*"

Actually, an entire scenario had popped into his head in the millisecond or so that it took to recognize the cop car for what it was. He'd imagined an escaped convict parachuting out of a hijacked plane into the mountains somewhere up the road a ways, and the police heading up to try and catch him before he caught a ride out and away. The whole story was there, bang, in an instant. He didn't know where it had come from; random firing of synapses in a panicked brain, probably. He'd read that some people thought that that's all dreams were, too, just random impulses that the brain interpreted in ways it could understand. Whatever, it didn't matter. What mattered was that the cop was gone.

They broke out over the top of the ridge and there, stretched out in the valley below them, was the river. The road angled down until they were in the valley floor alongside it, driving through the aspens and cottonwoods along the bank. The trees were mostly bare, but what few leaves remained were still brilliant yellow and orange. The river was running low and clear, clearer than they'd seen it all summer, with pools of slow-moving water like a giant's footprints leading upstream as far as they could see.

"God, I wish I'd brought the fishing poles," he said.

"I thought we were looking for meteorites today."

"You can look for meteorites in a fishing stream, too."

"True." She twisted around in her seat and began digging under the coats they had brought along in case the weather turned chilly, saying, "Of course, you could have forgotten to take them out of the car last time we went fishing."

He glanced over at her, about to tell her not to bother looking, but an approaching car distracted him for a moment, and before he could say anything she exclaimed, "Hey, what do you know, you did!"

"What?"

"You did forget to put them away. They're right here." She rattled the rods together to prove it.

He felt his heart give a twist in his chest, and suddenly it was pounding like crazy. He searched frantically for a pull-off, saw one coming up on the other side of the road, and braked hard, skidding into it and bringing the car to rest sideways.

"Hey!" She picked herself up out of the footwell. "What the hell was that all about?"

He had to take a couple of deep breaths before he could say, "I did too put them away."

She gave him a look that said clear as words, "You've blown a seam somewhere, bucko." But she didn't say it. She just reached back behind the seats and pulled out one of the three-foot sections of bamboo fishing pole.

"That doesn't make a bit of difference," he said, still struggling for control. "I remember putting them away not twenty minutes ago."

"Huh?"

"They were rolling around loose back there when I went to put the cooler in, so I gathered them up and put them on the workbench because I didn't want them rubbing on the Styrofoam and squeaking all the way up here. I remember doing that!"

She looked down at the pole in her hands, back up at him again. Her grin was a bit shaky as she said, "Want me to toss them out?"

There could have been no better thing to say at that moment. Under the force of her smile, the anger that had suddenly welled up in him, the fear; both went wherever laps go when you stand up.

"I love you," he said simply, meaning it.

"I love you too. Shall we go fishing?"

"I don't think I could handle it right now. I did put those poles away. I swear I did."

"Then how did they get here?"

After a moment he said, "You wished them here."

Another police car hove into sight back the way they had come, swished past with lights ablaze, and was gone, leaves fluttering along the road in its wake.

"I still don't buy it."

They were driving on up the canyon, the fishing poles back under the coats, but not forgotten.

"I don't know what else to say. I remember taking them out of the car. That memory is clear as can be."

"You think there's another pair of fishing poles back home in the garage, then?"

Instead of answering, he took a sip of the Coke she had taken from the cooler. He set the can back in its niche in the console between the seats, then with a sigh, said, "No, that'd be asking too much. Conservation of mass wouldn't allow it."

"But you would?"

He shrugged. "Love, I remember what I did. I did put them away. But you didn't know about it, so when you went to look for them in back you found them." Slowly, the first smile he'd smiled in minutes spread across his face, and he went on: "Or to put it differently, your luckiness collapsed the luck-on probability wave in your favor without regard for what I'd already done."

"So we're back to luck-ons, are we?"

"It's an explanation."

"And I suppose you'll drag out the multiple-universe theory to explain how you could remember it happening another way, right?" She was kidding, but there was an undercurrent of concern in her voice. They brainstormed together on wild ideas all the time, but never before had he

117

gotten so...intense...about it.

"The multiple-universe theory?" he asked, his mind still not up to speed yet after his shock.

"You know. The universe splits off with every decision, so everything actually happens both ways."

"Oh, sure. Yeah, now that you mention it; it makes sense. When you collapsed the fishing pole luck-on you made a universe where I didn't take the poles out of the car, and somehow I wound up in the wrong universe."

"Thanks."

"Sorry. I didn't mean it that way. Just that in the other universe there must be another me who did put them in the car, and he and I somehow got our universes crossed."

She laughed suddenly. "And over there you and I are having a conversation just like this one, only you're saying, `but I did leave them in the car!' and I'm saying, `Then where are they now?'"

He laughed with her, took another sip of pop, then said, "If that sort of thing happens very often, that could explain a lot."

"A lot of what?"

"A lot of arguments we get into about whose memory is right. Stuff like whether or not you told me you had to work Saturday, or what day we saw *Slaughterhouse Five* for the first time, or—"

"I haven't seen *Slaughterhouse Five,* and neither have you. We've been wanting to for years and we've never gotten around to it."

"Exactly. But I remember last month suggesting we go rent it, and you said you'd already seen it. We got into quite an argument about it. You even described some of the scenes to me."

"We didn't either have an argument about—did we?"

"I did. Evidently you didn't."

"How can that be? Why didn't you stay in the universe where we had the argument, if that's the way you remember it?"

"I don't know. Maybe we're attracted to each other." He poked her playfully in the ribs.

"Yeow! You think so, do you?"

"Oh, maybe a little. Just enough to keep us together even when the universes keep splitting us up." He whacked the steering wheel in excitement. "Yeah! Look, everybody in the universe but you is a robot, right?"

"Huh?"

"It's called solipsism. A solipsist believes that only he or she is real, that the rest of the universe is there merely to stimulate the self. The most powerful argument for solipsism is that it feels that way, that almost everybody already believes it deep down. You know everybody else is mortal, but you can't believe it about yourself; that sort of thing. Okay, suppose that's right, but in every universe, a different person is real. You're only real in one universe, and in all the other ones, the ones created every time something could go two ways, it's just echoes of yourself going through the motions for somebody else's benefit."

"So how does that—?"

"You and I are attracted to each other. Really. We're both real, here, in the same universe. And when the dividing universes split us up, we find our way back together. Maybe they naturally merge if there's not too much difference between the two, or—"

"Whoa, stop, wait a minute." She picked up the can of pop and took a long drink. "Look, this is all silly speculation. Luck-ons and multiple universes and arguments we didn't have. I don't believe it for a minute. I don't want to believe it."

"Why not?"

"Because if it's true, then we could get separated. We do get separated. And I don't know how to get back to you."

"But we do get back! That's the beauty of it. We're like magnets. We attract each other clear across multiple universes. All for the price of a few faulty memories."

They were driving through deep forest now. She looked away, watching the trees stream past, a blur of green, imagining each one a universe into which she could tumble.

"You're right, though," he said. "It's all speculation. We should experiment."

"No!"

"We can be careful. If we wish for something together, we'll both stay on the same side of the collapsing luck-on event. And then we'll know whether we can control it or not. It doesn't even need to be something all that unlikely. Like, there are lots of moose around here; we can wish for a moose out in the river when we come around the next corner. Okay?"

"You don't give me much choice. You've already wished for it." And now she found herself wishing for it too. Wishing for a great, big moose with a rack of horns just as big as whatever he had wished for, standing however he imagined it standing. As they approached the corner she reached out and grasped his hand, squeezing hard. Be there, be there, be there be—

"Son of a bitch," he said quietly.

A moose, big and black and real as ever, stood knee deep in the water, eating the grass along the bank. It eyed them dubiously as they passed.

"Quick, when did we see *Slaughterhouse Five*?"

"We didn't."

"Right. Are the fishing poles still there?"

"I don't want to look."

"I won't let go."

He couldn't have if he'd wanted to. She was gripping him as if her life depended on it, and she didn't think she'd ever let go of him again. But she twisted around and looked under the coats one-handed, and the poles were still there.

"Still there," she said. "So now what?"

"Once could be coincidence. We need another test to raise the odds against it happening by chance. If we can do it twice in a row, we'll know it's for real." He felt her tense even more, and added, "The better we understand it, the more control we'll have over it."

She knew he was right. Now that they were this far, there was no turning back. "So what do we wish for this time?" she asked.

"How about something different? Something we normally wouldn't want to see, like a beer can in the road. Just to test if we can control which fork in the path we take, or if it's always the lucky path. Okay?"

"Okay, a beer can in the road."

"Uncrushed," he added. "Just to make it less probable."

"Okay."

They were already going around a curve; she tried to imagine a beer can standing on the center line just beyond where it straightened out again. She got an image in her mind, and seconds later image and reality were the same. There it stood, tall, rectangular, shining blue and white and gold in the sunlight, almost twice the size of a regular can...

"A Foster's can?" he asked incredulously.

"Well, you said you wanted improbable."

"Ha, so I did." He flipped on the emergency flashers and began to brake to a stop.

"What're you doing?"

"Picking up our litter. After all, we did put it there." He stopped the car, opened the door, and picked up the can. He looked it over carefully, then said, "Looks like a Foster's can to me."

He held it out to her. She reached out with her right hand and took it from him, her left still holding on to his right. It certainly did look like a Foster's can, all right, right down to the improbably small flip-top hole on top. But where had it come from? Had their wish forced someone else to stop and set it on the road when they normally wouldn't have?

"You know," she said quietly, "this is what we get for subscribing to all those science magazines. We know just enough to be dangerous."

"I've got to find me a bush to hide behind," he said. They were driving slowly now, the road twisting and winding and switching back on itself as they neared the top of the mountain.

"I could use one too." She shook the empty Coke can, then tossed it behind the seat to join the Foster's can. It wasn't just the pop, though, she thought. This whole business with wishing themselves along different branches in the universe had scared it right out of her. They were playing with dynamite here, worse, and it didn't take a whole lot of foresight to see that they could screw up bad if they weren't careful.

"Hah, I can do better than a bush for you," he said. "There's a campground just ahead." He slowed down and turned off onto the gravel campground road, the car bouncing over the potholes until he got it into first gear and slowed to a crawl. They drove along beneath the trees, passing pullouts and picnic tables and fire grates, until they came to an outhouse. He stopped the car and said, "Go ahead. I'll park over there by the creek and just use a bush. There's nobody around."

She hesitated, not wanting to let go his hand, certainly not wanting to let him out of her sight, but she realized that unless they wanted to change their bathroom habits there were going to have to be times when they were apart. She nodded. "Don't make any wishes while I'm gone," she said, and she got out of the car.

The stream was even lower up here than it had been below. As he stood a few feet back on the bank, zipping his pants back up, he looked out into the pool where the main channel swirled around a good-sized boulder, trying to spot the fish that he knew had to be in there. He was careful not to wish for any fish, but if there were any there, he wouldn't mind seeing one.

He heard footsteps crunching on gravel and he thought, "Good grief, she was fast," but when he turned around he saw that it wasn't her after all. It was a tall, heavily-built man wearing some sort of loose gray coverall, carrying what looked like a Saturday Night Special in his shaking hand. The man's feet and legs were wet, as if he'd forded the stream.

"Get in the car," the man said. "You drive."

He looked up past the gunman and saw the outhouse door beginning to open. He couldn't make himself speak, not with the gun pointing at him, but he managed to nod, turn, and walk around the front of the car, keeping the gunman's eyes away from the outhouse, then open his own door and get in. The gunman got in the passenger side and held the gun to his head. "We're going to town. You drive real calm and normal like, and you live longer. Got that?"

"Got it," he managed to say.

"Let's go."

He started the car and put it in gear. In the rearview mirror he could see her running toward the car, shouting, and he tried not to think how she must feel as he let out the clutch and pulled out onto the gravel road again. He accelerated, got it in second, not caring about the potholes, only wanting to get this nut with the gun away from her, because he knew who the guy was. This was his escaped convict, the one the cops were hurrying up into the mountains to catch before he caught a ride out and away. He had wished this guy here.

Well he'd just have to wish him back out, first chance he got. He ought to be able to manage a sharp turn and a loose door, or something similar. He almost smiled at the thought, but then he realized what that would mean. If he wished this guy gone, without her beside him when he did it, would she still follow him down the right branch when the universe split? Were they magnets, always returning to one another even if they were separated? That was all speculation. And even if it were true, how big a change in the universe could he make before they got too far apart to attract each other again?

Damn! He'd reacted instantly, wanting to keep her out of danger, when what he should have done was wait for her to show up and then held her hand while the two of them wished for a tree to fall over on the guy. Now he was getting farther away by the second, and farther from including her in any plan he could come up with.

The outhouse was dark, as outhouses in the trees usually are. She expected to hear flies buzzing around inside, but it was eerily silent. Not until she'd sat down and looked up in the corner over the door did she see the reason for the silence: an enormous spider web dotted with the trussed-up corpses of the outhouse's aerial occupants.

Where was the spider? Let's hope it's in some innocuous corner, she thought. She began to look along the walls, then, suddenly realizing what she was about to do, she squeezed her eyes tight and covered them with her hands for good measure. Don't look! she told herself. If you don't look, you can't collapse the probability wave one way or the other.

She heard the car crunching gravel as he drove off, then the engine shut off and there was silence, broken only by the rush of the stream. She heard his door close.

Then, light as a spider landing on bare skin, she felt something touch her knee.

The universe seemed to shatter into fragments in that moment, and her with it. Part of her wished with all its might that the spider would crawl away, down her leg and out the door. Another part wanted no spider at all, but a stray bit of leaf or a pine needle instead. It could be; after all, she hadn't seen it yet. Still another part of her wanted only to scream, not in terror but in frustration, because another part, the dominant part, insisted on wanting nothing at all. Let whatever happens happen, she told herself, and with that decision made, the shattered pieces became whole once more.

She opened her eyes. The spider was as fat, as hairy, as ugly as she had feared, and it wasn't budging. She reached out and flicked it off her knee. That, at least, required no wish.

Pointedly ignoring the spider, she finished what she'd set out to do, pulled her pants back up again, and opened the door. She heard the car door open and close again, and when she looked toward the car she saw the man with the gun. For a moment she couldn't move, even to take a breath, and then it was too late to shout a warning, throw a rock, or anything else. The man climbed in the car, slammed the door, and the engine started.

She ran down the road toward the car anyway, shouting for them to stop, but he put it in gear and drove away before she could get there. She knew why he did it, but she still howled in frustration as she stood in the middle of the road and watched the car bounce its way out to the highway, then accelerate back toward town.

Now what? she thought as the dust settled. She leaned up against a tree for support, the craggy bark rough against her fingers. What do I do? Wish for a cop? There's at least two of them up here.

She tried to think it out. If she wished for anything, then she would likely wind up in a different universe than the one he was in. And despite his talk about being attracted to one another, she had no way of knowing if she could find her way back to him.

Okay, then. It was better to wait it out, not do anything, and hope that he managed to get away from the kidnapper. She supposed it would be safe to wish for that, since her wish involved him directly.

But what if he didn't get away? What if the kidnapper...well, what if he killed him? What if this universe, the one she was in right now, was a universe in which her husband got killed? He wouldn't die; he'd live on in a universe where the gun misfired, or where the kidnapper didn't even pull the trigger, but she would still be here with a dead husband. A dead copy of a husband, but somehow she didn't think any amount of wishing would bring them back together after that.

What then? Should she wish for something after all? Cast herself adrift in the universes and hope to meet him again somewhere else, sometime on down the line?

What would he do? He's got a man with a gun in the car, and he knows he can wish him away if he wants to; what would he do?

He'd try to decide what she would do. He wasn't in any danger, not from his point of view. The "real" him would never find himself in a universe where he died. He would get out of it somehow. So he'd try to

124

decide what she would do, and he'd act accordingly.

Well then, what should she do? From her viewpoint, the chances of him dying were greatest right here, if she did nothing. So doing nothing was out. Make a little wish, and thus just a little change? That seemed to imply a little change in his fate, too. No, what it came down to was a large change, a jump well away from the universe they were in now. Something very improbable, then, to match the very improbable something that would get him out of trouble.

What, though? What should she wish for?

In the car, his thoughts spiraled round and round the same subject. The kidnapper still held the gun on him, though in his left hand now and not all that threateningly. He seemed to be more concerned with squeezing as much heat out of the heater as he could get. He was shivering all over.

"Must be cold up there under a parachute, huh?"

"Don't talk, just drive."

He didn't like being told that at all. The way he figured it, the guy didn't want him to talk because he planned on killing him once he warmed up enough to drive the car himself. The less the kidnapper knew about his victim, the easier it would be to pull the trigger.

He was going to have to do something, and he was going to have to do it soon, before the guy warmed up. The easiest something would be to wish for the heater to break, he supposed. Or maybe for the whole car to break down. They guy wouldn't kill him if he couldn't get away from the body, would he?

He didn't want to find out. What he wanted was a sure way out of this mess, which meant a radical change. It had to be something plausible, something he could imagine happening so his belief in it could bias the probability wave toward collapsing in his favor, but it had to be unlikely. The likely thing in this universe was for him to wind up dead.

What, though? And would she realize what he had to do, and do something comparable? He tried to separate himself from his situation and see it from her viewpoint. She'd been afraid of getting separated; that was foremost in her mind. But she wasn't particularly religious. Surely she'd decide that death was about the biggest separation they could face.

The rest of the chain clicked into place. It wasn't hard to guess; they had always thought alike. Yes, she would know what he had to do, and what she had to do as well.

He turned his attention back to the kidnapper. The guy didn't look any warmer at all. In fact, his face looked as gray as a cloudy day, and now he was having trouble breathing, too. In fact, it looked as if he was having a heart attack.

A heart attack? a tiny voice asked, incredulous. A heart attack? Well, it could happen. The guy's been under stress, that's for sure, and he's got to be at least forty, and probably not in all that good a shape if he's been in prison for long. He's cold as ice, and probably had to walk at least a mile through the trees before he got to the campground, plus he's—

He stopped trying to convince himself. He didn't need any more convincing. The kidnapper was convincing enough on his own. The gun had slipped from his numb fingers and he clutched at his chest with his right hand, then slumped forward and struck his head on the dash.

There was a pull-off coming up on the right side of the road. He swung the car into it, reached across the kidnapper's lap and opened his door, planted a foot against his side, and shoved him out onto the ground. He opened the glove box and took out a pen, slid it into the gun barrel, and flipped the gun out on top of the body. Then he slammed the door, spun the car around, and headed back toward the campground.

Let her still be there, he thought. Let her still be there.

She was close to despair. She'd made her wish, imagined it in her mind a half dozen times until she believed with all her might that it could really happen, but nothing had happened. She walked along the campground road, her head bowed to the ground, looking carefully at every rock lest she miss the one important one, but it was all gravel here. Damn! She should have imagined it in the woods, where there weren't so many other rocks to worry about. But it was too late for that; she had imagined it this way, and she didn't want to change the scene in mid-wish. She had to stick with it, and she had to believe in it, force the probability wave to follow her will. She had to—

A flicker of motion out of the corner of her eye caught her attention. Something bright, high up in the sky. It winked out even as she turned toward it, and for long seconds she waited for something more, but nothing happened. She looked down to the road again, discouraged, just as the sharp Crack! of stone hitting stone reached her ears. Immediately after, the sonic boom from above finally rolled over her as well. About a hundred yards up the road, a black rock bounced and rolled to a stop amid the gravel, and as she walked, then broke into a run toward it, she smelled the scorched odor of her improbable wish drifting out to meet her.

It was a tiny lump of iron, about the size of a baby's fist. She stood over it, wondering if she should pick it up, when she heard the familiar sound of the car turning in off the highway. She watched it come along under the trees and pull to a stop beside her. He climbed out, reaching for her, holding her as if he never wanted to let go.

"Are you really here?" he asked. "Is it really you?"

"The one and only." She nodded toward the ground at their feet. "And look, I've found one!"

INTRODUCTION TO

SCHRÖDINGER'S KILN

Common events can have uncommon explanations. Who hasn't gone to stick a cup in a microwave only to find a cup already there? Maybe you just forgot the last one, but maybe you didn't.

SCHRÖDINGER'S KILN

When her finger caught in the smooth wall of red clay and the nearly finished stoneware mug ripped apart like a house under a tornado, Mary simply lifted her hands from the wreckage and watched it spin around and around atop the wheel's muddy disk. She didn't get angry. She was way past angry. This was the fifth mug she'd ruined today, and she'd used up all her mad after the second. All the same, it was more than simple fatigue that made her hands shake now. That was her livelihood spinning around on display before her.

She fumbled with her left foot for the power switch, finally kicking it with her big toe. The lump of clay coasted to a stop, and now that the electric motor's whine and rumble had quit, the only sound in the studio was the classical music coming from the radio on the drying table beside the wheel.

The table with only two mugs on it, where there should have been eight.

And of those two, only one was new today. The other had already been glazed and fired. Mary picked it up without bothering to clean the mud off her hands and tilted it to her lips.

Gah. Cold coffee.

Leaving the ruined mug on the wheel, she stood and carried the half-full one through the clutter of packing boxes and clay sacks into the kitchen, where she opened the microwave oven—and stopped. There was already another mug sitting on the glass dish.

Lord, she thought, how long has that been there? Since yesterday, at least, because she only used one mug a day. She took the old one out and replaced it with the new one, then closed the door and pushed the one-minute button. Her finger twitched and she got two minutes instead, but the light came on and the carousel began revolving slowly while the microwaves did their thing. Mary turned to the sink and washed out the old mug while she waited for the coffee to heat.

There was no denying it any more, she was falling apart. Age and arthritis had made her hands unsteady, and now her memory was failing, too. Pretty soon it wouldn't matter how many mugs she could make in a day, because she wouldn't be able to remember who had ordered them.

At least she hadn't started collecting cats, the way so many old women did.

She looked back into the studio—which used to be the dining room until she'd grown tired of carrying clay up and down from the basement—at the mess on the wheel. The lack of cats was little comfort when she couldn't even fill a simple order for a set of mugs. For that matter, the wheel itself was a constant reminder of her decline. She'd always hated electric wheels, hated them with the artist's disdain for mechanization, but her legs could no longer push a foot-wheel all day.

The microwave beeped softly, but the coffee aroma leaking out around the door drew Mary's attention even more. She'd overdone it. The coffee had boiled. Sure enough, when she opened the door, there sat the mug in a puddle of foamy brown stickiness. Sighing, she lifted it out by the still-cool handle—amazed as always at how the oven could heat the coffee but not the cup—then drained it into the sink and washed out this mug, too. To hell with coffee; she didn't need any more caffeine making her shake, anyway.

There wasn't room in the rack for the second mug. Puzzled, Mary turned around with it still in her hands, scanning the pottery-filled shelves that lined the studio walls. Had she taken it from one of the finished orders? No, each set was complete, plates and saucers and mugs stacked neatly in rows, waiting for customers to pick them up or for Mary to mail them out. She wondered if she'd accidentally shorted someone when she'd packed an order. Must have, she supposed, carrying the extra mug across the room to set it in a gap on the shelves. No telling which order; all her mugs were the same nowadays. Her trademark design hadn't changed in years.

Well, whoever it belonged to would no doubt call to complain when they unpacked the box. Disgusted with herself, Mary went outside to stand for a moment in the back yard and take a breath of fresh air. Late evening light filtered through the apple tree next to the house, and the breeze carried the scent of its blossoms. Ah, yes, that felt good. Maybe a walk would help calm her down even more.

She didn't exactly get lost. Disoriented was more the word for it. The neighborhood had changed so over the years, none of the landmarks she remembered were the same anymore. She knew she would eventually find her way home, though, and she did, if a bit later than she'd expected. The Sun was already down by the time she spotted her familiar white house with its daffodils lining the walk. Tired, and a little bit scared, she switched out the lights in the studio and went straight to bed.

She had to chisel the ruined mug off the wheel in the morning. She should have done it last night, but she'd been preoccupied and she'd forgotten. Determined to do better today, she set straight to work on the mugs, and she finished two in a row before her hands grew tired and she ruined the third. She'd been expecting that, so she switched tactics, making a few of the easier plates and bowls so she wouldn't have to do all the difficult work at once. It seemed to help, though she ruined a few of those, too.

Over the next few days she did manage to finish a few complete dining sets, but only by working late into the night. By the end of the week she was exhausted, yet when she compared her output against the incoming orders, she realized she hadn't even come close to keeping up with the demand. Nor even to making a living. At this rate she would barely be able to pay her light bill.

She sat at her shipping desk, rubbing her eyes and staring at the clutter of papers. She needed to eat. She was tired and hungry and she hadn't eaten since — when? She couldn't remember. Hadn't she heated up some leftover spaghetti for lunch? If so, she didn't remember eating it.

Good grief, no wonder she felt so wrung out. She went over to the microwave and opened the door. Sure enough, there sat the plate full of spaghetti, still cold, or cold once again. She gave it a couple of minutes on full power, watching the carousel spin slowly round the whole time so she wouldn't forget it again, then she set the plate on the counter and ate standing up. When she was done she put the plate in the sink—right on top of the one she'd used for lunch.

The hair on the back of her neck stood straight out. She *had* eaten lunch; she remembered it now. So where had the extra plate full of spaghetti come from?

The same place the extra mug had come from, no doubt. But where was that? Certainly not another shorted customer.

Nobody called to complain all next week, and after four more mugs and a bowl of soup showed up in the microwave, Mary reluctantly concluded that they were somehow appearing out of thin air. It didn't happen every time. Most of the time she got out only what she put into the oven, but every now and then —when she was most confused, it seemed—she would get something new. It was spooky. For a while she was afraid to go near the thing, but once when she finally forgot her fear and tried to warm up a cinnamon roll, she found half a dozen plates, three mugs, and a gravy boat all crammed inside the tiny compartment.

It apparently had something to do with her forgetfulness. On good days, when her memory was working the way it used to, she never got anything new out of the microwave, but on bad days, when the likelihood that she had forgotten something in there anyway went way up—that's when it happened. She tried experimenting with it, popping open the door whenever she went past, sticking things inside and leaving them for varying times, even putting in things she normally wouldn't put into the oven, but like a watched pot that never boils, the microwave refused to perform until she truly forgot what might be waiting for her.

By the end of the second week since she'd noticed the phenomenon, she had a complete dinner set, and the pace was accelerating. Her unsteady hands and her experiments had eaten into her production time so badly that she was behind on her orders, so she did the only logical thing: she packed up the newfound pottery and shipped it out to the longest-waiting customer.

After another week she had filled half her orders the regular way and half with the microwave, and in the process she had come to understand the rules, if not the theory behind these strange manifestations. There had to be at least *some* chance that she had left an object in the microwave, and she had to honestly forget whether or not she had, before it would happen. But with her failing memory, the odds of that being true had grown from a rare event to near certainty.

And now she began finding mysterious casseroles in the refrigerator, vases full of dead flowers in the breakfast nook, and even extra cash in the sugar bowl where she kept what she had always laughingly called her "mad money."

Life settled into a strange, but comfortable, new routine, one that could have continued indefinitely without further complication if curiosity hadn't eventually overcome her. On one of the rare days when her arthritis wasn't bothering her too much to get out and her mind felt too lucid to allow any spontaneous pottery, she went to the library, determined to discover how this could be. She spent an entire afternoon in the science section, starting with microwaves and progressing to waves in general, then to particles and the physicists who worked with them. She read about Einstein and Dirac— and Schrödinger. The man who had proposed the odd notion that a cat in a box might be both dead and alive at the same time until someone looked to see which it was, and therefore forced the universe to choose.

Change the conditions just a bit, with a forgetful person and a microwave oven, say, and Mary could easily see how her condition could force the universe to choose between emptiness or a piece of pottery.

She returned home that evening in a pensive mood, circling warily around the kitchen. She'd had enough strange physics for one day. She headed straight for the bedroom, kicked off her shoes, and collapsed on the bed without even removing her clothes. But she had hardly begun to relax when she heard a noise, a tiny scratching sound, from within her closet. She raised up, staring at the door. Was that a meow she heard? Could a cat have somehow gotten into the house, or was she just responding to the power of suggestion from reading about Schrödinger's experiment?

Slowly, carefully, she lay back on the bed, unwilling to get up and see.

INTRODUCTION TO

FERMAT'S LOST THEOREM

Anybody who studies math for long eventually has a go at proving Fermat's Last Theorem. I did, anyway, and one day the answer came to me in a flash of insight, just as it supposedly did to Fermat over 300 years ago. With four simple strokes of a pen, I drew it out for posterity—and immediately started writing this story. Who cared about the proof? I knew what it felt like to solve it, and that was infinitely more valuable to a writer.

Part way into the story, I took another look at my proof, and then I knew what it felt like to forget the brilliant chain of logic that led to my great discovery. Excellent! More story material.

I must have struck a chord. When the story was published in *Analog* magazine, people started sending me *their* proofs! And the Science Fiction and Fantsy Writers of America nominated the story for the Nebula award. It didn't win, but given the way the story turns out, that somehow seems appropriate.

FERMAT'S LOST THEOREM

When Rick Hopkins met the new math professor, he felt the sudden conviction that he'd slept with her. Trouble was, he couldn't remember when.

The faculty lounge was abuzz with people milling about, cocktail glasses and colored napkins in hand. Marsha Selwood stood amid a small knot of professors and assistant profs near the punch bowl while Vince Gardoni, the department head, introduced her around. Tall, blonde, with high cheekbones and green eyes, she would have been the center of attention even if she hadn't been the guest of honor. The only people in the room who weren't fawning over her were the other women, and the dozen or so grad students who hovered over the hors d'oeuvres, nervously packing away rumaki and canapés as if they were French fries. Rick didn't recognize half of them, but he supposed their formal clothing accounted for that. Put them in baggy jeans and flannel shirts and they would suddenly become familiar again.

Maybe that was the problem with Marsha. Rick must have met her under different circumstances, and he just wasn't making the connection.

Had he really slept with her? A moment ago he'd have sworn he had, but now he wasn't sure. There'd been that flash of recognition, a momentary glimpse of the two of them entwined in an unfamiliar bed, but nothing after that, and now even the flash was gone. He couldn't remember anything about the actual act, where it had been, or when. It couldn't have been

139

recently; he'd been away all through the holidays, and she'd been teaching halfway across the country during the fall semester. Maybe it had just been wishful thinking.

Then again, maybe not. That look on her face was unmistakable. She was waiting for him to say something, to acknowledge their special secret, and Rick had about two seconds to come up with the right response or he was dead meat.

When in doubt, go for the truth. Rick smiled at her and said, "I just had the strongest sensation of *déjà vu*," putting as much spin into the words as he could without alerting Vince to the subtext.

Marsha blinked her green eyes at him and said, "Now that's odd, so did I."

Not to be outdone, Vince said, "You're kidding. I did too."

Rick and Marsha exchanged a knowing glance, then Marsha turned to Vince. "Oh really? What about?"

Three more grad students entered the lounge, two guys flanking a woman, all three of them wearing the same style suit. Gray, wide lapels, red ties. They stomped the snow from their shoes—black running shoes, it looked like—and made straight for the punch bowl. When they drew close, Rick could see that the woman's oversized glasses had tiny winking lights around the rims, but facing inward, where she could see them better than anyone else could. Rick smiled at the odd trio and sipped his wine while Vince said, "It was really strange, but for just a second there I was sure we were holding an awards ceremony for Rick."

Rick tried not to snort Chablis through his nose. The idea of Vince awarding him anything was laughable. Vince had barely spoken to him since their run-in with the NSA over Rick's code-breaking algorithm. Marsha didn't seem to realize that, though, because she asked seriously, "Oh really, what for?"

Vince laughed. "Oh, nothing much. Just solving Fermat's last theorem."

"That's been done," Rick said. "Andrew Wiles, at Princeton."

Waving a green napkin in dismissal, Vince said, "No no, Wiles's proof was a big, ugly, 200-page thing. I mean *Fermat's* proof, the elegant one he didn't bother to write down."

Marsha's eyes glittered with mischief. "Well, Rick," she said, "Looks like we know what you'll be doing for the next couple of years, eh?"

"What?" Rick frowned. Both Marsha and Vince were watching him like vultures. Like mathematicians who'd just laid down a challenge. "Oh no," he said. "If you think I'm going to waste my time on that, you're nuttier than Fermat."

But as he said that, he felt a flash of insight, a tantalizing glimpse of the proof, as if he'd already solved it. The moment he focused his attention on it, though, it was gone, just like his night in the sack with Marsha.

On the way home, while he was giving a ride to Nigel, one of the other single men in the department, Nigel said, "I didn't realize you were so popular. I had three different people ask me about you tonight."

"Oh really?" Rick concentrated on keeping the Volkswagen from sliding on the icy streets. It had snowed on New Year's Eve, and traffic had packed it all down before the plows could clear it away. Now they would be stuck with it for months.

"Yeah, they kept asking about your work, and what you were planning next."

Rick groaned. "It wasn't those bastards from the NSA again, was it? I gave up cryptography over a year ago."

"No, I don't think so," Nigel said. "These guys weren't near as slick."

The National Security Agency people had definitely been slick. When Rick had inadvertently stepped on federal toes with his code-breaking project, they had materialized like dark wraiths. A few soft words to the dean of the college, a midnight visit to his office to clean off his hard drive— they'd even found his backup disks in the closet at home, though Rick had found no evidence of forced entry to the house. They had swept through his life in a single night, and Rick had suddenly found himself without a project. A whole year down the tubes, and strict orders from Vince to lay off cryptography.

Now he realized what tonight's little exchange had been all about. Rick hadn't picked a new project yet. He wasn't doing anything exciting, and he hadn't written any papers for over a year. Vince's little bit about Fermat's last theorem hadn't been one-upmanship in the presence of a beautiful new colleague; it had been a hint. Do something interesting or wind up teaching remedial algebra for the rest of your life.

An oncoming car seemed to materialize out of nowhere, sliding into their lane. Rick dodged to the right, narrowly missing a parked delivery van. "Jeez, where did that guy come from?" he said as the headlights swept past, but as he spoke, his mind was already leaping off on a tangent.

"Graphically," he whispered. "I can solve it graphically."

"What?" Nigel asked.

"Nothing," Rick said.

He lay awake that night, the yellow sodium vapor glow from the streetlight casting shadows of tree branches on the wall. They curved and zagged in the illuminated square, and Rick tried to envision them as lines on a graph. How could they illustrate Fermat's last theorem?

Fermat's was one of the oldest—and simplest—unproved theorems in mathematics. Pythagoras had proved that the sides of a right triangle added up by the relationship $A^2+B^2=C^2$, and it was easy to show that there were an infinite number of integer solutions to the equation, but no one had been able to find an integer situation in which $A^3+B^3=C^3$, or for any higher powers either. Nearly everyone believed that no such solutions existed, but nobody had been able to prove it.

Nobody except Pierre de Fermat. He had been more of a hobbyist than a mathematician, but he was good at it. He had made some big advances in probablilty theory, and had nearly invented calculus. And in the margin of Diophantus's *Arithmetica*, beside the section discussing integer solutions to $A^2+B^2=C^2$, he had written his theorem, adding, "I have discovered a truly remarkable proof which this margin is too small to contain."

Mathematicians had been trying for over three centuries to figure out what the Frenchman had had in mind, but so far without success. Andrew Wiles had come up with a proof in 1993, but it wasn't elegant and it used semistable elliptic curves and hyperbolic planes—math that Fermat couldn't have known about. Fermat's proof had to be simpler, maybe even visual.

Rick tried to recall the insight he'd had in the car, but it was gone. Vanished as completely as Fermat's own proof, which Fermat had never bothered to write down even though he'd had another twenty-eight years of life to do it after scribbling his tantalizing note in the margin.

Marsha came by his office the next day to borrow his stapler. "I've got to tack up a few spreadsheets to make it feel like home," she said.

"I know what you mean," Rick said, uncovering the stapler from the piles of notes and student papers on his desk. He wondered again where he could have met her before. It bothered him that he'd misplaced the memory of an entire romance, if that's what it had been. Maybe it had been a single drunken revel at a convention somewhere.

Marsha took the stapler from him, but instead of leaving she sat down in the chair beside his desk and said, "So are you actually working on Fermat's last theorem?"

Rick laughed. "I wasn't until Vince brought it up, but since then I've had a couple thoughts I might pursue. I doubt if it'll come to anything, though."

She shrugged. "You never know."

There was a moment of uncomfortable silence; she said, "You never told me what your *déjà vu* experience was last night."

He felt himself blushing. "I, uh, well, I suddenly remembered that we'd met before."

"Oh," she said. "Have we?"

That settled that. She didn't remember it either, so they must not have. Not that he'd have minded; she was a striking woman, and a genuine memory of a night with her would have been a great discovery to dredge out of the dark corners of his mind. He sighed. "I thought so, but then a moment later I wasn't sure."

"That's the way with *déjà vu*."

Rick thought back to the party. "Didn't you say you'd felt something, too?"

"Yes, I did. For a second there, I thought I'd been an instructor here before."

"Wow, Vince had a flash, too. What do you suppose the probablity is of that happening to three people simultaneously?"

Marsha laughed. "Well, how often do you get *déjà vu*? Once a week, maybe?"

"Who knows?" Rick leaned back in his chair. "I suppose that's a fair ballpark figure, though."

"And the experience lasts for what, a minute at the most?"

"Sure." He could see where she was going now, so he said, "One minute out of let's see...fourteen-forty in a day, so just about exactly ten thousand minutes in a week. Jeez, for three simultaneous events, that's one in ten thousand *cubed.*"

"One in ten to the twelfth," Marsha said. "One in a trillion. Holy cow."

Rick whistled softly. "Mysterious forces are about."

"Yeah, sure." Marsha shook her head. "Now figure the odds of *some* mysterious coincidence out of the thousands of things that happen every day, and suddenly it doesn't seem so surprising. It'd have to happen again before I'd believe there's anything going on."

Rick held up his left arm. "We'll have to synchronize our watches, so we can compare our experiences. Or—" he paused, considering his next words carefully. "Or spend more time together."

She tilted her head. "Oh? What did you have in mind?"

"Well," Rick said, wiggling his watch. "It's about lunch time. Have you tried the faculty dining hall yet?"

"No, I haven't."

Rick stood up and pulled his coat off the stand by the door. "By all means, then, let me show you where it is."

The sidewalks were even icier than the streets, and since Marsha was wearing smooth-soled shoes Rick offered her his arm. That was his excuse, anyway.

"So tell me about your ideas for Fermat's last theorem," she asked him as they crossed the open quad from the math offices to the dining hall.

He told her about the sudden flash of inspiration he'd had on the drive home the previous night, how he'd thought of solving it by showing the relationships among A, B, and C visually, but how he'd lost the thread before he could write it down.

"Maybe that's why Fermat never wrote it down either," Marsha said, laughing. "Maybe he forgot it after he wrote his note in the margin."

"God, that'd be terrible," Rick said. "I just had a glimmer of hope, but imagine having the whole proof in your head and forgetting—" He stumbled, and Marsha had to help him stay on his feet, but he didn't start walking again.

"What is it?" she asked.

"Quick, do you have something to write on?"

She patted her coat pockets. "No. Why?"

"Arrgh! Neither do I, but I've got it. I know how to solve it!"

"You do?"

"I—think so." He turned half around, contemplating a sprint across the ice to his office, but he knew he'd never make it. Not before the memory faded. It was fading already. "Here," he said, gripping Marsha's arm fiercely. "Listen. In order to get an integer solution, you've got to have three integers whose squares or cubes or whatever are close enough together that two of them *can* be added together to make the third, right?"

"Okay," Marsha said, nodding.

"All right, we know it works for squares, so let's look at cubes. Three cubed is twenty-seven, and four cubed is sixty-four, so their sum is ninety-one, which *is* less than five cubed. So we know that three and four don't work. So now look at the general case, where you try it with *any* three consecutive integers. If you can show that no solutions exist for any of them, then you've proved the theorem."

"What about three cubed plus, oh, seven cubed?" Marsha asked. "Or ninety-seven cubed. Wouldn't you have to test every possible combination of integers?"

"No, no," Rick said excitedly. "You just look at consecutive ones, because they're the limiting case. You don't test for three and ninety-seven, because you test for ninety-*six* and ninety-seven, and if the sum of *their* cubes is less than ninety-eight cubed, then you know the sum for three and ninety-seven is going to be less."

"Sure," Marsha said. "But how do you show that for all cases? There's still an infinite number of consecutive integers."

"Graphically," Rick said immediately. "Yes, of course! Graph all the cubes of all the possible A's and B's and C's, and—and—damn."

"What?"

"I've lost the thread."

"No, no, think. Graph all the possible sums of consecutive cubes, and..." she trailed off hopefully. "And...?"

Rick shook his head. "And I've lost it. It blinked out like a popped soap bubble."

She tugged him into walking again. "Come on, let's get back to your office and think this through. You had something; we'll track it down."

Rick let her lead him back while he tried desperately to remember his thought. He squeezed his eyes shut, opened them again, and saw three students standing beneath one of the bare trees to the side of the path. Were they—? Yes, they were the same grad students who'd arrived late at the party last night. Great; he'd drawn a crowd. Before the day was out, Vince would no doubt hear about his newest professor and Rick brainstorming arm-in-arm in the middle of the quad.

They tried all afternoon to reconstruct his train of thought, using his computer to graph every combination of squares, cubes, fourths and so on they could think of, but whatever spatial relationship he had visualized in that moment in the quad refused to materialize on the screen.

What *did* happen, though, was that Marsha edged her chair a little closer and a little closer to his over the course of the afternoon, until she might as well have been sitting in his lap. As Rick's frustration with Fermat's last theorem grew, he began to pay more attention to the woman by his side. A sudden rumble made them both look down at their stomachs, then Rick broke out laughing. "Guilty," he said. "And I'm guilty of making you skip lunch, too. Would you let me take you to dinner?"

She rubbed her eyes and leaned back in her chair. "Sure. But this time bring a notebook and a pen."

Over steak and shrimp in a quiet corner of the Bayview Inn, Marsha said, "You know, I forgot all about it in the excitement, but when you had your flash of inspiration there in the quad, I had another shot of *déjà vu* myself."

"Impossible."

"No it's not. The odds for two of us are just a hundred million to one."

"Hah. What did you remember?"

She got an impish grin and rolled her eyes toward the ceiling, but she finally said, "Well, I saw a whole chain of events leading up to my asking you up to my apartment for the night."

"You're kidding."

Marsha toyed with a shrimp on her plate. "I usually don't kid about that sort of thing."

"No, I didn't mean it that way. I meant, That's wild, because that's the flash I got *last* night."

"What?"

"Last night, at the party, when I said I'd just had a moment of *déjà vu*, that's what I'd seen. You and me going to bed in an upstairs apartment. Yellow curtains on the windows, and flannel sheets with little sheep printed on them."

"That's my bedroom!" Marsha said. "Do you remember anything more about it?"

He shook his head. "Not about the room, but, um, you've got a couple of freckles just to the side of your left breast."

She dropped her fork to the plate. "This isn't really *déjà vu* we're having, is it?"

"I don't think so. It's more like precognition or something."

"Does that mean you're going to solve Fermat's last theorem?"

Rick shrugged. "Who cares? What I want to know is whether or not you're going to invite me up to your apartment tonight."

Her impish grin returned. "I don't know. You haven't kissed me yet. I never invite a man up to my apartment unless he's a good kisser."

"Well," Rick said, leaning forward and puckering his lips, "I'm willing to take the test."

Rick woke in the middle of the night with the answer fully-formed in his mind. He reached for the note pad he always kept on the nightstand, but his hand met something cold and hard that didn't belong there, tipping it over with a crash. Oh, right. Different bedroom.

"What was that?" Marsha asked sleepily.

"Sorry," Rick muttered. "I think I tipped over the lamp."

"S'all right," she said, snuggling up against him. "Worry about it in the morning."

"But I—" need a note pad, he almost said, then he realized he didn't after all. Whatever his thought had been, he'd lost it again.

He lay back down and stared at the ceiling. What the hell was going on? Marsha was right, this wasn't just *déjà vu*. Something was happening to their minds.

Everything in the room had a silvery tint; the Moon had risen while they slept, and was now shining on the bed. A shadow drifted slowly across the foot of it, and Rick thought for a moment that it must be from a passing car's headlights, but then he realized the angle was all wrong for that. It had to be something up in the sky.

He looked out the window and realized there was a third possibility: Someone was walking along the flat-topped roof of the next building over, and the Moon behind him threw his shadow directly into Marsha's bedroom. It looked like the guy was carrying something on his shoulder, something that glinted in the Moonlight.

A gun? No, it was too big for that, unless it was a bazooka. It looked more like a telescope. Oh, sure. The night was clear and the moon was bright as could be; it was probably just an astronomy student out there.

Or a Peeping Tom. As Rick watched, the person on the roof set the telescope on a tripod and pointed it straight at Marsha's window. When he bent down to look through it, Rick raised his hand into the shaft of moonlight, middle finger extended.

The person with the telescope leaped back as if Rick had punched him in the nose. Rick slid out of bed and stepped to the window, just to let the guy know for sure he'd been spotted. He was about to open it and shout at the son of a bitch when the man took another stepped back, tripped over something, and disappeared.

"Oh shit," Rick said.

Marsha sat up. "Now what?" she asked.

Rick swept his hand around in the darkness at the foot of the bed, looking for his clothes. "I think somebody just fell off the roof over there."

"What?"

"Somebody was looking at us with a telescope. When I flipped him off, he backed up and dropped out of sight."

"There was somebody looking at *us*?" Marsha asked.

"Don't worry, he just got there." Rick tugged on his pants and shirt, found his shoes and put them on without socks, and said, "Keep an eye on the roof. I'm going over there and look for a body on the ground."

"Shouldn't we call the police?" Marsha asked.

"Not until we know there's a reason to," Rick said. "It'd be better for both of us if we didn't have our names in the paper."

Marsha nodded. "Good point."

Rick grabbed his coat on the way out. It was cold as hell stepping into the winter night straight from a warm bed, but he tugged the zipper up to his neck and stuck his hands in his pockets while he jogged across the courtyard, the snow squeaking beneath his shoes.

There was nobody on the ground on either side of the building. No tracks, either. The guy hadn't gone over the edge, then, and he had to be still in the building. Rick tried the front door, but it was locked, so he went around to the side with the fire escape and leaped up, caught the counterbalanced ladder with one hand and pulled it down. Then, hoping nobody else had called the police either, he crept up the iron staircase three flights to the roof.

The telescope was still there, but Rick couldn't see the guy who'd set it up. He approached the scope cautiously, looking for tracks in the snow, and sure enough, he found some. A semicircle had been trampled down behind the telescope, and four distinct prints led backward away from it where the peeper had retreated. But they didn't go anywhere. They vanished into smooth snow, as if the guy had leaped into the sky.

Rick looked for the other end of the trail of footprints, the ones whoever it was had made when he approached, and he saw the same thing. Footprints suddenly appeared in the snow, leading a dozen feet or so up to the telescope.

Too strange. Rick turned once around, looking for anything he might have missed, but he was alone on the rooftop. Alone and cold. With a shrug, he waved at Marsha's silvery form behind her window, then picked up the telescope and carried it back down the stairway. Let the Peeping Tom come after it if he wanted it back.

"It doesn't have any lenses," Marsha pointed out when they'd set it up in her living room. "Mirrors either." Rick looked down the front of the tube and realized she was right, but when he aimed the telescope at the Moon and looked through the eyepiece, he saw a heavily-cratered surface that looked close enough to touch.

"Something's certainly doing the job," he said. He aimed it down toward the one lit window in the building across from them and looked again. He could see into the room—a kitchen, it turned out—as clearly as if he had his face up against the glass, and now he heard a woman's voice saying, "Come on, honey, get up or you'll be late for work."

"What did you say?" Marsha asked.

"I didn't say anything," Rick said, stepping aside so Marsha could have a look. "It sounded like it came from the telescope."

"No way." She peered into the eyepiece. Rick saw movement in the window, and Marsha said, "A woman in a blue bathrobe just walked past."

The voice said, "I'll cook you a couple of eggs. How do you want 'em?"

"Scrambled," a male voice said.

"This is bizarre," Marsha whispered, backing away from the telescope.

"It's the NSA again," Rick said disgustedly. "They're the only people who could possibly have access to something like this."

Marsha looked at him with wide eyes. Every mathematician lived in dread of the NSA. "What do we do?"

"Damned if I know," Rick said. He examined the telescope again. "Nikon?" he muttered, reading the label on the side of the tube.

"Yeah, right."

"No, really, that's what it says."

Marsha bent over to look, and that motion triggered another flash of *déjà vu*: Rick clearly remembered seeing her bend down to look at his proof of Fermat's last theorem, the one where he graphed $A^n+(A+1)^n$ and $(A+2)^n$, and the graphs proved that the two functions never intersected. But exactly what was being plotted against what?

Marsha gasped. "They're going to break in," she said.

"Who?"

"*Them*." She pointed toward the roof across the way, where three figures had appeared. They were black silhouettes against the Moon, and each one turned around a couple of times, evidently looking for their 'scope. Rick pointed it toward them and heard a man's voice say, "The doot must have come up and grabbed it."

One of them turned and looked toward Marsha's apartment. Rick reached out and switched off the light, but it was too late. The voice said, "Yada, there they are."

"Now what?" another voice said.

"Rewind?" the third one, female, said.

"Nodo. I've already crossed myself twice," the first voice said. "I do it again and I'll spring a twonky a month long."

"Bort that," the woman said, "Let's just go take it back."

"But won't that snark his discovery? We trang that up and the department'll send us all back to the Cretaceous."

"We've *already* tranged it. If he's figured out how to work the scope, he's probably—"

"Like it's really tough to point it at something."

"—listening to us right now."

"Oh skrot, you're right. Let's bounce before we snark it up any worse." One by one all three figures disappeared again, and this time there was no doubt about them falling off the roof or hiding behind something. They simply vanished.

"That's not the NSA," Marsha whispered.

"No, I don't think so," Rick whispered back. "But whoever they are, you were right; they're coming here."

"What can we do?"

"Have you got a gun?"

Marsha shook her head. "Just pepper gas," she said, taking her purse from the table by the door and removing the leather-covered spray canister from inside it.

"Good," Rick said. "Get ready to use it." He went into the kitchen and grabbed the broom from the corner by the back door, busted off the bristled end by stomping on it, and swished the ragged broken end back and forth in the air. "This ought to do," he said. "Now we stand back to back in the living room and wait for them to make their move."

They took up their positions. "Don't hesitate," Rick said. "Spray 'em all the moment you see a target."

"Right." Marsha held out the pepper canister. "Shouldn't we call the pol—"

But it was too late. With a flicker of light and a whuff of displaced air, the three figures from the roof materialized right beside them. Rick felt a moment of intense *déjà vu*; he could hardly see their black-clad shapes through the sudden vision of the elegant graph proving Fermat's last theorem, but he swung around with the broomstick and flailed away at the shadowy figures beyond it.

Marsha spun and sprayed with the deadly accuracy of a city-bred woman, and all three intruders dropped to the floor, coughing and choking. A beam of blue light shot out from one of them and struck the wall beside Rick, and he leaped aside and whacked at the source of it with the stick. He felt wood strike flesh, and the light winked out. Holding his breath and blinking to regain his sight, he reached down and picked up a wide-barreled pistol-gripped flashlight and backed away again.

"Got any rope?" he asked.

It took fifteen minutes before any of their captives recovered well enough to speak. Rick and Marsha had tied them to kitchen chairs, and stood back to wait. In the bright overhead light, their stealth-black oversuits looked less threatening, almost silly.

"I recognize all three of them," Rick told her. "They were at your welcoming party, and in the quad when we both got hit by that *déjà vu*. And I'd be willing to bet they were in the car that came at me from nowhere on the way home, too. Weren't you?" He pointed the blue light gun at the most-recovered of the intruders.

"Hey, watch that," the kid said, still sniffling from the pepper spray. "You pop me with that, you'll twonk the whole connie."

"You want to put that in English?" Rick asked.

"What part didn't you snag?"

"Twonk."

"Twonk? You're tranged. I'm sure that's a twencie. From way before your time, in fact. Means screwing up the time flow. Leaving a twonky, like a magnoscope on a rooftop."

Marsha said, "I think he means an anachronism."

"Straight! You twonk the connie—that's *continuum*—and you cause all sorts of problems downstream."

Rick leaned back against the kitchen counter. "Are you trying to tell us you're time travelers?"

"Ain't trying to tell you nada. You asked."

Rick wouldn't have believed a word of it if it hadn't been for the telescope in the living room, and the way his head filled with future memories every time these guys showed up. Did time machines leave some kind of wake that caused *déjà vu*?

"What are you doing here?" he asked.

"What do you think? We're here to dock you solving Fermat's last theorem."

"Dock?" Marsha asked.

"Doc-u-ment-a-rize," the kid said. "It's a field lab in historical vidding."

Rick laughed. "You're nuts. You're *tranged*. I haven't solved it. I wasn't even interested in it until you guys showed up at the party last night and gave Vince the idea."

"We didn't give nobody zot."

"Ah, but you did." Rick tugged a paper towel off the roll beneath a cabinet and drew a quick XY axis on it with a pen from the cup by the phone, then he swept two curves upward from the origin. "That's it, right?"

The kid's eyes bugged. "Torrie, you get that?"

The girl coughed. "You skrottin' me? I can hardly see." Rick wondered how she could see anyway; her glasses—as lensless as the telescope—blinked from the frames with a dozen different colors, all aimed inward.

The kid said, "Skrot, that would've been maxie. The whole concept swished out in four lines on a napkin. Maybe we can get him to do it again. Will you?"

"Weren't you listening?" Rick said. "I got the idea from *you*. Every time you show up, I see it in my head."

There was a long silence, then the woman, Torrie, said, "Uh oh."

"It's leakage," Vrank said. He was the talkative one, the narrator for the "dock." He explained what Torrie and Shil, his camera and sound ops, were doing as they spread the guts of their time machines out on the kitchen table. Rick and Marsha had finally decided to let them go once they'd promised not to snark anything up.

The time machines looked like fanny packs until Shil unzipped their flaps and unfolded them into flat, floppy panels of circuitry. Vrank said, "There's supposed to be suppressors in there to keep down the ripple effect when we chrono, but evidently one of em's tranged. Sorry about that."

"Sorry?" Marsha said. "You've put Rick through the wringer."

"It's worse than that," Vrank said. "We've evidently twonked his whole life. You honestly weren't even thinking about Fermat's last theorem until last night?"

"Nope," Rick said.

"What about the journal?" Torrie asked. "You wrote in your journal that you got a flash of inspiration at the reception, and again on the drive home, and you described how you worked on it for days after you met Marsha here, 'cause you wanted to impress her."

"What journal?" Rick asked.

"Twonky," Shil said, poking at a couple of bumps and a squiggle in the dark fabric. "The journal's a—yada, sure enough, here's the prob. It was yours, Vrank."

"Skrot. Now what?"

"Can't you go back and undo it?" Rick said, leaning over the table to look at the offending circuit. It looked like someone had doodled with a laundry marker on a piece of gray nylon. "Can't you tell yourself to fix your time machine before you leave?"

Vrank shook his head. "For one thing, looping like that's a good way to trang your brain, but even if I tried it, that'd just dox it up even worse. We came back here to dock your discovery, which means you *do* figure it out."

"Or at least he gets the credit for it," Torrie said.

Shil looked up from the time machine. He and Vrank and Torrie exchanged knowing glances. "It'd work," Shil said.

"It would, wouldn't it?" said Vrank.

"What?" Rick asked, backing warily away and getting ready with his broom handle. "What would work?"

"Going with it. Docking your discovery the way we originally intended to."

"It's not my discovery," Rick said. "You guys planted it."

"Yada? Then where did it come from?" Vrank asked. "*We* got it from you."

There was a long, pregnant silence, then Rick pulled out a chair and sat down. "My head hurts," he said.

"It's not a proof," he said the next morning. Torrie and Vrank and Shil and Marsha were gathered around Marsha's computer, where Rick had displayed a graph of his brainstorm, but on the screen where the two curves were supposed to diverge and thus prove that no integer solutions existed, they crossed.

"That's not right," Vrank said. "You're missing something."

"Obviously."

"Cheer up," Torrie said. "You'll get it soon. Your journal said it took you just a few days."

"No pressure," Marsha said, giggling.

"Yeah." Rick stared at the screen for a few minutes, then said, "So Vrank, why don't you jump forward and back again, give me another hint."

Vrank laughed. "Sorry. Shil fixed the chrono, so it wouldn't do any good."

"Besides," Torrie said, "we need to get some good shots of you thinking. It wouldn't do to have you spring it right off, or people downtime would know for sure what happened."

"Couldn't have that," Rick said sourly. He tapped at the keyboard, changing the display from fourth to fifth power integers, but the parabolas still crossed.

"Actually," Marsha said, "isn't their intersection a counterexample? Maybe you can prove the theorem *wrong*. That would be just as big a deal."

Rick thought about that, then said, "The intersection points aren't necessarily rational numbers. Besides, Wiles proved the theorem true already. I'm just looking for a more elegant way. And trying to impress you, of course." He put his arm around Marsha. She was the one good thing to come of all this.

A week later, he was getting used to having people from the future popping in and out of his office, his living room, even his bedroom. He drew the line at his bathroom, demanding at least one safe refuge, but that didn't help him either. The theorem and his flawed proof of it haunted him no matter where he went, and *that* was what was driving him nearly crazy.

He called a halt to it the next time Vrank and his crew showed up in his office. "Look," he told them, "it's not going to work. The whole concept is bogus."

"No, no," Vrank assured him. "You're close. I can tell."

"Yeah, why don't you?"

"What?"

"Why don't you tell? Just give me the solution, I'll write it down, you can finish your documentary, and I can get back to my life."

Torrie frowned. "That wouldn't make for good drama."

"You want me to climb in a bathtub and shout 'Eureka?' Fine. Write me a script. But I'm tired of trying to validate your mistake. I never wanted to work on this stupid theorem anyway."

Shil looked up at the clock and grinned. Rick said, "What's so funny?"

"Twenty minutes from now you won't be saying that."

"Oh?" Rick looked from Shil to Vrank to Torrie. All three had big grins on their faces. "What, this is the big moment?"

"Yada," Torrie said. The telltales around her glasses winked red and yellow.

Rick looked back to the mess of papers on his desk. He'd given up on the graphical route, and was trying to come up with a completely new paradigm. "No way," he said. "I'm completely at sea here. I couldn't prove the Pythagorean theorem in twenty minutes."

"Come on," Torrie said, "try."

Rick turned back to his desk, conscious of her glasses recording his every move, and tried to concentrate on the problem. What was he missing? He shuffled through the pages of graphs and the tables of logarithms, tapping his pencil on the tiny corner of bare desktop. Out of perversity, he picked his nose. If he concentrated, he could hear the clock humming, the second hand sweeping around and around.

When twenty minutes had come and gone, he looked up again and said, "I think it's time for plan B."

The proof from the future was no better than his own. Rick had called Marsha into his office to see it, but the two of them read the article in the futuristic plastic unibook with growing confusion. "It's not a proof," Rick said, using the recessed toggle on the side to flip back to the abstract on the first page. "It says it is, but it's got the same problem I have with mine. Doesn't anybody do peer review in the future?"

"That's your article," Vrank said, his voice worried. "I downloaded it straight out of the archive."

"It may have my name on it," Rick said, "but I'd never try to publish something with this basic a mistake in it."

"Then it's twonked," Shil said. "Our little snark-up here must have rippled down the connie and changed it."

"Oh, skrot," Vrank said, grabbing the door frame for support. "Rick, you've got to solve it. If you don't, we're doxed bad."

"Sorry," Rick said. "I've given it my best shot."

There was a moment of silence while everybody scratched their heads, then Marsha said, "Why don't we go to the source?"

"We're *at* the source," Vrank said.

"No, I mean Fermat. Why don't you go back to 1650 or whenever it was and get the proof from *him*?"

Vrank and his companions shuffled back and forth nervously, and finally Vrank said, "Well, uh, actually, we already did. He didn't have a proof either."

"You're kidding." Rick laughed. "He didn't have a proof?"

Vrank shook his head. "We docked his life before we got to yours, just for a prologue, you know, but it turned out he was wrong when he wrote that note in the margin. He had a flash of inspiration, but it turned out to be—"

Rick's laughter drowned him out. "Your time machine!" Rick said when he got his breath back. "The one with the bad filter. You did the same thing to him that you did to me."

Vrank blushed. "Yeah, I guess so."

"Then there never *was* a proof. Never was, and never will be. Except for Wiles's semistable elliptic curves."

"Yada." Vrank sighed and turned to his companions. "We're snarked, dooties."

"What happens now?" Marsha asked.

"Nothing, at least from your point of view. We, on the other hand, get to bounce back downstream and see if anybody's filed a complaint."

"And if they did?"

"Then we have to pay a fine and make resti to anybody whose life got screwed up. Not to mention re-taking historical vid."

"You don't just go back and undo the mistake?"

Shil laughed. "Define 'mistake.' We came back to dock Rick solving the theorem, which he wouldn't even have tried if we hadn't. But we wouldn't have come back here in the first place if he hadn't done it already, so maybe we should trang the ripple suppressors in Vrank's chrono again and bounce back and forth across the herenow until he twigs to it, hey? Which is the 'real' connie?"

"This is," Rick said after a moment's translation. "You've screwed with my head enough already; just leave well enough alone and go pay your fine."

157

Vrank nodded. "That's the way the judges usually figure it, too. Well, wish us luck." He tapped his forehead in a mock salute, reached down to touch a control on his fanny pack/time machine, and vanished. Torrie and Shil blinked out a moment later.

"Whew," Marsha said, leaning back in the chair beside Rick's. "I was afraid they were going to undo everything all the way back to me getting hired here, and I'd never have met you."

Rick gave her a hug. "I'd have given them the proof before it came to that. I was just holding out to see if I could get them off our case entirely."

"What?" Marsha stared at him with wide eyes. "You *did* figure it out?"

"That's right." Rick shuffled through the papers on his desk. "Hmm, that's strange," he said. "I had it here a minute ago."

Author's note: In order to properly research this story, I of course had to find an elegant solution to Fermat's last theorem. It is indeed a truly remarkable proof, which the margin of this publication is also too small to contain. Fortunately, the editor has graciously agreed to print it in a separate appendix, which can be found on page 251.

INTRODUCTION TO

BATTLE LINES

A friend of mine was editing a literary magazine, and he had a cool piece of artwork with no story to go with it. The artwork shows a winged woman and a naked man in tight embrace miles over a city that is itself built on an arch over a deep chasm, in which tiny flying figures can just barely be seen. I didn't actually see the artwork before I wrote the story; Ken just described it to me over the phone, but that was enough to generate the idea. I loved the fact that the woman had the wings and the man didn't, and I wondered what could make him take such a risk. It's a question the parents of teenagers must ask themselves every time their kids go out on a date.

BATTLE LINES

"If you love me, you'll do it." Zofia's soft, sultry voice filled the patrol plane's bubble cockpit, warming Gordon like sunlight pouring through a gap in the clouds. He looked over at her in the seat beside him and she smiled, her lips open slightly, a hint of teeth behind them. Her irridescent silver wings, held tight to her body, rustled softly as she tilted her head sideways and turned to look at him out of just her left eye. A wisp of dark hair fell forward to partially hide her face.

God, how he loved that coy look. She knew just which buttons to push. Still, what she was asking him to do...

"Love don't have nothin' to do with it, darlin'," he said, falling into the pilot's cant that he knew turned *her* on. "We're talkin' survival here. I don't have those pretty wings of yours."

"But I do," she said, extending them as far as she could in the narrow confines of the cockpit. They touched either side of the double-wide cabin, and wrapped around to nearly block his view ahead. "I will catch you. And then—" her voice grew softer " —then we will make glorious love in mid-air."

"Fallin' like bricks the whole time." He banked the plane around in a slow circle, looking for more of Relig's warriors, but the battle was over. It had been a rout; even bio-enhanced warclones were no match for a squadron of battleplanes. Zofia's people were free—and now she wanted to celebrate.

So did Gordon, but on the ground.

"I won't let you fall," she insisted. "I love you."

"I don't doubt that," he said, doubting it immensely. The two of them had spent twelve hours a day for four days on patrol in a crowded airplane without killing one another, but that didn't mean it was love. He didn't say that, though. What did it matter if she loved him? That wasn't the issue. He said, "What I doubt is whether you can keep an extra ninety kilos in the air. Like as not we'd both go splat if you tried it."

"Thanks for the compliment," she said sarcastically, and he realized he'd just belittled her secondary sex characteristics. Accipitan women might not have breasts, but their chest size was still a matter of importance to their lovers. Vital importance, if Zofia's description of their mating habits was true, for those shapely mounds that mimicked a normal woman's breasts were the powerful muscles that drove their wings.

"I'm sorry," he said. "I didn't mean it that way. You have wonderfully big, rippling—one could even say heaving—pectorals. But I won't be any help at all in keeping us aloft. Not like an Accipitan man."

She laughed. "Hah. Our men are no help either. How could they be? They're upside down!"

Gordon supposed she had a point. He'd never seen an Accip fly inverted. The way their wings attached, he doubted if they could. Did the women actually carry their mates during sex? He supposed it was possible.

"All the same," he said, "I'm heavier than they are."

"Maybe, but not by that much. You certainly don't weigh ninety kilos." Her voice held a note of reproach.

"I do with my flight gear on."

"Silly, you won't be wearing flight gear."

He laughed at the image. "You want me to bail out of my plane with nothin' on, hopin' you'll snatch me before I get to fallin' too fast for you to keep up, and then you expect me to—to perform—while I'm hangin' on for dear life? I hate to disappoint you, but human physiology doesn't work like that."

"How do you know? Have you ever tried it?"

He looked out at the ground two kilometers below. The cavern leading to Relig's underground warren was smaller than the thumbnail of his outstretched hand. The city on the arch spanning the cavern was smaller still. And tiny specks of flyers above it were just visible if he squinted. It was

162

a long way down. In his warship Gordon felt invincible, and the thrill of victory for a just cause was a powerful aphrodisiac, but the thought of stepping out of his metal cocoon into all that empty air cooled his fire. The plane could fly fine without him, but without it he was a ballistic projectile. "I don't have to try it," he said. "I can imagine it just fine."

"I won't be wearing anything either." She rubbed her hands over his shoulders and chest, leaned close and nuzzled his ear.

Her voice and her caress brought the response she wanted, but Gordon took her hands in his before they could stray far enough to find that out.

"You want to make love in flight?" he asked. "Okay, let's do it. Right here, in the plane. If we unbuckle and twist around a little, we —"

"That's too restrictive," she said petulantly. "I want to feel free!"

"Okay, then, let's land and do it on the ground."

"It doesn't feel natural on the ground."

That line seemed so familiar Gordon had to laugh.

"What?"

How could he tell her that he recognized her come-on? It suddenly struck him how strange it was for him to be fighting her advances. Him, Gordon DeLinn, the interstellar rake of a fighter pilot. Usually he was the one who tried to talk hesitant women into having sex with him, not the other way around.

"You're being a tease!" she pouted, leaning away from him and looking out the side window.

"I'm not," he said. "I'm just not ready to risk my life for sex."

"You're not risking your life! I said I'd catch you."

He shrugged. "You'll try. But accidents happen. Turbulence, or a bug in your eye, or you might sprain your wrist bailing out."

"You think I'm ugly, don't you? I'm too alien. You think it'd be bestiality."

"What?" That had come out of nowhere. "Where'd you get that crazy idea?"

She turned her head again to face him, her lips full and red in a pout. "The missionaries have been preaching that it's a sin. That we Accipitans have been genetically altered until we're no longer human."

"Missionaries," Gordon snorted. Half the battles he had fought were against missionaries and their repressive agendas. He leaned toward her and kissed those soft, inviting lips. "Don't listen to those idiots," he told her. "You're plenty human enough for me." He didn't tell her that it was her differences that turned him on, that he liked his women exotic.

She kissed him hungrily, and her hands returned to his shoulders and back. He reached out and ran his fingers around her powerful muscles, along the soft, rippling skin at the edges of her wings, down the long ridges at her sides where they attached. She reached under his flight suit, tugging open the zips and running her hands over his chest, his sides, down into his pants. She began peeling his suit off of him, and he didn't stop her. He couldn't. He didn't have enough hands to do that and continue touching her, and now her wings themselves were caressing him, their silky softness enfolding him.

"Oh yes," she murmured. "Oh yes, let's do it."

"We *are* doing it," he said, unfastening the complicated straps that held her brief clothing in place.

"I want more." She kissed his right nipple, her tongue circling around and around until it was hard as a berry. "You drive me crazy," she whispered. "I want you."

He recognized those lines, too. Whispered in the heat of passion, they always worked. And now that he was on the receiving end, he knew why. It doesn't matter how many times a person hears them, or even uses them himself; they're incredibly flattering, and if someone wants to believe them, they will.

He was running out of protests. The plane was flying itself, would even return to the hanger if he told it to. And Zofia was playing his body like a bard plays a harp.

She pulled off his jacket, and the liner beneath it. Every inch of skin she exposed received a kiss. Gordon protested feebly, but he knew if she stopped he would finish undressing himself. He had to have her. His sense of self-preservation had given way to more primal urges; he wanted to make love with this woman right now, no matter what. Even if he had to do it her way.

"Do you promise to catch me?" he asked.

She smiled, knowing she had won. "Trust me," she said, as she reached for the lever that would blow the canopy and pitch them out into the air. "Trust me."

INTRODUCTION TO

THERE GOES THE NEIGHBORHOOD

In the mid '90s there was an explosion of what I call "feel good fantasy," in which the characters were overly nice to one another and solved their problems way too easily. Some friends and I decided to counter that trend with an anthology called "Spatterfairies," in which fantasy creatures behaved a little more realistically.

Several of us wrote stories for it, and we made T-shirts with garish, blood-spattered lettering to advertise it at conventions, but the anthology never really got off the ground. Most of us sold our stories elsewhere, adding to the resurgence of dark fantasy that was already springing up in response to the glut of "feel good" stories. We didn't start a revolution, but we did have a lot of fun.

I still have the T-shirt.

THERE GOES THE NEIGHBORHOOD

The drive-by charming caught Mary completely by surprise. Over the years she had grown used to machine-gun fire in the night, to squealing tires and sirens and flashing lights, but the sudden fey attack was something new.

She was sitting in her recliner in the living room, re-reading her tattered copy of *Gone With the Wind*, when she heard the soft tinkle of tiny bells in the distance. Fairy bells, hundreds of them growing nearer and louder until they drowned out the television that she kept on so she wouldn't have to hear every small-caliber altercation in the neighborhood. The bells passed Mary's house like a carillon tumbling down a staircase, then suddenly stopped two doors down, at the Fraleys' house. Of course the Fraleys didn't live there anymore—hadn't for years, since the neighborhood had started to decline—but Mary still thought of it as theirs.

The bells were only a new twist in an old wound; Mary had grown used to loud cars arriving at all hours of the night, their drivers only staying for the few minutes it took to make a deal. She supposed it was only a matter of time before someone brought a souped-up, magic-powered vehicle by to pick up their fix. She got up to see what it looked like.

But this was no simple drug deal. In the silence, a high-pitched, piercing voice shouted, "This is for Boldershanks, ye dust-skimmin' scum!" Then came a sound like the hand of Oberon clawing the strings out of a harp, and a flash of light that drove Mary—just peeking out around the curtain—back against the wall. She blinked away afterimages of an improbably tall, slender figure with his hand outstretched toward the house, standing beside a gleaming chrome twelve-foot pumpkin on wheels, drawn by hundreds of mice.

Darkness and high-pitched laughter, then the bells began again—loud at first, then fading into the distance.

Mary had been sure this latest set of neighbors were up to no good, but this clinched it. For fairies to be involved, they had to be dealing pixie dust, the strongest hallucinogen ever discovered. Rumor had it the dust came from the desiccated bodies of actual pixies, but Mary didn't know if she believed that. All she knew was that the apparition outside looked like something straight out of the Brothers Grimm.

She risked another look. There, across the street and down, stood the result of the fairies' work: Where before a tin-sided, double-wide trailer had besmirched the weedy lot, now stood a two-story Victorian complete with gabled roof, shutters, and a front porch. The yard was groomed to perfection, its grass flatter than a golf green and sporting dozens of rose bushes in full bloom. A white picket fence surrounded the whole affair. It was hard to tell in the blue glow of the streetlight, but the house looked pink.

"Oh my," Mary whispered, her breath nearly taken away by the beauty of it. She hadn't seen such a wonderful house in decades, and never on this street.

The tenants didn't share her enthusiasm. The front door banged open and all four of them rushed out, the three tuxedo-clad men cursing and waving their walking sticks at the departed fairymobile while the woman— the Slut, Mary had always called her—tugged off her full-length evening gown and flung it to the ground. For a moment she looked as if she were about to pull the slip off, too, but she settled for jumping up and down on the dress.

One of the men threw his stick down the street, where it bounced end over and end and clattered to a stop against one of the burned-out cars near the corner. Mary wondered what they'd been doing with sticks, then she realized that until a few moments ago those had no doubt been guns, and the tuxedos and dress had been her neighbors' usual ripped T-shirts and baggy pants.

Come to think of it.... She reached into the middle shelf of the bookcase by the window and with the unerring accuracy of long practice picked up her binoculars and brought them to bear on her neighbors. They were hardly recognizable. The one with the scruffy beard now sported a well-trimmed Vandyke, and the woman's stringy black hair had been permed. All four of them looked as if they'd been recently bathed, probably for the first time in months, and by the fit of their clothes it looked like they'd been shaped up, too.

They turned away from the street and the long-vanished fairies, speaking among themselves in words too indistinct to carry all the way to Mary's ears. Then, to her horror, they began to attack the house and grounds, ripping out rose bushes, kicking over the fence, and pulling trim off the building.

"Of course," Mary said, lowering her binoculars and turning away from the window. "They couldn't be caught living in a *pretty* house."

She understood why a few minutes later when a loud car, its stereo thumping and bumping even over the engine noise, pulled onto the street, slowed down near the Victorian, then suddenly roared away and vanished around the corner with a squeal of tires. The driver obviously didn't want to get involved with someone who'd been marked by the fey.

The dust dealers renewed their efforts to destroy the evidence, but the fairies' work proved tougher than the dealers. No matter how fast they worked, the uprooted roses would amble back to their beds, the picket fence would right itself, and the house would grow back within minutes whatever they pulled loose.

When Mary looked out again in the early morning light, the house was still there, and still beautiful. And yes, it was pink; the softest, rosiest shade of pink she had ever seen.

The police arrived not long after dawn. One of them spotted Mary peeking around her curtain and came to her door. He was a big, rough-shaven man who smelled of smoke and cologne, and he wore a crooked grin as he said, "Excuse me, Ma'am, I'm Officer Connely from the third precinct. Sorry to disturb you, but did you by any chance witness what happened here last night?"

Mary considered saying she hadn't, as she'd said to the cops so many times before when the guns started up, but this one's obvious amusement made her pause.

"It must've been something," the cop went on. "I've seen dozens of these after the fact, but I'd give anything to watch it happen."

"Well," Mary said, opening the screen door to let him inside, "there wasn't really that much to see. It all happened in a flash. But the noise, now, that was a caution." She sat Officer Connely down on her couch and offered him tea, and after he'd accepted a cup she sat in her recliner opposite him and described what she'd heard.

"Boldershanks?" he asked when she got to that part of her tale. He scribbled the name into his notebook with a short stub of pencil from one of his uniform's pockets.

"That's what it sounded like," Mary said, "but I could be mistaken."

"Oh, you heard it right." The cop shook his head. "Boldershanks. Wow. Your neighbors are messing with big magic. It's a wonder they're still walking on two legs."

"Oh." Mary sipped her tea. "Is he a major player in fairy circles?"

The cop flexed his fingers in an absent-minded sort of way, and his pencil pirouetted neatly over each knuckle, back and forth. "No ma'am. He was just a small-time street charmer somebody shook down for his pixie dust. But his godmother, now, *she's* not somebody you'd want to mess with."

"No, of course not," Mary said. "Who might she be?"

"You ever heard of Titania?" Officer Connely asked.

Mary had. Long after the officer left, she stood by the window and watched as her neighbors — evidently not arrested for lack of evidence — tried in vain to erase Titania's work. They were using shovels and spray paint now, but that had no more permanent effect than their earlier attempts. When the queen of the fairies charmed a place, it evidently stayed charmed.

Mary looked out at her own yard, slowly going to weeds since her back had started bothering her. Her house was falling apart, too, but her social security check barely paid the taxes, let alone upkeep. She looked back at the shiny new Victorian and wished the fairies would come do the same for her.

She said as much to Flora, her neighbor, when they met at the mailbox that afternoon.

"Oh no, dearie," Flora said, resting her wrinkled hand on Mary's. "You don't want anything from the fey folk. Even when they mean good, their gifts always come at a price."

So Mary had heard, but she wasn't convinced. If Titania were willing to give, outright, a perfectly good remodeling job to her enemies just to embarrass them in public, Mary didn't see any reason why she couldn't do the same for a confidant who provided her with information on the other pixie-profiteers on her block. Mary had been watching her neighbors for years; she knew everyone's business.

Reaching the queen of the fairies turned out to be more difficult than she expected. Mary hadn't supposed Titania would be listed in the phone book, but now that the wee folk had come out of hiding she had assumed someone in her acquaintance would know how to find one. But if anyone did, they weren't telling. Mary found herself snubbed by every one of her friends as soon as she mentioned fairies, and by the end of the day she was no closer than before.

She went to bed early, exhausted by her effort, and fell into a deep sleep. Suddenly she found herself standing in an open meadow, ankle deep in yellow and blue wildflowers, facing a throne of orange and white mushrooms upon which sat the queen of the fairies. Titania was a bit on the plump side, with silver hair that wound sinuously down to her waist, and dressed in nothing more than a bright blue scarf draped around her body. Beside her stood the unnaturally tall elf who had charmed the Fraleys' house, and surrounding them all stood dozens of dwarfs and goblins and sprites of various sizes and hues. A few pixies hovered silently on diaphanous wings, their arms crossed over their bodies and their wide almond eyes focused unblinkingly on Mary.

"We hear you've been looking for us," Titania said lazily, inspecting her long red fingernails as she spoke.

"Um, yes," Mary said. "I—"

"Most people don't look forward to an encounter with the supernatural."

Something in her voice sent a chill down Mary's spine, but Mary forced herself to say, "I saw what you did to the dust dealers' house on Jefferson

Street last night. There's three more dealers on that block, and I'll tell you their names in exchange for the same job on my house."

Titania snickered, and her subjects echoed her like a laugh track on a TV sitcom. "We already know who they are," the fairy queen said. "We supply them with their product."

Mary gasped. "You what?"

"We sell pixie dust to your dealers. Where else did you think it came from?"

"I—I—" Mary stammered. "I thought—I've heard it comes from dead pixies."

Titania frowned, and her retinue shifted nervously. "It can," she said. "We use more...benign ways of extracting it, but some people get greedy."

"And you give them new houses for it?" Mary asked incredulously.

"We deal with them thoroughly if they actually hurt someone," Titania said, her voice ominously low. "But your neighbors were just doing a little freelance skimming on the side, so we let them go with a warning."

"Oh," Mary said. "I—I didn't know."

"Well, you do now, and you only get one warning yourself: Lay off our operatives or you'll find yourself living in a shoe."

Titania swept her arm out as if waving away a fly, and Mary felt herself tumble over backwards—to land with a thump in her bed.

She sat up, wondering if she had imagined the whole encounter, but when she switched on the lamp she found her bedspread covered with flowers. She picked up a couple of them, held them to her nose, and inhaled their sweet fragrance. Then, still clutching the flowers, she leaned slowly back against her pillow and schemed.

The next morning she waited until she saw activity in the Fraleys' house—it was nearly ten before the dust dealers got up—then walked across the street and down and knocked on the front door.

The Slut answered it. She had ripped the sleeves off a ruffled blouse and tied the tails together below her bosom, exposing a generous stretch of shapely stomach and waist above a pair of black tuxedo pants ripped off just below the crotch.

"Yeah?" she asked.

"I—I want to talk to you about buying your house," Mary said. "Well, trading, actually."

The Slut laughed, and a wad of chewing gum flew out of her mouth and hit Mary on the chest. Mary dabbed at it with her handkerchief while the Slut shouted into the house, "Hey Frank! There's another one wants to swap for the pixie palace."

Frank stepped into the entryway behind the Slut. He had formerly been a paunchy, greasy slob of a man, but now his darkly handsome features could have graced the covers of romance books. Unfortunately, his manners hadn't been improved along with his looks. "Piss off, lady," he growled. "We've already traded with the crone up the street." He pointed toward Flora's sagging, dispirited cottage, right beside Mary's own.

"What?" Mary gasped. "You've moving next to *me?* You can't!"

"Oh yes we can," the Slut said. "By tonight we'll be like peas in a pod." She smiled sweetly as she slammed the door in Mary's face.

Mary stormed back up the street and banged on Flora's door. "How could you do this to me?" she demanded. "We've been neighbors for forty years!"

"Listen, dearie," Flora said through her screen door, "I may be old, but I'm not senile. An opportunity like this doesn't come along every day."

"Opportunity!" Mary said. "You told me you wouldn't accept anything from the fairies because there's always a price."

"That's if you ask for it. This is a straight trade, a perfect chance to pick up a charmer without any strings attached." Flora shook her finger at Mary. "Besides, you were going to do the same to me, weren't you?"

Mary had no answer to that, save to turn around and walk stiffly back to her own house.

The next two weeks were purest hell. The dust dealers played their stereo loud enough to drown out Mary's TV even at its highest volume, and within days they had built up a new set of late-night customers who rattled her windows with their hopped-up cars. They came and went at all hours, save during the mornings, when the dealers slept in. Only then was the house quiet enough for Mary to relax, but after such long, nerve-wracking nights she couldn't sleep even so.

She kept track of her new neighbors' comings and goings, just as she did with everyone on the block, but it wasn't until they returned late one unusually quiet night that she saw anything interesting. She had her binoculars out and focused on their car the moment they pulled up to the curb, and she saw one of the men clutching a mysterious bundle wrapped in a coat. The coat wiggled in his grasp when he got out of the car, and Mary didn't need to see the iridescent blue wing slip out through the neck hole to know what they'd captured. They were going to render down another pixie for its dust.

She rushed for the door, no plan in mind except to rescue the poor creature, but she stopped with her hand on the knob. What could an old woman do against four healthy dust dealers?

She considered running to Flora for help, but even if that two-faced witch were to cooperate, they would only be two old ladies against the four. The entire neighborhood's honest population—Mary could only think of six—wouldn't be enough to do any good.

No, she needed help from another source. She locked her door again and went into the bathroom, where she swallowed two sleeping pills and stuffed the cotton from the top of the jar into her ears. Then she opened the jar of fairy blossoms that she had collected off her bed and scattered the now-withered petals over the spread, then lay down in their midst. It seemed to take forever for the pills to take effect, but she finally felt herself drift away.

The Queen was not pleased when Mary appeared in the midst of her nocturnal frolic, but she was even less pleased at the news Mary bore.

"Goldenrod, Lightfoot, see to the rescue," she commanded. Her long, skinny elf and a winged sprite of some sort both vanished in a shower of silvery glitter, then Titania turned back to Mary. "I suppose you want some kind of reward."

Mary tried not to wither under her intense gaze. "I—well, yes, I think that would only be fair," she stammered.

"Something like a *charming* new house?" Titania asked. "Maybe just a little bit bigger and nicer than the one your friend cheated you out of?"

Mary swallowed. "That—would do fine, yes. Provided there isn't a catch," she added quickly, remembering Flora's admonition about asking for things from fairies.

Titania smiled, showing an abundance of teeth. "Oh, I wouldn't think of it," she said. "The house will be perfect." She swept her arm toward Mary, who once again tumbled backward, to land on a soft down coverlet in a canopy bed in the most adorable bedroom she'd seen outside of a *Better Homes and Gardens* magazine.

She lay there for a moment, luxuriating in the wonder of dreams made real. Then, excitement burning away the effects of the sleeping pills, she got up to explore her new house. It was everything she'd hoped for, from the attic all the way down to the basement. She spent hours peeking into every nook and cranny, oohing and aahing at the flowery wallpaper and the elegant carved trimmery and the cabinets full of fine china, and it wasn't until dawn that she thought to go outside and check what it looked like from the street.

Titania hadn't skimped. Mary's house was bigger and more elaborate than Flora's. Than either of Flora's, since the elf had charmed the dust dealers' new residence as well.

Of the dealers themselves there was no trace, save for some pig-like hoofprints crossing the flower bed next to the street.

While Mary stood admiring her new house, Flora came walking up the sidewalk, a sheepish expression on her face. "Nice remodeling job," she said. "I like it. I like 'em both."

"You going to move back?" Mary asked.

Flora nodded. "As long as there's no hard feelings."

Mary laughed. "All's well that ends well, I always say." She threw her arms around her long-time friend. She could afford to be magnanimous, now.

So she helped Flora move her belongings back into the house next door, and they got together for lunch in Mary's new dining room, then they had afternoon tea at Flora's, and so on visiting back and forth for weeks on end.

Having three fancy houses suddenly sprout up on the block put a damper on the pixie dust business, so the evenings were considerably quieter than before, too. Some of the other residents along the street took a chance and renovated their houses the old-fashioned way, and pretty soon the entire neighborhood began to recover some of its former, natural charm.

And all the people there lived happily ever after, at least until the revised tax assessments arrived in the mail and everyone living on fixed incomes — Mary included — had to move away.

INTRODUCTION TO

THE DIFFERENCE BETWEEN SCIENCE FICTION AND FANTASY: A MATHEMATICAL ANALYSIS

When this was published (appropriately enough in *The Magazine of Fantasy & Science Fiction*), it generated a flurry of fan mail, all of it containing modifications to my theory and further calculations supporting those modifications. Then the article was translated into Russian, and it generated another round of research. I felt a little like Einstein after the publication of his General Theory of Relativity. I may have started a new branch of science!

The Difference Between Science Fiction and Fantasy: A Mathematical Analysis

By Jerry Oltion
Department of Bibliostatistics
Oregon Fictional Institute
Eugene, Oregon

Introduction

Writers, editors, fans and critics of science fiction and fantasy have long argued over a precise definition of the two respective genres, mistakenly assuming that such definitions will permit them to establish a strict delineation between the two and thus determine the relative superiority of one genre over the other. This effort is doomed at the outset due to the immense difficulty in agreeing on the rigorous set of criteria necessary for the establishment of literary definitions. Mathematics, however, bypasses that hurdle by providing terms whose value is already known and whose relative magnitude can be easily compared. This paper explores the mathematical approach to determining the precise difference between the two genres.

Method

The greatest obstacle to the mathematical approach was in converting the terms "science fiction" and "fantasy" into numerical values upon which the ensuing analysis could be made. Fortunately, data transmission techniques over the last few decades have provided a convenient method of

179

numerical encoding, namely the simple substitution of digits for letters. The American Standard Code for Information Interchange (ASCII) was briefly considered for this project, the encoding begins at an arbitrarily high number (65), and makes an unnecessary distinction between upper and lower case letters. The fundamental underlying principle of ASCII encoding, however, remains valid: i.e., a sequential substitution from A to Z, with A receiving the lowest value and Z receiving the highest. The only possible non-arbitrary choice for a starting point is to begin encoding with the cardinal number 1, and proceed sequentially through the standard English alphabet to a value of 26 for the letter Z (table 1). From there it is a simple matter to sum the values of the digits representing the words "science fiction" and "fantasy" and to compute their difference (table 2).

Table 1

A	B	C	D	E	F	G	H	I	J	K	L	M
1	2	3	4	5	6	7	8	9	10	11	12	13

N	O	P	Q	R	S	T	U	V	W	X	Y	Z
14	15	16	17	18	19	20	21	22	23	24	25	26

Table 2

S	=	19		F	=	6
C	=	3		A	=	1
I	=	9		N	=	14
E	=	5		T	=	20
N	=	14		A	=	1
C	=	3		S	=	19
E	=	5		Y	=	25
F	=	6		SUM	=	86
I	=	9				
C	=	3			134	
T	=	20			-- 86	
I	=	9	DIFF		48	
O	=	15				
N	=	14				
SUM	=	134				

Results

After encoding and summation, "science fiction" was found to have a value of 134 and "fantasy" was found to have a value of 86. Subtraction produces the result: 48. This may be taken as the definitive, rigorously mathematical difference between the two genres.

Interpretation

This value at first seems reasonable. However, as Adams[1] has hypothesized in his groundbreaking work, *The Hitchhiker's Guide to the Galaxy* (a work that straddles both genres under question and therefore must be accepted unquestioningly by both camps), the answer to the ultimate question about Life, the Universe and Everything should be 42. This means that the calculated result is 6 off from the theoretically obtained value, a deviation of over 14 percent.

Could there be an error in the calculation? Since the author of this article is primarily a writer of science fiction, not fantasy, the chance of that happening is so insignificant as to laughable, but the two terms were re-encoded and the addition and subtraction were performed again on the back of a new envelope, and the answer remains 48. The correct spelling of "science fiction" and "fantasy" has also been checked.

Could Adams' value be in error? That is equally laughable. As anyone in the publishing business know, no one who sells more than a million copies of each of his books *and* who spends over five months on the *New York Times* bestseller list[2] can be wrong.

Perhaps the question, "What is the difference between science fiction and fantasy?" is not the ultimate question. This seems unlikely, however, given the immense attention this conundrum has garnered from nearly every professional in the field. At conventions and on the computer networks, more time is spent arguing this question than any other, including just what sort of story will win the Nebula and Hugo Awards.[3]

Nor could the discrepancy be explained by agents taking their customary 15 percent commission, as that would skew the data in the other direction, producing a result of 35.7. Moreover, both science fiction and fantasy authors use agents, and this their effects cancel out.

Hence the discrepancy between the calculated and theoretical results must lie within the science fiction and fantasy genres themselves.

Discussion

As science fiction is the larger term (the minuend) and fantasy the smaller (the subtrahend), and as the calculated value for their difference is larger than the theoretical value, it is obvious that either science fiction is somehow too large or that fantasy is too small to deliver the proper result. This realization leads to the next question: is this a qualitative or a quantitative value?

Fortunately this can be answered with a simple *reductio ad absurdum*. If the difference were quantitative, then there would have to be either too much science fiction or too little fantasy; however, a review of market listings[4] for the major magazines and book publishers indicates that editors are reporting a relative lack of science fiction, which would hardly be the case if there were too much of it. Also, no fantasy magazines or book publishers report a similar lack of material, which should be the case if there were too little fantasy.

In fact, anecdotal evidence suggests just the opposite. respected critic have publicly stated that fantasy — particularly the most prevalent form of it known as the "trilogy" or "endless series" — is stealing the rack space from the real (i.e. science fiction) books. This could not be the case if there were too little of it.

Therefore, the difference between the two genres must be qualitative.

Conclusions

We began by demonstrating that the difference between science fiction and fantasy could be solved mathematically. Our result (48) unexpectedly led us to another conclusion: that the difference must be qualitative.

Despite the near perfection of many works in the science fiction genre[5], no one can reasonably argue that the quality of science fiction is too high. Sturgeon's Law[6] also precludes that notion. Therefore we have reached the inescapable conclusion that fantasy is qualitatively deficient. The degree of deficiency has been shown to be 6, or 14.3 percent.

Further Implications

Since the mathematical method has proved so successful in answering the science fiction/fantasy question, its use is indicated in any similar argument. For instance, a comparison of apples (69) and oranges (79) reveals that they are actually more similar than different, their difference (10) being only 13.5 percent of their mean value (74).

Acknowledgements

Review of an early draft of this paper by L. Goodloe is gratefully acknowledged.

References

1. Adams, A. *The Hitchhiker's Guide to the Galaxy*, Pocket Books, 1979.

2. Information from the cover of *Life, the Universe and Everything*, Pocket Books, 1982. Current figures may be larger.

3. Statistical analysis by keyword search of communications on the Genie computer network between January 1992 and October 1994.

4. *Gila Queen's Guide to Markets*, annual science fiction and fantasy issue, April 1994.

5. Oltion, J. *Frame of Reference*, Questar, 1987; Oltion, J. "The Pandora Probe," *Analog Science Fiction & Fact*, December, 1994; Oltion, J. and Goodloe, L., "Waterworld," *Analog Science Fiction & Fact*, March 1994, etc.

6. "Ninety percent of science fiction is crap*, but then ninety percent of everything is crap."

*Many critics dispute the word "crap," insisting that Sturgeon said "crud" instead.

Introduction to

The Moon Tree

A great deal of this story is based on fact. There really is a Moon Tree on the University of Oregon campus, the town around it is filled with old hippies, the Republican party has...I'll be kind and simply say that it has embraced a less tolerant, more militaristic approach to world problems than is appropriate for a civilized nation.

The Moon Tree's effect on the local citizenry is a little harder to corroborate, but Eugene, Oregon does seem to be an unusually friendly town, and this story seems as good an explanation as any.

THE MOON TREE

The Moon Tree lost its top last December. Six feet of perfect Douglas Fir, callously hacked off by some selfish idiot out for a Christmas tree. The branches left behind look like the fingers of an open hand, reaching up to cradle a crown that's no longer there.

So said the newspaper reporter who covered the story. According to him, whoever did it probably had no idea that he'd vandalized a national treasure. The campus gardeners hadn't put a plaque or anything special around the tree, probably because they were afraid that somebody would vandalize it on purpose if they knew what it was. Not everybody loves the space program, after all, and Eugene, Oregon, where the tree resides, is a hotbed of political unrest.

No, the reporter figured that the person who topped it was probably just some cheap, selfish bastard who didn't want to pay $25 for one of the local farm-grown trees. I'm glad that's the official explanation. It would be a shame if if people thought it was done in protest, or worse, in anger.

Especially since we did it to save the world.

I knew it was special the moment I saw it. I don't spend much time on the University of Oregon campus, but I needed to find a magazine the public library didn't have, and it was a sunny autumn day so I'd decided to take the long way past the flower gardens. Stop and smell the last of the roses before winter set in, and all that. I'd forgotten that sunny weather brings out the coeds, too. I wound up watching them more than the flowers, and wishing I were two decades younger so they might look back at me with interest instead of curiosity. One dark-haired, pale-skinned young woman with a tight black T-shirt and long, bare legs was sitting on the grass and staring at me with such puzzlement that I felt like walking up to her and saying, "No, your eyes aren't deceiving you. I'm a genuine relic of the sixties. This shirt is indeed tie-dyed, my vest does indeed bear fringe, and these are real beads around my neck. Get used to it; a lot of people still dress this way in Eugene." But then my eyes focused beyond her, and I instantly forgot her.

The tree was about twenty-five feet high, but its aura rose twice that; a great, billowing silvery-blue cloud of light, dancing and twisting in the ethereal breeze. I thought at first I was witnessing some sort of lightning discharge, but when it went on and on without dissipating I realized I was seeing a true aura, the strongest one I'd seen since 1972, when a Moon rock had come to SWOMSI—our local science museum—as part of a travelling exhibit.

The lawn had been heavily landscaped, with contoured ridges four or five feet high in places. I stumbled through the miniature hills and valleys toward the tree, not caring where I placed my feet. I must have brushed right past the dark-haired girl, but I felt nothing until I reached the tree and touched a branch, running my fingers over the soft, flat needles. The last three inches or so of each tuft was a lighter shade of green from this summer's growth. The aura seemed brighter at the edges, too.

"Hey, you kicked me!"

I turned away from the tree. The girl had followed me. I noticed now that she had a pierced eyebrow, the silver ring standing out as she glared at me with her brown eyes. Normally I don't like piercings, nor the butch, tattooed and booted look she affected to go with it, but the tree's aura was already working on her, softening some of her features, enhancing others. It was entirely subjective, I'm sure, but that's the nature of physical attraction.

She smelled nice, too. Lilac, I guessed.

"Are you all right?" she asked, and from her expression I could tell she hadn't expected those words to come out of her mouth.

"I'm fine," I answered. I smiled, wondering if the tree would make her see the character in crooked teeth. Hoping so.

Its influence might have made her look beautiful, but she didn't look convinced. "You brushed right past me," she said. "Like you were in a trance."

"I'm sorry. I saw something that startled me, and I guess I kind of spaced out."

She looked at the tree, then back at me. "What did you see?"

"You don't see anything?" I reached out to touch a branch again.

"I see a tree. A fir tree." She seemed proud of knowing what kind it was.

"No aura around it?"

"No what?"

"Aura. Like a big glowing halo."

"No." Her frown just drew my attention to her lips. Naturally pink against her pale skin.

"How about me? Do you see anything...unusual about me? Besides the clothes?"

"All men are unusual, but..." She made a big show of squinting and looking me up and down. "You still look kind of spacey, if that's what you mean. Are you on something?"

She was starting to glow herself, now. I had to look away in order to concentrate. "I think this tree was planted under a full Moon," I said. "Or maybe some of the soil it's growing in has Moondust in it. Something about it has a lunar influence, anyway."

She looked beautiful when exasperated, too. "You mean like astrology? You don't really believe that stuff, do you?"

"Well, yes, I do actually." Before she could run away, I added, "In an intellectual sort of way."

Only a student—someone trained to ask questions—would have stuck around to argue the philosophy of astrology, but she was game. She crossed her arms beneath her breasts (making their allure even stronger as my attention was drawn to them) and said, "An intellectual belief in astrology is an oxymoron, isn't it?"

I laughed. She was perfect. "Where have you been all my life?" I asked. "Yes, it's an oxymoron. It also happens to be true, to a limited extent. The Moon, at least, has a definite influence on our lives."

"Sure it does," she said, ignoring my compliment. "Tides. Light when it's full. Menstrual cycles."

"Ah, yes. Menses. Doesn't it seem a little too much coincidence that the cycle governing birth is tied so closely to the celestial symbol of love?"

She smiled a *gotcha!* sort of smile. "I thought Venus was the symbol of love."

That took me by surprise. It took me a moment to think through the implications before I answered. She waited, clearly enjoying my dilemma. At last I said, "You're right, but the Moon is a symbol of love, too, and it's a lot closer to us. It probably has more chance to shape our lives than Venus does."

"Probably?" she asked, still grinning. "I never heard of an astrologer saying 'probably' before."

"That's why my interest in it is more intellectual than most. I'm willing to admit it's mostly conjecture."

The tree was definitely doing its thing for her, now, too. She looked me over again, gave me a genuine smile, and said, "You know, I was starting to think all the old hippies around here were kind of pathetic, but you aren't. Different, that's for sure, but I think I kind of like that." She nodded toward the yellow backpack on the grass where she had been sitting when I first saw her. "Let's go sit down and you can tell me what the Moon and astrology have to do with this tree."

I looked beyond the tree toward the library. I'd been planning to spend the afternoon reading up on Oregon politics, trying to find a chink in the armor of Don Ravon, our fundamentalist senator from Portland whose intolerance for anything other than his own lifestyle was making life hard for people like me, but the prospect of an afternoon in the grass with an interested college girl — even if that interest was brought on by external forces — seemed much more attractive. Ravon could wait.

So we walked back to her spot on a high berm in the heavily landscaped lawn and got comfortable, she lying long and sinuous on her left side, me sitting cross-legged before her.

"The connection between the Moon and the tree," I told her, "is that the Moon influences lovers, and the tree is making us fall for each other." I held up my hand to stop her embarrassed protest. "No, I mean it. Would you normally talk to a complete stranger the way you've been talking to me?"

"Maybe," she said. "If he was interesting."

"But you thought I was pathetic at first. Spaced out."

"And I asked if you were okay. Then I found out you were interesting."

"But if that tree weren't here, you wouldn't have done anything, would you?"

"I don't see what the tree has to do with it. I wasn't thinking about it when I saw you."

"You still don't see the aura?" I asked. "To me it's like a big silver-blue flame all around it. And some of it has spread to you, too."

"What?"

"You've got an aura now too."

She looked down at her body, then held out the arm that wasn't propping her up so she could sight along it. "I can't see anything."

"Most people can't," I said with a sigh.

"But you can." If we'd been anywhere else but next to the tree, her tone of voice would have left no doubt that she thought I was insane, and that our conversation was over. But it didn't come out that way, quite.

I weighed my words, then realized what I was doing and tossed away the scale. I gave that up years ago. "Yeah," I said. "I think it was some bad acid I had back in '68. I was barely a teenager at the time, but I wanted to see what it was like. After that I was seeing auras around practically everything. Most of 'em went away after a year or so, but some of them stayed, and I started to notice things about them. Like, when the Moon is out they seem to make people fall in love. Or maybe people falling in love under the Moon make auras, I don't know. It's hard to tell."

She was quiet for a long time before she said, "You really believe this, don't you?"

"I really do. And I notice you're not denying anything either."

She blushed. "Look, I like you well enough, but I'm not falling in love with you, okay?"

"Give it time," I said. "Or not. I'm at least twenty years older than you; it could be kind of inconvenient. For you, I mean. You may not want to have an old throwback to the flower days following you around. I don't think we're so far into it we couldn't get out if we wanted to. If you want, I'll go on over to the library and let you get on with whatever you were doing." I felt a real pang of regret at those words. We weren't head-over-heels yet, but we were definitely bonding.

191

She didn't look all that happy, either. "You mean that, too, don't you?"

I nodded. "But if I go, you'd better move a little farther from that tree or you'll just fall for the next guy who comes along."

She glanced back over at the fir, warily, as if it might be sneaking up on her. "You make it sound like I don't have any choice in the matter."

"You don't. Not much, anyway. The longer we're together under its influence, the less choice either one of us will have."

"You don't seem too upset by the idea."

I shrugged. "I thought you were pretty even before I got within range of the tree. You're intelligent and curious as well. I could easily fall for someone like you without help."

"Thanks." She sat up and hugged her knees to herself. "Look, no offense, but this is getting a little too strange. Maybe you're used to this sort of thing, being from the sixties and all, but I don't even know your name."

"Arthur," I told her. "But my friends call me 'Jade.' Because I have green eyes."

"I noticed. All right, Jade, I'm Megan. And I'm a little confused right now, okay? I need a little time to myself to think about this. But I don't want you to just go away. Could we meet again in a couple of hours or something?"

"Sure." I didn't know if the lightness I was feeling came from me or the tree, but at that point I didn't particularly care. We were making a date.

"Right here?" she asked.

"Okay," I said, but a glance at the still-glowing tree made me say, "No, wait a minute. Let's make sure it's really our idea if we decide to see more of each other. How about we meet over in the student union? Neutral ground."

"All right. The student union in two hours."

"Shall we synchronize our watches?"

She looked down at her wrist before she realized I'd been joking, then looked back up at me and grinned. "Get out of here."

I got. But I was whistling the whole way.

I spent the two hours in the library, but not looking up dirt on Don Ravon. I dug through the computerized card catalog for information on the campus trees, and eventually came up with an identification guide for a botany class. It had a map of campus with all the trees and shrubs marked, and when I looked at the listing for the one with the aura I saw a (17) and an (18) beside the label: "Douglas Fir, *Pseudotsuga taxifolia*." Endnote number 17 talked about how to tell a Douglas Fir from other firs, and how it isn't a "true fir" because the cones hang down instead of point upward. Number 18 said, "This particular fir is often called the 'Moon Tree' because it was grown from a seed that rode to the Moon and back in the Apollo 16 space capsule."

Ha! I'd been right. I checked out the book and walked back past the tree (still glowing) to the student union, where I bought a paper cup full of coffee and took a table out in front. While I waited for Megan to show up, I amused myself by watching the flickering auras on some of the students sitting at tables around me. Three of them, all sporting the same silver-blue glow I'd seen on the Moon Tree, were sitting together. Two guys and a girl. A green Frisbee rested on the table between them, also glowing silver, and I guessed they had been tossing it back and forth near the Tree. I wondered how the triangle would work out, and bet myself one of the guys would be the other one's best man. Or maybe they would all move in together.

One aura farther back toward the wall was different. It was red instead of silver, and so faint I could hardly tell it was there. It barely reached beyond the clothing and hair of the buzz-cut neo-Nazi radiating it. He was sitting alone at a table in the corner, his back to the wall, and he kept glancing up nervously from the book he was reading. He kept catching my eye before I could look away, and after about the fourth time he got up and stalked toward me. I thought he was going to demand why I was staring at him, but I held his gaze as he came toward me and he looked away first. He brushed past my table, nearly spilling my coffee, and I glanced at his book as he swept by. Between his fingers I could just see the title: *Wartide*, and a picture of an over-muscled guy with a gun in his hands and a bandolier full of bullets over each shoulder.

I'd seen red auras before, usually on people stuck in traffic or banging on stubborn vending machines. I'd never seen one on a person reading for pleasure. I wanted to catch up with him and ask him why he cultivated that mindset on purpose, but I couldn't think of a good way to broach the subject. Besides, he was leaving the building and I had to stay and meet Megan.

She stepped up beside me a couple minutes later and set her backpack and a can of orange pop on the table. "Hi," she said.

"How're you feeling?" I stood up and pulled out a chair for her.

She looked as if she'd never had anyone do that before, but then she smiled and sat down. "Not bad, actually. I walked around and tried to think of all the reasons why I shouldn't get involved with you, and I couldn't come up with one. I've got to tell you right up front that I don't believe in auras or that some tree made me fall for you, but I do want to find out more about you."

"Look at this first," I said, showing her the footnote in the botany book.

Her eyes grew wide when she read it. I could actually see her beliefs shift. Just a subtle change in the colored glow that surrounded her, like heat lightning seen out of the corner of your eye, but it was there.

"Wow, it really *was* influenced by the Moon."

"And now it's influencing everybody who gets near it."

She giggled. "I always thought this was a friendly campus. Now I know why."

"Yeah."

"And—" She tilted her head sideways. "Do you suppose that's how the whole free-love thing in the '60s happened? All that attention the country was paying to the Moon?"

I looked down at my tie-dye and love beads. "I prefer to think it was a lifestyle choice we made out of respect for the Earth and the people we share it with, but if the Moon had some effect on us, I guess that's okay with me."

She got a dreamy look in her eyes. "And maybe that's why all the astronauts are such hotties, too."

I shrugged. "I'll have to take your word for it that they are, but sure, it makes sense. The ones who were youngest when they went are probably the best looking today. The Moon supposedly has its greatest influence on young things."

"Like seeds," Megan pointed out. "And babies." She frowned. "I suppose that's where astrology came from. Ancient people must have noticed a connection between what was in the sky when a child was born and the way the child grew up. Then people kept claiming more and more connections until it became the mass of contradictions we've got today."

"Most myths have at least a little basis in fact." I took a sip of my coffee. "If we ever make it back there with a permanent base, the kids born there are going to be stunning. They'll be like a whole new race compared to us."

"Think of the movie stars they'd make." Megan leaned back in her chair and sighed. "Unfortunately, we're not headed back to the Moon anytime soon."

"No?" I asked. "Not even with the space station?"

She shook her head. "Nope. The government wants another spectacle to sell the public on space again, so they're planning a mission to—" she stopped. "Uh-oh."

"What?"

"They're planning a mission to Mars."

I thought of the red aura I'd seen around the angry student just a few minutes earlier. Mars's influence? I had no way of knowing for sure, but I knew what would happen if we actually brought back samples from the god of War.

We've got samples already, of course, in the form of meteorites, but they're thousands—maybe even millions—of years old. Their influence has faded over the millennia, but even so, it was strong enough to set the scientific community at each other's throats when one group of researchers thought they'd found evidence of life in one. I imagined what fresh Martian samples would do; or worse, what something like a Mars Tree could do if it were planted in Washington, DC.

"We've got to do something," I said.

Megan held out her hands. "What can we do? Blow up the rocket?"

I looked at her in alarm, saw that she was kidding, but still said, "No, no, we can't go around blowing things up or we're as bad as what we're trying to prevent."

"Maybe we could show the President what the Moon Tree does to people. If he knew the danger of going to Mars, maybe he'd cancel the project."

I shook my head. "We could never get him to come here. And even if we *could* convince him, he would probably be even more eager to go than before. He might mellow out a little near the Tree, but once he got back to Washington he'd go right back to being his old self. He'd probably want to drop Mars samples all through the Middle East to push them over the edge

195

and end his troubles once and for all."

She narrowed her eyes and pursed her lips in thought. "You're right, but there's got to be somebody we could convince. The head of NASA, maybe?"

"I can't think of a good way to get him out here, either." Then I remembered why I'd come to campus today in the first place, and laughed out loud.

"What?"

"I just thought of one person we *could* bring here, and it might do us more good than the President anyway."

"Who?"

"Don Ravon. Oregon's very own proponent of intolerance and hatred."

"Him? He's worse than the President."

"Precisely. But he's also the top runner for the Republican nomination in the next election. If we could get to him..."

Life is more complicated than that, of course. You can't just invite a senator out for a picnic on campus, especially in the fall. That late in the year it's cold and rainy most of the time, and senators are busy in Washington anyway, trying to finish up the last of their wheeling and dealing before breaking for the holidays. And Ravon was too busy gearing up for next year's election campaign, thinking up the most efficient way to slander his liberal opponent.

We researched them both before we made our move. After all, we didn't want to help put someone even worse than Ravon in office. Irene Moldoya had her faults, but we were mostly concerned with her stance on the space program, and that was just what we'd hoped for. She proposed cautious advancement with a space station, then a base on the Moon, using the ice deposits on the south lunar pole to help set up a permanent base there before we went onward to Mars. Under her plan, the effect of the Moon on living things would be known long before we got to the other planets. That might not keep us from going, but we would at least know what to expect, and maybe we could prepare for the effect it would have on us.

Megan and I spent most of October and November making our plans. Every few days we took our umbrellas and a tarp and sat on the grass not far from the Moon Tree, watching as other people came under its influence, paused a moment in their hasty course across campus, and walked away a little slower, smiling. Often they walked away in pairs, which confirmed what we already knew.

In early December we made our move.

Like I say, someone topped the Moon Tree. A few days later, after the furor died down, two people representing themselves as a private timber baron and his young wife made a contribution to Senator Ravon's campaign fund. As a personal gift, they brought a Christmas Tree for campaign headquarters, where they knew Ravon and his all-volunteer staff—composed primarily of young church-going college girls—would be putting in a lot of long hours through the holidays and would appreciate some midnight cheer.

We didn't alert the media. There will be plenty of opportunities for scandal to get out, and Ravon has political enemies far more devious than us who can figure out the maximum use of the indiscretions that must surely be playing out in his office over the holidays.

No, we used the time to atone for our own sin. I've got some property outside of town, the remains of a commune that didn't work out. I doubt if Senator Ravon will notice that his office Christmas tree is missing all its cones, but we saw no reason to waste them. Christmas trees are big business around here, and my acreage—now Megan's and mine—is prime tree growing land. It will take a few years for Moon Tree Farms to produce anything tall enough to stand in anyone's living room, but we figure the timing should be just about right. Even if Ravon's opponent can't stop America from going straight to Mars, people all over the country will be feeling exceptionally fond of one another just about the time the first mission comes back with samples. With any luck, the feeling will overpower anything a few red rocks can do to the national spirit.

As we used to say when I was younger, make love, not war.

INTRODUCTION TO

FICTION

I've heard it argued that reading is a form of self-induced insanity, because you intentionally put yourself into a state where you hear and see things that aren't really there. I decided to play with the idea of what would happen if that were actually true.

This story made its debut in an appropriate venue: at a convention where I was the writer guest of honor. What better place to question the validity of the very concept of writing?

Those who have already read "The Love Song of Laura Morrison" (and you probably should before you read "Fiction") will notice that the version quoted here is not the same as the version at the beginning of this book. That's what happens when you start playing around with alternate universes.

Fiction

Roger knew the doctors were approaching by the squeak of their soft-soled shoes on the waxed floor. Damn. Just when he was getting to the good part. He read faster, hoping he could at least make it to a scene break before they interrupted him.

They discussed him as they approached, as if he weren't there. Roger was getting used to that. He tried to tune them out and concentrate on the perils of Laura Morrison, who was putting on her spacesuit, not knowing the fabric under the arms had weakened with age.

The new one, no doubt a fresh intern, had a penetrating voice. "Why does he hold his arms out like that?" he asked. "Does he think he's driving?"

"No," said the regular doctor, Williams. "He says he's reading."

"Breeding? He thinks there's a woman—"

"No, no. *Reading*. He claims he's holding onto a bunch of thin sheets of wood all bound together on one edge, and he's looking at some sort of marks on them."

Teigh and Laura stood in the airlock while the pressure dropped to zero. Laura's suit bulged with the strain, but held.

"How strange. Is he responsive?"

Doctor Williams snorted. "Barely. He's usually quite reluctant to give up his delusion. Let me show you. Roger?"

Teigh led Laura out of the airlock, and Laura, seeing the stars for the

201

first time in decades, leaned her head back and said, "Hah, hasn't changed much."

"Roger."

"Do his eyes always flick from side to side like that?"

"Only when he's 'reading.' Roger, this is Doctor Gordon. Can you say hello to him for me?"

They climbed into the rocket car for the five-minute journey to the starship under construction. Laura's suit creaked ominously as she stretched to reach the seatbelt.

"Roger."

Roger sighed and lowered the book. Doctor Williams and the intern (his name already forgotten) stood before him, their white lab coats spotless, their faces contorted in artificial smiles. Roger said, "Could you maybe come back in a few minutes? I've just got a couple of pages to go, and—"

"Pages?" the intern asked, ignoring Roger's request.

"Pages." Roger rattled the one he'd been reading. His eyes caught the line, *...drowned out in the hiss of escaping air...* and he knew he'd been right. Her suit hadn't held.

"And what do you see on those...pages?"

Roger sighed. "I see a great story about an old woman who lives on a space colony. Right now she's outside for the first time in years, and her spacesuit is about to blow. Now if you wouldn't mind, I'd like to—"

"He seems quite coherent, other than the obvious delusion," the intern remarked.

Doctor Williams sniffed. "Oh yes. But I'm nearly convinced that this 'reading' of his, these imaginary 'books' he examines, are symptoms of a much deeper disturbance. For instance, many of the stories he describes to me, supposedly from the pages of these books, involve murder and death. Others show an obsession with sex. They nearly always concern people in dire circumstances."

"Blowout!" Teigh shouted into the radio. "I've got someone with a suit blowout! Help me!"

"Do they indeed? How intriguing."

The shoes squeaked as the two doctors walked away. Doctor Williams said, "When you've got the time, you should have him read aloud to you. It's incredible. He can go on for hours without repeating himself, spinning new fantasies as fast as he can talk."

Teigh watched helplessly while the medics forced air into her lungs...

"Astounding."

"Oh, indeed. It's one of the most elaborate delusional systems I've ever encountered. He's not only come up with a whole new — though admittedly farfetched — method of information transfer, but he imagines a whole industry established to support it."

"Does he now?"

At last Laura was breathing on her own; horrible, bubbling breaths that made Teigh sick to listen to, but she was alive again.

"He described it to me once. The mechanics of it alone are incredibly complex. But what I'd like to know," Doctor Williams said as they rounded the corner at the far end of the hall, "is where he gets all those *ideas*."

Introduction to

Gems in the Rough

A few years ago I started wondering what would happen if time travel became so cheap that people could go back and revise even the most trivial parts of their lives. I decided there would probably be two different approaches to the situation: some people would tinker with their past until everything was perfect, while others would leave well enough alone and only use the technology for emergencies.

Then I thought, "What would happen if two people—one of either type—went out on a date?"

Gems in the Rough

Derek felt a moment of Déjà New just before the doorbell rang. A moment of disorientation, a split second wherein he felt two sets of memories crowding his mind before reality asserted itself again. He got up from the couch where he had been reading the *Rolling Stone*, switched off the magazine and draped it over the arm of the couch, and went to answer the door. Déjà New before the date even started wasn't a good sign. Especially on a first date. It meant something had gone so disastrously wrong that he and Gardenia had decided to backspace and try it again.

Except he had no memory of the faux pas. Usually when you backspaced you remembered why you'd done it, at least until you'd had a chance to make whatever change you'd gone back for. Gardenia must have done it on her own. But was it his mistake or hers she'd come back to undo? He had no idea. It made him decidedly uncomfortable. Did he have spinach between his teeth? Had he left his fly open? Had he said something offensive? How could he fix it if he didn't know what it was?

He opened the door. Gardenia stood there, her blonde hair curling down past her oval face to touch her shoulders. She was dressed in iridescent blue bodypaint that shimmered with flashes of green and yellow when she moved. It showed off her designer physique to perfection, and as Derek said, "Come in," and stood aside for her, he wondered if he had lost control and molested her right there in the living room.

Except in cases of date rape it was usually considered the man's duty to backspace and undo it, to spare the woman the unpleasant memory.

Maybe she had raped him? Or perhaps she was a murderess, and now she would spend the rest of the evening telling him in detail how she had killed him the first time around. He hated dates like that. If that's what had happened, he would backspace a few hours and cancel the whole date, claiming a headache.

He wished he could just ask her, but most people considered that a worse breach of etiquette than murder. Derek didn't share their opinion, but you were supposed to pretend you hadn't noticed the moment of discontinuity when someone you were with backspaced, so he merely smiled and said, "You look lovely."

She did, too. She always looked nice at the bank where they both worked, but she never dressed like this. Wendy, their supervisor, would never have allowed it. Gardenia would have outclassed her in a potato sack—a fact that no doubt fueled Wendy's hostility—but in bodypaint Gardenia would have made her look even more like the witch she was.

Derek was glad he hadn't elected to wear paint; he took good care of himself, but he would never match her attractiveness either, not even in a gay bar. As it was, his black and white casual suit would blend in with everyone else's and allow people to admire her without distraction.

Now that she was in the room with him, he smelled the flowery aroma of her perfume. Apple blossoms? He couldn't tell.

"So where are we going?" she asked.

They had agreed to go out for dinner when he'd asked her that morning, but they had never settled on a place. Now it looked as if that decision was up to him. He'd been imagining someplace dimly lit and intimate, but a woman didn't dress like that to go sit in the dark. "How about Thai food?" he asked. "I know a place with a rooftop garden."

She narrowed her eyes. "Thai food? I've never tried it."

"Then you should." He held out his hand and led her through his apartment and up the stairs to the roof, where they watched the sunset for a few minutes before he hailed an aircab.

At the restaurant the headwaiter took one look at Gardenia and seated them at a table on the edge of the building, where everyone in the passing cars could see her and know that Thai Heaven was where the beautiful people dined. The weather attenuation field let just a whisper of sound through from the traffic, and only enough of a breeze to waft her hair gently into the air from time to time.

The menus were six pages long. "Pad Thai is the most traditional dish," Derek said as he scrolled through with the thumb slide in the left margin, "but I've never had a bad meal here no matter what I pick."

"That's encouraging," Gardenia replied. She looked at the choices for a minute. "Have you ever had the Three Kings Crown?"

Derek scanned through his menu for it, found it under "specialties" with four stars beside it. "Never had the courage," he admitted. "You want to try it?"

"Sure," she said. But a moment later Derek felt another wave of Déjà New and she said, "On second thought, let's not. It's too—well, it's probably too spicy."

Derek looked at her glittering green eyes as she spoke, and she glanced away. "Don't 'probably' me," he said, smiling to show her he was more amused than mad. "You backspaced just now, didn't you?"

She blushed. Just her cheeks—her bodypaint didn't allow him to see more. "Um...yes. I'm sorry, but my lips were *hot*, and..."

"This is a problem?" he asked, and she blushed even redder.

"I suppose I should have asked you first," she said, "but I didn't think you'd mind."

"It's all right." He looked down at his menu again, wondering how long she had let the peppers burn before she'd excused herself from the table on the pretext of going to the bathroom and used the restaurant's backspacer instead. But his curiosity faded quickly, like a dream after a person wakes. It was hard to focus on a lost reality after the new one asserted itself. Only the person who went back remembered the way things were before, and even their memory faded over time.

No hot entrees, though. He remembered that much.

He played it safe and ordered Prig King. She ordered Massaman, then changed her mind at the last moment and got the Pad Thai instead.

"Was Massaman too hot, too?" he asked when the waiter left.

She shook her head. "No, it just wasn't what I wanted."

"Ah." He hadn't felt any more discontinuities, so maybe that's all it had been.

He looked down through the passing traffic to the grassy street below, where pedestrians walked hand-in-hand in the last light of evening. A couple of kids were chasing a stray dog. The dog barked at them, staying just out of reach until one of the kids picked up a stick and swung it in a wide arc, but instead of hitting the dog he wound up hitting his companion.

"Ow," said Derek, wincing in sympathetic pain.

"What?" asked Gardenia.

He pointed. "One of those kids down there just whacked the other one with a stick by accident."

"Oh. Then we're on borrowed time." She grinned at him. "Got any thirty-second fantasies you want to try out?"

He looked at her painted curves, at her mischievous smile. "Is that a trick question? But there's really not much point, is there? We won't remember it. Besides, it looks like they're not going to backspace." He nodded toward the kids, who were chasing the dog again.

"Wow," said Gardenia. "I sure would have."

"I gather you backspace a lot."

She shrugged. "Not as much as some people. But I don't see any reason to live with a bruise when it's so easy to go back and eliminate it."

"Hmm." He picked up his fork and twirled it in his fingers. "I guess for me it depends on how bad the bruise is. I've actually still got a couple of scars from my childhood. Even after the backspacer was invented, I didn't figure it was worth going back that far to fix stuff that had already healed."

Gardenia's eyes widened. "You have *scars*?"

"Yep."

"Where?"

"Let's just say if I showed them to you here, we'd *have* to backspace or get kicked out of the restaurant."

"Oh."

The waiter came back with their drinks, sweet ice tea with cream swirling through it. Derek mixed his up with his straw until the tea resembled rusty water; Gardenia held hers carefully in her hands, watching the cream drift downward like jellyfish tendrils slowly invading the bottom of the glass.

"So how bad does something have to be before you'll backspace?" she asked.

He shrugged. "Not that bad, really. Just last week I caught a cold at a party, so I went back and took an immune booster before I got there."

"You still went to the party?" She set her glass down. "I'd have found one that didn't have sick people."

"It was my sister's party. I didn't want to offend her."

"Oh." Gardenia smiled knowingly. "Family is still the one thing you can't change, isn't it? My father drives me crazy sometimes, but no matter how many times I go back and try to fix things, he still manages to put a blotch on an otherwise perfect life."

"Is that what you're trying to do?" Derek asked. "Make a perfect life?"

She looked at him with a puzzled expression. "Of course I am. Doesn't everyone? What else is the backspacer for?"

The waiter brought their food, the aroma of curry and peanut sauce filling the air. As they piled rice and noodles and chicken and vegetables on their plates, Derek said, "I don't know if it's *for* anything in particular. I doubt if the guy who invented it figured on a tenth of the use it gets. He probably thought he was saving lives."

"He is," Gardenia said. "He's saved us from having to live with all the rotten luck and bad memories that people used to be stuck with."

Derek watched the way she moved when she picked up the plate of Pad Thai. He could see every muscle at work. With only a layer of iridescent paint between her and the world, she was as good as naked. So were half a dozen other people in the restaurant. They were all slender and good-looking, and none of them considered the consequences of being miles away from home with nothing to protect them from the weather or from other people. If something went wrong, they would go back and fix it.

"I've got to admit," he said, "I like the way it's made people relax."

Gardenia flinched, then looked away.

"What?" he asked. "I said something wrong, didn't I?"

"No, it's...well...I just wouldn't call it 'relaxed.'"

"No?"

She hesitated, then took a deep breath and plunged ahead like a swimmer into icy water. "I worry about everything. Is my hair right? Is my paint thin enough? Is it too thin? Did I say something stupid? Could I have said something more intelligent? Now that I've got the chance to go back and re-do everything, it feels like I'm obligated to do it. It's not easy being perfect, you know."

"Actually, I don't know," he said. "I've never tried."

"You should."

He looked down at his plate, for a moment seeing not noodles and rice but a writhing mass of worms. He looked back up at Gardenia. "Sorry. I'm getting too personal for a first date. And you're answering because you plan to hit the backspacer the first chance you get and make a polite apology when I asked you out this morning. Right?"

She made a little shrug. "We don't have to undo the whole date. I kind of like you. We could still have a lot of fun together."

He smiled. "Thanks. Somehow that means more coming from someone on borrowed time than it would if we were still on the main track."

She laughed. "Isn't it strange how a person can only say what they really mean when it doesn't matter?"

"Yeah."

She picked up her fork. "As long as we're backing up, let's check the food first and see if we want to re-order."

"Sure." Derek tasted the Pad Thai. Thai Heaven's version was light and delicate, the eggs and noodles and bean sprouts blending smoothly into one wonderful flavor. The Prig King was stronger, the peanut sauce and the curry fighting for dominance but neither quite overpowering the other.

"It's perfect," Gardenia said.

"You use that like a technical term."

She tossed her hair back away from her forehead with a casual flip of her head. "It is."

"Tell you what," he said. "Let's do something really crazy. Let's finish the meal before we backspace. In fact, let's finish the whole night first. Linear time all the way to the end. Just for curiosity's sake. If we're going to backspace at the end of it anyway, let's see what happens when it doesn't matter."

Gardenia colored slightly, no doubt thinking of all the ways the evening might progress. "All right," she said. She picked up a forkful of noodles and brought them to her mouth, but one slithered off her fork at just the wrong moment and landed on her left breast, where it draped itself over her nipple and dangled there like an organic pasty while she gasped, "Oh no! You've got to let me undo that."

"Nope." He grinned and reached across the table to remove the noodle, which he slurped slowly into his mouth while he wiggled his eyebrows lasciviously at her.

"But—"

"No revisions, not for the entire night."

"But I've got sauce on my boob!"

"Want me to lick it off?"

"We'll get kicked out of the restaurant."

"Good point. Better use your napkin."

She did, wiping off some of the iridescent paint in the process. Bodypaint normally wouldn't come off with casual rubbing, but something in the sauce must have acted like a natural solvent.

Her pink nipple seemed all the more red peeking through the field of blue. "Well," she said, "this is certainly turning out to be an interesting date, that's for sure."

"I spent months choreographing it."

She looked up at him so quickly her hair flew forward for a second before falling back down around her shoulders. "What? How could you—?"

"I'm kidding."

"Oh." She took another bite. "You sure know how to keep a woman off guard."

"Natural talent," he said. They ate in silence for a few minutes before he asked, "So how many times have you murdered Wendy?" Wendy delighted in making her workers miserable with stupid new rules; the tellers and loan officers sometimes took out their frustrations the old-fashioned way.

Gardenia rolled her eyes and swallowed. "Who knows? The memories fade. But I'm pretty sure I poisoned her coffee last week, and I sort of remember pushing her down the stairs a month or so ago. How about you?"

"Shotgun," he said. "About three months ago. Marched into her office and let her have it right in the chest. At least that's how I remember it. Funny thing, nobody backspaced for over an hour afterward."

"At the *bank*?" she said incredulously. "We kept working? Why? We'd just have to do it over again."

213

"I think we were just so happy to have her out of our hair that we were willing to put in the extra time before we brought her back. But I don't know for sure. Like you said, the memories fade."

She stirred her tea and drank, then said, "I've always wondered why she stays at a job where everyone hates her."

"Same reason we stay at a job we hate, I suppose," he replied. "No amount of backspacing will find us a free lunch. And even with Wendy, the bank isn't really that bad."

"I suppose not," she said. "I keep thinking I ought to go back and try for a better job, but I've put so much work into the rest of my life I'd hate to wipe it all out just for that."

Derek knew what she meant. The psychological toll of a major edit could be extreme. Reworking the bad times was one thing, but losing all the good times that went with them was too large a price for most people to pay. And paradoxically enough, the more a person fine-tuned their day-to-day life, the less likely they were to throw the entire thing to the winds and start over.

Gardenia, he suspected, would stay at the bank, waiting on surly customers and poisoning Wendy's coffee to relieve stress, until Hell froze over.

It was like polishing a diamond. Once you made the rough cut you couldn't whack off any more big chunks. From then on you accepted the general shape of it and just polished it with finer and finer abrasive until every facet glittered.

Except tonight. Derek wondered how it would work out. Not that it mattered, of course, but it was kind of interesting in a retro sort of way.

After dinner they went down to the street to walk off the excess food they had eaten. They strolled hand in hand, Gardenia wearing Derek's jacket to protect her from the chilly evening breezes, until they saw a chocolate shop and ducked inside for dessert. It turned out they both liked dark chocolate, and since they were on borrowed time anyway they bought a whole pound of truffles and ate them in the cab on the way back to Derek's apartment.

"Oh man," Gardenia said as she staggered down the stairs, holding her stomach. "I ate waaaay too much."

"Me too. Want some Alka Seltzer?"

"Alka Seltzer? You actually have some?"

He shrugged. "No matter how many times I try it, my cooking never seems to improve. I've pretty much given up."

She dropped onto the living room couch. "At least you're prepared for the results. Well, as long as we're going linear tonight, bring on the seltzer."

He went into the kitchen and fixed two glasses, bringing them both into the living room. They sat side-by-side on the couch and sipped at the fizzing water while the quarter-sized tablets dissolved, but before they got to the bottom she started to giggle and he began to laugh with her.

"Nobody would believe us if we told them about this," she said. "I mean, the very idea of letting it go on this long. Without having sex or doing anything really outrageous, either. We should at least leap off the roof into traffic or something."

"That would make it kind of hard to backspace," he pointed out.

"So it would."

"We could rob the bank."

"Done that," she said. "They made me give it all back."

"Yeah, that's the problem." He set his glass down on the coffee table and put an arm around her. "You know what I'd really like to do?" he asked.

"What?"

"Just hold you. You're soft and warm and beautiful and I like being close to you. If you don't mind."

She looked at him in surprise. "Mind? You want to cuddle instead of leap straight into the sack and you think I'd mind? Good grief, where have you been all my life?"

He smiled and drew her into his arms. He felt goosebumps on her skin and said softly, "You're cold."

"No I'm not."

"Oh."

Her hair smelled like apple blossoms. That's what he had noticed when she first came into his apartment.

"Hey," he said suddenly. "Just before you rang the doorbell I felt a shot of Déjà New. What happened?"

If she was offended by the question, she didn't show it. She laughed softly, leaned back so she could see his eyes, and said, "Nothing, really. I was wearing black and white, too. We looked like a couple of penguins, so I went back home and put on paint instead."

"Ah. I'm sure you looked stunning in black and white, too, but I can't say I'm sorry you changed." He put his arms around her again, brushing his hands lightly over her iridescent skin.

Some time later, her head resting on the bare triangle of his chest where she had unbuttoned his shirt, she said, "We're not going to undo this, are we?"

"I don't know. What do you think? Can you live with all the night's memories?"

She nodded. "I wouldn't give them up for anything. Except..."

"Except what?"

"Now I wish I'd stuck with Three Kings Crown."

"Next time," he said. "Assuming you're willing to risk going out with me twice."

She snuggled in closer to him. "It's a date."

Introduction to

House Calls

Some of my best stories come from shoving two completely different ideas together and seeing what emerges. I got the first half of this one about twenty-five years ago, when somebody spiked a water cooler at school with vodka. The second half came considerably later, after Alzheimer's disease rose into the public's awareness.

"House Calls" originally appeared in an audio anthology called *Frequency*. This is its first time in print.

HOUSE CALLS

It was three in the morning when the drunks banged on my door. Of course it was three in the morning; it's always three in the morning when people come to me for spiritual help. That's when they finally admit they're not going to get to sleep because of whatever it is that's bothering them.

I wasn't asleep either, but that's not so much from a guilty conscience as it is a consequence of age. So I put down my book and trudged wearily into the entryway to see who it was this time, wondering as I clicked on the light if Buddhist leaders ever had this problem.

Two men stood on my porch, both wet as dishrags from the rain that had been falling all night, and both drunk as lords. The smell of alcohol hit me like a slap in the face before either of them spoke.

The smaller of the two said, "We beg your pardon, Father, but we are in need of your assistance." Raindrops beaded on his bald head and ran down the sides to drip off his nose, cheekbones, and chin. He didn't sound drunk, which cheered me a bit, but the odd, almost imbecilic grin on his face made me nervous. Axe murderers wear that grin. But this man was as old as me, and he looked even feebler.

His companion, a heavier, hairier man with tight black curls atop his head and on his chin, said, "Ya, 'as ri' Fadder. Ya godda make it sop." He clutched the porch railing beside the door as if he were on a ship in a storm.

"Make what stop?" I asked, fearing some drunken revelation of tormented guilt after a murder, or worse.

But the old man said, "He cannot stop the alcohol."

Ah. I had let my imagination run away. This was a simple drinking problem after all. I had counseled many an alcoholic. And despite the hour, I knew that you must set them on the path to recovery the moment they ask for help, for when they sober up they often change their minds. So I opened my door wider and ushered them in.

They shook like spaniels just inside the door, spraying water everywhere. The short, bald one removed his jacket and hung it on the coat rack. His companion was in no shape to remove anything, so I simply led them through the living room and into the kitchen, where he could sit at the table and drip on the tile floor while I made coffee.

"Tha' won' work," he said when he realized what I was doing. "I been drinkin' 'spresso all night, bud it don' work."

Could that be possible? This poor wretch looked and smelled like he'd been bathing in vodka. And recently. I looked to his cherubic companion for enlightenment, but his face now bore an expression of puzzlement. "Who are you?" he asked when he saw me looking at him.

"I'm Father Murray," I told him. "Who are you?"

The question clearly upset him. "I know who I am!" he said hotly. "I'm...I'm...just a minute."

"You're Ivan Wright," the drunk told him. To me he said, "S'all ri'. He forgets things, b' they come back. I'm Egger...*Edgar* Clawson. An' I figured out how Jesus did it."

"Did what?" I asked. I scooped coffee grounds into the machine anyway. I needed a cup, even if nobody else wanted one.

"Changed water into wine," said Edgar.

"Ah. The original act of transubstantiation. And you say you know how he did it?"

"'As ri'. Id isn't hard. 'Sjust like when you turna wine an' crackers into the blood an' body of Chris'. Olny differnt."

"Of course." As I ran water from the tap into the pitcher so I could pour it into the coffee maker, I was trying to decide whether to humor him or be stern with him. But he removed the choice.

"Here, lemme show ya." He lurched to his feet, and would have fallen if Ivan hadn't caught him. Ivan was grinning again now, I noticed.

Edgar steadied himself against the countertop and reached for the coffee urn, which I held out gingerly toward him. He didn't take it; just put his hands around it, then he licked a finger and dipped it in the water. When I frowned at that, he said, "Sorry, but it works bedder if I touch it d'recly."

I said, "I'm sure it—" and then the smell of alcohol hit me even stronger than before. I sniffed the water in the urn and recoiled as the acrid bite of hard spirits burned my sinuses.

"Cool, huh?" he asked.

Living proof that Jesus could have actually performed the miracle reported by his disciples? Yes, indeed it was cool.

Or a trick. Perhaps he'd had a flask up his sleeve.

But the water level hadn't changed. I took a cautious sip directly from the urn to see if it could still be mostly water with just some flavor added, but it flashed to vapor in my mouth and burned all the way down. I'd tasted everclear in my younger days; this was the real stuff.

"How did you do that?" I gasped.

"How do I *stop* it?" he wailed. "I'm drunk 's a skunk, an' ev'ry time I try to drink somethin' I get drunker. And thirstier, 'cause it keeps makin' me hafta pee."

"I see." I had always believed that indiscreet experimenting with religion could be dangerous, but this was unusually direct evidence. "Have you tried just *not* doing whatever it is you do before you drink something?" I asked.

"Of course I have," he said indignantly. "Can't. Try not thinkin' of pink efelants."

"Ah," I said. "I think I see the problem. And you've tried coffee. Juice?"

"Yep. Jus' as bad."

"Have you tried something that doesn't have water in it?"

"Like wha'?"

Hmm. Indeed. What could a person drink that didn't contain water? Besides alcohol, of course. I looked to Ivan, but he was lost in la-la land again. He was apparently at that stage with Alzheimer's when the memory switches in and out like a Christmas light blinking on a tree.

I was on my own here. Edgar had come to me for help, and he certainly needed it, but I was afraid I might have to take him to a hospital if I couldn't

221

come up with something. The thought rankled; I was the religious healer here, I should be better equipped to handle this than a doctor. But what could I give him that he couldn't transubstantiate?

I felt a glimmer of an idea. What about something that had already been transubstantiated? It seemed absurd to give him *more* alcohol, but then according to doctrine, by the time it crossed his lips it wouldn't be alcohol anymore, would it? The only question was whose power was stronger: my holy consecration or his lay experiment gone wrong.

"All right, let's try something," I said. I took a bottle of burgundy from the wine rack by the refrigerator and a cracker from the box in the cabinet. Not the official stuff, but it's not supposed to matter.

"Holy, Holy, Holy," I said to begin the process, then opened the wine.

"Fightin' fire with fire?" Edgar asked hopefully.

Before I could answer, Ivan blinked on again. "Blood of Christ," he said. "Of course. Yes, that will work."

"Glad you think so," I told him.

"I know so," he said, beaming beatifically.

"Uh huh." I dispensed with all the prayers and the pax and cut straight to the fraction rite, pouring a tumbler full of wine, mixing in a few drops of water, holding up the cracker and blessing it, then breaking it in half, breaking off a tiny fragment, and putting that in the wine.

"This is the Lamb of God who takes away the sins of the world," I recited. "Happy are those who are called to his supper."

Edgar looked at me quizzically until Ivan told him, "You should say, 'Lord, I am not worthy to receive you, but only say the word and I shall be healed.'"

"Oh." Edgar stumbled through it. He sounded sincere.

So I ate half the cracker and washed it down with some wine, then said, "The body of Christ" and put the other half of the cracker on Edgar's tongue. When he'd swallowed the cracker I said, "The blood of Christ," and gave him the tumbler.

"Okay." He sipped cautiously. Swallowed. Then he smiled and drained the whole works. "Yeah!" he said. He filled the tumbler from the sink and took a sip of that, then laughed out loud. "Back to normal!"

That was a bonus I hadn't counted on. I felt brief disappointment that my proof of Jesus's miracle was now gone, but then I felt hot shame color my cheeks. Since when do we need proof?

"Wunnerful!" said Edgar. "You're one hot Fadder. Maybe you can even help ol' Ivan here."

I looked over at him. Not home again. "I don't know," I said to Edgar. "It looks like Alzheimer's to me. Not much I can do about that."

"Damn shame," said Edgar. "Pardon my French. But he spen' twenny years medivatin' unner a bo tree, and just when he asheefed—achiefed—true enlight'ment he started to forget stuff. Every now 'n then he 'members, but it's fadin' fast."

I looked at Ivan again. True enlightenment? When he was lucid, he *was* pretty lucid. And that haunting smile...

That haunted smile. The frustration he must feel, to know the meaning of life, the answer to everything, and then to lose it, over and over again.

Hubris almost made me think I could solve his problem as well, but I knew when I was out of my element. "Sorry," I said. "I'd like to help, but this is a job for a Buddhist. And I know just the one. Hold on." I went into my study and rummaged around among the flyers I keep until I found the one for the temple over on Orange Street.

Edgar was still drunk, and insisted on going right away. Ivan was in no shape to protest, so they headed out into the rain again. I checked the clock on the mantel on my way upstairs: four fifteen. I smiled a wicked little smile as I prepared for bed. The Venerable Omi Otaru was about to lose a night's sleep.

Introduction to

Winners

I consider lotteries a tax on the mathematically challenged. I mean, who in their right mind would pay a dollar for a chance to win a million (or ten million, or fifty million) when the odds are over a hundred million to one against them? It's the biggest scam since P.T. Barnum painted "This way to the egress" on the exit door. Yet I still buy a ticket on occasion, and I generally feel like I've gotten my money's worth even when I don't win. Why? Maybe because there are more important things in life than money.

WINNERS

Judy was halfway through her second glass of beer, idly watching the bartender in the mirror and trying to ignore the TV overhead, when the man next to her said, "Hey, didja hear that? What a rip!"

"What?" Judy asked. She turned to look at the guy. He was in his mid-thirties, had curly brown hair thinning on top, and wore a smudged green jersey with the name "Gordy" stitched over the breast pocket. She hadn't seen him here before, but then she wasn't exactly a regular. She'd only been in a few times since the miscarriage; the few times when Phil was away and the house had gotten too lonely.

"On the TV," Gordy said. "This guy won ten thousand bucks in the lottery last week, but some kid stole his ticket before he could cash it in. Snatched it right out of his hand."

"Bummer," said Judy.

It was evidently the wrong thing to say. "Bummer?" Gordy said incredulously. "*Bummer*? Ten thousand bucks is *way* worse than a bummer."

If she hadn't had a couple of beers already, Judy probably would have let it slide. As it was, she thought it over a moment and then said, "No, it's just a bummer, because the guy didn't lose ten thousand bucks. He lost a lottery ticket. Paid what, a dollar for it? That's what he lost."

Gordy cocked his head to the side and wrinkled his forehead. Judy drained off another quarter of her glass of beer before he said, "But that ticket was worth ten grand!"

"What if it was?" Judy asked. "The guy still didn't lose more than a buck." Gordy looked like he was going to protest some more, so she held out a hand and said, "Look, I've got a ticket right here." She reached into her jacket's inside pocket and fished around for the flimsy receipt with her six numbers printed on it, and held it out in front of her. "How much is it worth?" she asked.

Gordy grinned and nodded toward the TV. "We won't know for another five minutes."

"Right. It could be worth what—thirty million? Far more likely it's not worth anything. But either way, it cost me a buck. Got a match?"

"Huh?"

"Got a match? Or a lighter?" When Gordy shook his head, Judy turned around on her stool. "Does anybody here have a lighter?"

Four college guys seated at the table behind her looked up. A man and woman next to them did as well. The woman was just lighting a cigarette; she finished the job and handed Judy a green Scripto.

"Thanks." She flicked the flame to life and held the lottery ticket over it.

"What, are you crazy?" Gordy demanded, grabbing the ticket from her hand before the flame could reach it.

"I'm perfectly sane," Judy told him. "My counselor told me so." She grinned. "I've played those same numbers for six months, and never won a dollar. Never cared, after the first couple weeks. I buy lottery tickets for the cheap hope, for the daydreams I get just knowing I've got one in my pocket. I've already got my dollar's worth out of it." She took it back from Gordy's unresisting fingers and held it over the flame again. Every eye in the bar was on her now.

"Don't!" Gordy said. "Not until the drawing."

"Tell you what," Judy said. "You buy it from me for two dollars and I won't burn it."

Gordy actually reached for his wallet, but then he shook his head and said, "Wait a minute. You can't scam me like that. I've got my own damned ticket, and it only cost me a buck."

Judy smiled. "So my ticket isn't worth two dollars to you?"

"It...hell, I don't know. No, probably not."

"Anybody else want to buy it for two dollars?" asked Judy.

Nobody spoke.

So she lowered the ticket into the flame. The flimsy paper caught quickly, curling brown, then black in a wave toward the corner she held. When her fingers grew warm she dropped it in the ashtray between her and Gordy, then handed the woman her lighter.

"I just burned a dollar," she said. "Except I already got my good out of it, so I didn't lose a thing, really."

She finished her beer and stood, then extended her right hand out to Gordy. "Good luck," she said.

Gordy looked up from the pile of ash and shook her hand somewhat hesitantly. "Aren't you at least going to stay and see if you would've won?"

Judy looked up to the television mounted over the bar. The announcer was standing in front of the ball-juggling machine, just beginning his spiel. Judy shook her head and turned away. The truth was, she would never have burned her ticket if she hadn't been in the mood for an argument. But she'd realized it was an argument she could win, and she'd needed that one small victory. After the miscarriage, she needed every victory she could get.

Whatever the cost.

She walked slowly to the door, aware of everyone's heads turning to follow her. As she opened the door and stepped out into the cool autumn air, she heard the announcer call out, "Thirteen!"

What do you know? she thought. Got one. Then she closed the door firmly behind her and walked on into the night.

INTRODUCTION TO

BIG TWO-SIDED RIVER

One of my friends used to call me up in the afternoons and talk me into dropping whatever I was doing to go fishing with him. I would grumble guiltily that I should stay home and write instead, but I would always go. Finally Matt said, "Look, just write a story about fishing and then this will all be research."

It took me quite a while to come up with a good science-fictional setting for a fishing story. There aren't many rivers in the Solar System, besides those on Earth. I was paging through an atlas of the planets when it dawned on me that I was thinking too narrow. Way too narrow.

The title came to me before anything else, and once I'd thought of it there was no way I could make it anything but a Hemingway pastiche.

BIG TWO-SIDED RIVER

I

The ice tug dropped down into lower orbit, pulling ahead as it did until it disappeared around the curve of the planet. Jack drifted alongside the netted bundle the tug pilot had released from its clamp on the outer hull. There were no settlements here, nothing but space and the flat expanse of ring below him. The fragments of Tenner Station had long since merged with the ring. The reactor core would be a lump big enough to find with binoculars if he knew where to look, but it could be a thousand kilometers away for all he knew. Or fifty thousand. Things drifted in the rings.

Jack took his binoculars from the net bundle and looked down at the ring anyway. By naked eye at this distance it had a smooth texture like that of a high-speed photograph. Just a little bit grainy. With the binoculars it showed its true nature: a jumble of pebbles and rocks and boulders. Some were as big as ships. In between them, keeping station with the largest of the boulders, drifted the ring trout. They were pale gold in Saturn's reflected light. Pale gold torpedoes with long whip tentacles. The tentacles were pellet launchers for moving in space. Most of the ring's inhabitants had them. Some had hydrogen-oxygen rockets. The trout had both. Jack looked down into the ring and watched them maneuver with their pellet launchers. He watched one flick a tentacle to toss a pebble and drift in reaction into the shadow of a rock, only to toss another pebble and come to a stop there.

Deeper in the ring were the big trout. Jack tried to ignore the surface of

233

the ring and see down into it a ways. It was hard at first, but eventually he was able to subtract the ice from his field of vision and see only the trout. They were there, twenty meters or so into the ring—a ring only a hundred meters or so thick despite its enormous breadth—lurking in the shadow of an irregular chunk of ice the size of a tug's external fuel tank.

Jack smiled inside when he saw the big trout. Research, he thought, and he laughed out loud. He lined the cross-hairs in his binoculars on a big trout and triggered the message pulse. The comm laser was invisible to Jack, but the trout either saw it or felt it and launched itself away with its rocket. It moved much faster than the one that had been throwing pellets. Even startled as it was it had picked a destination before it launched, bouncing off another ice rock and killing most of its velocity without having to use its rocket again to slow down. It slipped into the shadow of another ice chunk and launched a pellet to stop.

Jack turned away to look at Saturn. It was a yellow-orange wall beside him. He gripped his oversize net bundle backpack for an anchor and twisted around until Saturn was above him, then behind him, then below. He put it back where it was, to his left side with the ring below. He was looking downstream. He liked it best that way.

Left alone, Jack and his bundle of supplies would eventually drift down into the ring plane, through it, and out the other side. That was the way orbits worked: everything had to cross the equator twice on its way around the planet, unless it was *on* the equator. The rings were the equator. Crossing through and coming to a stop on the other side would take about five hours; half an orbit. Jack enjoyed drifting over the ring with Saturn off to his left but he didn't want to wait that long. He put his binoculars away and pulled himself part way around his bundle until he found the straps, slipped into them and tightened them against his arms and legs. The rocket motor on the other side was pointing straight through his stomach if he had packed everything right. He took the firing control in his hand and pushed the handle slightly to the right. One of the tiny attitude nozzles fired, tipping the tied-together spaceship until Jack faced the ring flat on. He pushed the control the other way to stop his movement. He held his breath a moment, savoring the excitement rising in him before he touched the main firing button. As far as he knew, right now he was captain of the simplest piloted ship in space. The ice asteroids that he and the other miners sent on their slow journeys toward the habitats in Earth orbit didn't count. They were remotely piloted, by computer.

He pushed the button. The rocket pushed against the bundle. The bundle pushed against him. It was a light push, lighter than he had expected. His pack was too massive. Still smiling, Jack held the fire button down for another few seconds. Part of that extra mass was fuel.

When the ring began to rise visibly toward him, he let off the button and coasted. Without the binoculars the ring was a grainy photograph again. He was still too far from it to see individual particles with the naked eye, but he was too close to see the macroscopic patterns, the gaps and spokes made by tidal interaction and by the tiny moons orbiting within the rings themselves. Off to the right he could see where the plane humped up a few hundred meters in a gentle wave, possibly part of one of the braided rings but just as possibly a Periscope Heron enclave or even just the result of some mining tug's exhaust.

As he drifted closer, a flake of something drifted onto his leg and stuck. He watched it fluttering against the tight fabric of his micropore skinsuit, fluttering exactly as if it felt the breeze of his passage. It was probably attracted to the heat. Another landed on his left forearm. Jack unstrapped that arm and slowly reached down until the two creatures saw one another and tumbled off together toward the ring again. Flutterbies, they were called.

The miners had made up their own names for the life they had found so unexpectedly in the rings. Flutterbies and Ring Trout and Periscope Herons and a hundred others, all evidently living off the coal-black Nightoplankton that slowly concentrated the Sun's weak radiation into a useful form of energy. That was one theory. Nobody knew for sure if that's the way it was. When the biologists made it out from Earth they would know. Until then they only knew what miners are always quick to learn about the local fauna. Some of the creatures, properly cooked, could be eaten. Some were harder to catch than others.

The first of the ring particles drifted past. It was the size of his fist and moving about as fast as a gently-tossed rock. Below, the ring had resolved into individual particles. He had drifted close, engrossed in the flutterbies.

The sunlight was at his back. Even here, less than a kilometer from the ring, Jack felt that he should be able to see his shadow against it. It was that opaque. He knew that from the other side he would be able to see through it, see the Sun and even some of the stars about as easily as if he were looking up through a forest canopy, but from here it looked opaque. Off in the distance it still looked grainy, but opaque there, too.

He was getting close. It was time to turn around. Jack pushed the firing control sideways and felt the tiny attitude rocket swing him around until he was facing away from the ring. He had to look to both sides and down through his feet to make sure he was pointing the right way. He pushed the control again and stopped his rotation. Another ring particle, this one as big as his head, spun past only a few meters from his feet.

He pressed the main firing button. He felt the rocket pushing against him again, slowing him now. Another ring particle drifted past. Space seemed to be getting foggy around him. It looked as if he were about to dip into a big bank of fog. That was the ring surface coming up. The ring was mostly tiny particles; dust, really; the big ones were rare by comparison. The dust stayed in the plane better, though. Dust particles didn't have enough mass to plow their way through the rest of the dust every five hours like the bigger chunks did.

Jack let up on the fire button. He was still drifting ringward, but slowly now. He twisted the control to turn sideways so he could see. He was in the ring. He watched the boundary slide past, the ring surface fuzzy and indistinct close up, but sharp as a knife edge farther away. It closed over him like a wisp of cloud. Now the sky was slightly overcast. Cirrostratus.

Jack felt a heavy bump through the pack. He had hit an ice boulder. He rebounded from it, spinning gradually from the impact. The boulder was big. It was probably ten meters across, though very irregular. It had a deep depression in one face, hollowing it almost like a drinking cup. It was probably a nest of some sort, but it looked abandoned now. It would make a good camp. The high walls would protect his bubble from more boulders except for those coming straight in, and if he gave the whole camp a gentle motion through the ring then there wouldn't be any coming straight in.

He unfastened the wire pistol from his belt and aimed at the rim of the depression. The pistol fired a dart trailing a spun diamond monofilament. Jack pulled the trigger and the recoil spun him back slightly, but the dart hit the ice and stuck and he pulled on the pistol to arrest his motion again. He pulled the trigger a second time and the reel began to wind up, pulling him and the pack in toward the ice. His suit had maneuvering rockets built into the waistband, but the wire pistol was less wasteful.

By the time he reached the surface, Jack was ready with a handhold. He stretched out with his arm and triggered it just as its tip touched the ice, and the compressed air charge inside drove the barbed spike deep into the boulder. He unfastened another handhold from his equipment belt and anchored it an arm's reach away, then slipped out of the straps holding him to his pack. He used the straps to tie the pack to one handhold and he clipped his safety line to the other. He worked the wire pistol's dart free from the ice and put the pistol back on his belt. Then he advanced down into the depression, pulling himself along against projecting pieces of ice until he stood in the hollow looking back up at his pack on the rim.

The surface of the ice was bumpy. Jack put in another handhold to anchor himself and chipped at the ice with his boot until it was smooth enough for the bubble floor to rest against. It didn't have to be terribly smooth, since there was no gravity to pull him against the floor when he slept, but he wanted it smoother than it had been. It wasn't a camp unless you smoothed the ground.

When he was satisfied he pulled himself back up to his pack and removed the collapsed bubble from under the net holding everything in. His sleeping bag tried to drift out with the bubble, but he shoved it back in and tied off the net again. With the bubble out of it the netting looked much emptier. Half the mass had been the bubble.

He shook the bubble to unfold it. Half a dozen more handholds lay rolled up inside. He took them from their loops and went back down into the depression and anchored them to the walls, spacing them evenly around. He removed the handhold he had put in the very bottom and recharged its air tank from his suit. He hung that one back on his belt.

The bubble had straps tied to each of its six corners. Jack tied one to each handhold, cinching them down tight until the floor was stretched like a drum head. When the bubble was anchored he went back for the rest of his equipment and pushed it inside piece by piece through the tiny door. The clear fabric of the dome lay in folds over it all. The rocket engine stayed outside; Jack pushed it and its fuel tank ahead of him back out of the depression in the ice boulder and set it so that its flat base rested snugly against the ice on the side of the boulder facing back out of the ring plane.

He had to guess where the boulder's center of gravity would be from that point. On the job he had an ultra-sensitive gravitometer to do it for him so he could position the rocket exactly. Precision was important for the ice to make the long trip to the habitats in Earth orbit, but for this a good guess would do. He guessed that the center of gravity would be about two or three meters beneath the bubble. He aimed the rocket so it would push toward that point and anchored it firmly to the ice with a handhold on either side. Then he pulled his way around to the other side of the boulder, the side opposite the rocket. His safety line snaked back the way he had come, still clipped to the handhold there, but he attached another one where he was and held onto it while he pushed the firing button for the engine. Better to be safe, he thought. Normally the rocketeer didn't ride the ice.

He couldn't feel the thrust, not against so massive a chunk of ice, but after twenty seconds or so he let off the firing button and looked at the other ring particles around him. If he steadied himself and watched for half a minute he could just see their relative motion. That was about right. He didn't want to drift too far, just enough to make it through the rings and a little ways out into emptier space while he slept. He was wasn't sleepy yet, but he knew he would be. He'd been up for nineteen hours already, first working his shift and then waiting for the ice tug and then riding it out here to where old Tenner Station had been before the accident. It hadn't been difficult to hitch a ride; Tenner was still in the autopilot's route menu. The pilot had laughed at Jack's enormous pack and at his stated intention to camp in the rings, but he had taken extra care in stowing the net bag and he had stayed to talk for a few minutes before he left him there alone.

"Let me know how it goes," he had said when Jack stepped into the airlock.

Jack had smiled inside, feeling the man's wish to come along. "I will," he had replied.

The ice boulder was moving slowly toward the night side of the ring. The depression with the bubble in it wasn't at the very aft end of the travel axis, but it was aft of the equator and that was good enough. Jack pulled himself toward it again with gentle tugs on his safety line. On the rim again he chipped off a big chunk of ice and carried it down with him to the bubble. He pushed it in through the door of the bubble and followed it in, then remembered that his line was still fastened to the rim. He backed out again and ducked under one of the bubble's guy lines before he went back to unclip himself. When he unclipped himself from the handhold he clipped the line end to his waist again, the loop around the bubble line still holding him tied to the ice boulder and all his gear. He pulled himself back down to the bubble and crawled inside, then unclipped his line one last time and let the line reel draw it all back in.

The door seal took a little tugging to get closed all the way. The fabric of the bubble kept getting in the way. Jack finally stood erect with it draped over his head like a ghost costume at a Halloween party and pulled the zipper closed that way. He rummaged through his gear until he found the air bottle and cracked the valve. Air pressure inflated the bubble fast. The fabric stretched tight with only a fiftieth of an atmosphere, but Jack let air hiss out of the bottle until he had half an atmosphere. That was plenty for breathing. He knew people who had trouble with half an atmosphere, but he had never had any problem. He could sleep well at that pressure without the smothering dreams.

He turned on the air recycler and the heater while he waited for any leaks to make themselves apparent. The tight bubble skin was nearly invisible now. Through it Jack could see the ice surrounding him and the other ring particles above the horizon of his camp. He watched them drift gently in their separate orbits around the planet while he waited for the bubble to leak if it was going to. By the time he was satisfied with it the inside was warm enough that he could take off his helmet.

It was good to take off his helmet. He let it float free and scratched furiously at his scalp and neck and his right eyebrow. For some reason he had never been able to fathom, his right eyebrow always itched. It started itching the moment he put his helmet on and it didn't stop until he gave it a good scratching at the end of the shift. It was bearable if he didn't think about it. He didn't think about it or about the other itches that he couldn't scratch, but it was always there and scratching it at the end of the day was always a great pleasure. Only the right one was that way.

He peeled off the rest of his suit and shook it out like a rag. His lower body didn't have persistent itches because the suit was thin enough that he could scratch through it when he needed to. But it was still nice to be out of the suit.

Equipment floated everywhere in the bubble. The ice boulder didn't have enough gravity to hold anything to the floor. Jack made quick work tying everything to the walls, everything but his sleeping bag which he unrolled and stuck to the floor with Velcro. He didn't tie the ice block to anything either. It had started to melt, so he herded it into the middle of the bubble and left it there to melt the rest of the way while he got his cooking equipment out.

He didn't have much to cook. He wanted to cook, though. Cooking was important. He had scrounged in the shelves of the station commissary until he found cans that didn't heat upon opening and he had brought those. "Why do you want those?" the cook had asked. "You'll have to take extra stuff with you to heat them."

Jack had merely nodded and said, "That's why. Haven't you ever been camping?"

The cook had thought about it for a moment, his eyes misting over as he remembered some half-forgotten trip into the back country with his father or a favorite uncle, and he had given Jack the cans without further words.

Now Jack took a can opener and slit the top of a rabbit stew can and emptied it into a cooking bag. He put the bag into the tiny compartment in the stove and connected the air bottle to it and cracked the valve to let more air into the cooking chamber until it was at one atmosphere. It would heat much faster at two or three, but he didn't want to rush it. There was a right way and a wrong way. His stomach rumbled in anticipation. Even at one atmosphere the stew only took a couple minutes to heat all the way through, but it seemed that he got twice as hungry as he had been before just waiting for it to cook. That was the way it should be.

Finally Jack decided that the stew was hot throughout. He bled the pressure out of the stove and opened the door. There wasn't any food smell yet. He pulled the bag out by one corner and burned his fingers on it getting it open, but when he broke the seal he heard a soft hiss of escaping steam and then he smelled the stew. His stomach growled loud enough to hear.

He had let the stew get too hot. While it cooled he took another bag and coaxed about half the slushy ice glob into it and put a small net bag of fresh ground coffee into the cold water. He had never made fresh coffee in a bag before, but the cook had told him how and he followed the cook's directions to the letter even though it didn't seem right to him. He would have heated the bag at this point, but the cook had told him to just seal it and squish it around in his hands until it looked like coffee, the darker the better. He did that. It took a while to look like anything more than weak tea, but he kept at it until it looked like it might be coffee. By then the stew was cool enough to eat so he left the coffee bag to steep some more while he ate the stew. It was just thick enough that he could use a fork on it. It tasted better than he remembered stew tasting. It was even better than his mother's stew that she made in a big steel kettle over the sterilizing furnace in the lab. He remembered other meals he had cooked over a campfire and decided that they were almost as good as this, though. Everything tasted better when you were camping, he supposed. That was good. Even the station cook wouldn't mind that.

The coffee looked good and dark by the time he finished his stew. Jack shook his head at the next step but he followed the cook's instructions and removed the bag of used coffee grounds and put them in the dirty stew bag. The bag of strong, cold coffee went into the cold pouch in the bubble's side, outside the regular skin and the infrared blocking layers in it. Now it would lose heat to space.

In a few minutes it had frozen solid. Jack brought it back inside the bubble and whacked it against the top of the stove until it broke into shards. Two of the shards went into a cup-sized drinking bag. The bag with the rest of the coffee shards went back into the cold pouch for later. Jack swept enough water from the melting glob to fill his drinking bag and put that back into the stove. He let it heat at half an atmosphere for a few more minutes, then took it out and shook it gently to mix it well. It looked like coffee. When he opened the bag to get the straw in he could smell it and it smelled like coffee, too. He tasted it. It was coffee. He would have to tell the cook that it worked.

An enormous yawn caught up with him while he was drinking the cook's coffee. He finished the coffee quickly and sealed the bag again and put the rest of the water in the stew bag and put both bags away in the bigger bag that held all his food. He stretched his arms out over his head and leaned back to get the kinks out of his spine, then unzipped his sleeping bag and crawled in. He lay on his back in the bubble and watched the ring overhead. The ice boulder was nearly through it now and on the night side, though it wasn't really that much darker. Just a little cloudier. Regular stratus clouds now. The Sun was behind the ice wall to his left, but he could see where it had to be by the light on the ring particles. Earth would be out that way too. Earth and all the camping and all the fishing streams he had ever known. It was almost a billion and a half kilometers away.

He looked away from the brightness where Earth would be. He didn't want to think about Earth now.

Straight overhead, something alive drifted down toward the bubble. It was like a flutterby but smaller. Jack didn't know what it was. There were so many new species here in the rings, things that biologists back home would never believe possible. The ice miners tried to catalog them but there was never time. There was never time enough for anything but work and sleep. Work and sleep and thinking about how far they were from home.

Jack watched the tiny living mote land on the bubble fabric. He almost wished it could get in the bubble with him. If it did he would probably wind up swatting it, though, to get some sleep. It would almost surely wind up going for the heat of his face. Better that it stayed outside.

Sleep was catching up with him. Jack felt as if he could sleep if he just closed his eyes. He closed his eyes and slept.

II

When he woke he saw that the ice boulder had carried him down through the ring and back up through it again to the day side. He was above the ring by a kilometer or so. It was a grainy photograph again below him. Jack smiled at a thought. He was thinking that he was lying on his back in the bubble, looking out at the ring below him. The ring was so big and so flat that it could only be down no matter what attitude his own body was in. There was no disorientation near the ring. It was always down.

Jack sat up. The walls of the ice depression around him were covered with flutterbies. They were attracted to the heat of the bubble, but evidently the bubble was too hot even with its infrared shielding for them to land right on it for very long.

He had intended to make breakfast. Breakfast was part of camping. It was important, but now that he was awake and saw the flutterbies there on the ice he thought about the ring trout waiting for him and breakfast didn't seem as important as it had. He would skip breakfast. He packed half a dozen food bars into his helmet where he could reach them later on when he got hungry, then slid out of his sleeping bag and pulled on his micropore suit. The fabric was a little cold from being next to the bubble wall. It was invigorating.

When he put the helmet on, his right eyebrow began to itch. He tried not to think about it. He turned off the air recycler and the stove and made sure the air bottle was sealed tight, then opened the valve in the top of the bubble and let the air out. The fabric loosened without air pressing out on it, but without gravity it didn't collapse.

Some of the flutterbies had launched themselves away into the air stream, but most of them were still on the wall. Jack took a cooking bag with him and unsealed the bubble door. More flutterbies scattered when he stepped toward them. A few remained on the ice wall, trembling softly. He picked them gently off the ice and put them into the bag until he had a couple dozen of them. That would be plenty. He left the bag outside and went back into the bubble for his fishing pole. The pole was a half-wave ten-meter collapsible antenna off an ice tug, with twists of wire for eyes. The reel and line were straight off a wire pistol. He had bent the barb at the end of the wire pistol line into a hook.

He made sure his suit belt was stocked with handholds and that the fuel tank for the maneuvering rockets was full. He took a large net bag and tied that to his belt as well. When he was satisfied with his equipment he backed out of the bubble and sealed it so that the flutterbies couldn't get in while he was gone. He picked the bag of flutterbies out of space where he had left it and clipped it to his belt. Then, with a light push from his toes, he kicked off to go fishing.

The ice boulder dwindled behind him. It would soon be lost in the distance, but Jack knew that the transponder in the bubble would lead him back home when he was ready to come back. The bubble was a standard emergency survival bubble from one of the tugs in for repairs. All the emergency bubbles had transponders.

When he had drifted down until he was only a few meters above the ring surface he used his belt rockets to bring him close to another ice boulder about the size of the one he had camped on. When he reached it he anchored two handholds in the ice and tucked his feet into the loops. He positioned himself so that he was facing just inward of downstream, about at the edge of Saturn's disk. He watched the ring for a minute or two to get the feel of it. Inward toward the planet the particles were moving in a faster orbit. Outward they moved slower. The difference in speed was not great, but if he watched long enough he could see the relative motion. The effect was of a river flowing past him in two directions at once. It flowed away from him on his left and toward him on his right.

Jack threaded the hook through the eyes on his rod. He had put an eye on the end of each of the six sections of the antenna. When he got the hook through them all he pulled the sections out one by one until the pole was extended. He pulled some more line from the top until he could hold the butt end with the handle in one hand and the hook in the other. He let go the hook and the pole and they stayed where he left them. Then he opened the bag holding the flutterbies and waited until one crawled to the opening. He picked it out by its single wing and reclosed the bag. He spent a moment looking at the flutterby, wondering how to hook it. His excitement to be fishing waned a little. He had never liked hooking grasshoppers or worms, either. He remembered that from before. You always did it because that was part of fishing, but Jack had never liked it. His father had been pleased that Jack didn't like hooking the bait, but he was even more pleased that he still did it. Jack had never understood that, not really until now.

There was a thickening in the wing that had to be the rocket. He plucked the hook out of space and threaded the hook around the rocket, weaving it through the wing that was really the flutterby's body. The two legs at the wing tips thrashed. Jack let the hooked flutterby float free and took the pole in his hand and began stripping out more line and waving the pole back and forth until he had a lot of it out. He was careful to move slowly and not whip the flutterby off the hook. When he had fifty meters or so out he made his first cast. He brought the pole back and waited until the line had all looped back behind him and come to a stop, then brought it forward about halfway and gave a good tug on the line with his other hand at the same time. The line shot forward over his head, the flutterby trailing at the end of it, and stretched out until the flutterby was just inside the ring ahead of him. Jack let it drift.

He waited a few minutes. The flutterby was just visible at the edge of the ring. It wasn't moving much. No ring trout seemed interested in it. Jack couldn't see any ring trout from this angle. You had to be looking directly into the ring to see the trout. He waited a while more. His arm holding the pole began to get stiff.

There was a big chunk of ice just ahead of the flutterby. The trout would probably be in its shadow. Jack tried to roll cast so the bait would flip over toward it, but the line just pulled back toward him and went slack. He pulled it back for another cast.

His second cast went downstream of the ice chunk. He waited a while to see if anything would strike, then pulled it back. His third cast was high and didn't make it to the ring. He tugged it back but didn't wait long enough before he pulled the rod forward to make his fourth cast and when the hook sailed by the flutterby was gone. He had whipped it off on the back-cast.

This wasn't the way it was supposed to work. Jack wondered if this trip had been a good idea after all. It had seemed to be working last night, but now he didn't know. Not catching trout was very frustrating. He told himself that he had to be patient, but he didn't feel patient at all. He felt frustrated and angry.

He took a few deep breaths. On the job when things went wrong he would always take a few deep breaths to calm down. Give it a chance, he told himself. The first guy to try this on Earth probably didn't catch one on the first cast, either.

Feeling a little more patient after the deep breaths, he reeled in the line and baited the hook with another flutterby from the bag. He stripped out line and cast again, this time deeper into the ring. He cast almost straight down. The flutterby went deep into the ring before it hit a tiny chunk of ice and stopped. Jack reeled in some line to get the slack out of it.

There was a flash of motion near the flutterby. Jack felt the line surge as the trout hit it. The pole dipped down in an arc. The trout was firing its rocket to get away. Jack pulled on the pole, but instead of pulling the trout out of the ring, the tug on the end of five meters of pole and another couple meters of Jack simply spun the ice boulder around until he was holding the pole straight overhead toward the trout. Momentum took the boulder on past that point until he was bent over almost backwards, then it slowed to a stop under the pull of the line and swung back again. The trout was still trying to get away. It had quite a lot of thrust for a biological rocket, and a lot of fuel. Besides just spinning the boulder Jack had anchored himself to, the trout was pulling it deeper into the ring.

The trout finally ran out of fuel. It continued trying to get away with its pellet launcher, the reaction surging up the line in waves as it threw pellet after pellet, but the real fight was over. Jack began reeling in line. The trout came thrashing out of the ring. The ice boulder continued in the slow spin left over from the trout's last tug. The trout seemed to leap sideways each time Jack pulled on the line, and it took him a moment to realize what was happening. The trout was going into orbit around him. The trout was at the end of a line tied to a spinning ice boulder; what else could it do? Jack was glad that the boulder was as massive as it was, or conservation of momentum would start it spinning faster and faster the more he reeled the trout in.

The trout ran out of pellets to throw. All it could do now was wriggle at the end of the line. If it had enough time to generate more fuel, breaking down water into hydrogen and oxygen, it could put up another fight with its rocket, but for now it was exhausted.

Jack used his own maneuvering rockets to stop the ice boulder's motion. The trout at the end of the line kept going in its arc, and Jack had to reel it in fast to keep it from whacking into the ice. He reeled in line and the trout swung wide and then toward him. Jack held the pole high and the trout swung by just over his head and back out again. As he reeled it in the trout made three more orbits around the tip of the pole.

Jack could feel a laugh building in him. When he'd gone fishing with his father, his father would laugh because Jack was always too eager to land his fish and he would pull it clear onto the bank just in setting the hook. Jack would always wind up with the line tangled around a tree branch and the fish dangling out of his reach overhead. His father would have to climb the tree to untangle it and he would laugh all the while.

Jack laughed with his father. He wasn't frustrated anymore and he wasn't angry. And neither was he lonely. He felt deep into his soul but he couldn't feel the loneliness there at all. It was gone.

He reached out and caught the trout as it swung by on the end of the line. It was as long as his arm and twice as thick. Its tentacles grasped his suit and held on. Jack removed the hook from the trout's mouth. He pulled the net bag from his waist belt and put the trout into the bag, pulling the tentacles free and tying the bag closed. He anchored it to the ice with another handhold. The trout reached out through the net and gripped the ice as well.

Jack thought about trying for another trout. It was tempting. This first one had definitely been a thrill. His heart was still beating hard and he was still smiling from the experience. He had plenty of time, though. There was no reason to rush it. If he could catch a small one he could try it for dinner, but he only needed one to eat and one to take back to the station and he still had all day ahead of him.

He pulled his feet from the handholds and let himself drift away from the ice boulder. He was hungry now. Catching the trout had made him hungry. He turned his head to the side and bit a food bar from its clip and began to gnaw on it. Food bars were tough going. They weren't bad, though. In fact they tasted pretty good out here, out in the rings with a trout in the bag and camp not far away. Jack chewed on the bar and drank water from the suit nipple and savored them both. He wished he had thought to bring some coffee with him. He would have some soon enough when he got back. When he got back he would take a couple more fragments of the coffee ice and heat them with water in the stove and have fresh brewed coffee. He could taste it already.

He would tell the cook that his coffee had worked. He would tell the others that fishing had worked. He would come back relaxed and holding his trout up with pride and the others would know that it had worked. He looked up toward the Sun. Earth was out there too. It was a long ways away, but not so far as it had been.